WIN
SE
AL

C000234198

THE ONLY WELL LIFE IS A TRUE LIFE

i

Bcarhing hot wishes,
with weastle Smile For
Life Zumbathon, then
W.H. Smith 6oshorte,
Brook end Zac!
22/4/23

# Endorsements

'Barry Stone achieves the almost impossible: he writes from the point of view of a dog and makes me care about the canine and the people he comes into contact with. My tail's wagging!'

*Ian MacMillan. Barking At Winston. 2010.*

'Really, really powerful. A poignant tale of love and family life, with all its imperfections, frustrations, sadness and humour. Full of memorable characters with a heart warming feel-good end. Someone should make this book into a film.'

*Richard W. Hardwick. Winston And The Canny Lass. 2014.*

'Can dogs read our thoughts and emotions? Most certainly! Dogs can also share our hopes and fears, experience our joy and rescue us from the pain of living. That's the premise of Barry Stone's celebration of the mysterious bond between canine and human. An entertaining but thought-provoking book that takes a deep look into love, family and the destructive forces that drive lost young men into fatal behaviour against themselves and others.'

*Pauline Hadaway. Winston Sees All. 2023.*

'Barry Stone's novel offers a great account of the impact that sexuality can have on people when society tells them that they must live in a certain way; the raw emotion pours out of this book in a way that will touch anyone, not only LGBTQ+ people.'

*Jack Mowatt. Winston Sees All. 2023.*

# WINSTON
# SEES ALL

Barry Stone

**BERRY
PRESS**

First published 2023 by Berry Press
Berry Press
Green Door Workshop
NE25 0NB

Copyright © Barry Stone 2023

ISBN: 978 0 9566932 9 7

Typesetting and Cover Design: Mike Davis

Cover illustration: Ellie Whitworth/Ben Stone

Printed and bound in the UK by
Martins the Printers,
Sea View Works,
Spittal, Berwick Upon Tweed,
TD15 1RS

*With love for Paul Simpson-Stone and with gratitude to Hazel Orme.*

## RESCUE DOG

'A dog that has been placed in a new home after being abused, neglected, or abandoned by its previous owner.'

*Collins English Dictionary*

'A rescue dog is born out of a sorry canine on the day of his true saviour by human kindness. All at once he is elevated, all-seeing, all-knowing, carried by a tide of love going back to the earliest humans in need of rescue from themselves. His purpose is noble. His obligations immense. His challenges often insurmountable.'

*Anon.*

'Fight! Fight to become a rescue dog!'

*Her Hoityness, council kennels, 23 August 1972.*

## Author's Notes

I turned thirteen in late 1971. Not long before this I met
an academically gifted boy who was sixteen. His initials
were B.D. and he lived in a different part of the country.
Shortly before Christmas of that year, I was told that
he'd taken his life. I was not upset. After all, I hardly
knew him – but this suicide would sit within me like a
travel bag left by a stranger who knew that, one day, I
would need to unpack it. Even before my chance
meeting with B.D., I was aware of the pressure on boys
to be 'normal' and it was a dead cert that in time I
would see a link between this and teenage suicide.
Much has changed since the early 1970s and with all
my heart I hope things are easier for boys today. All I
offer is a glimpse of how things were. Rest in peace,
B.D.

Part one of the novel incorporates the first Winston
'tail' *Barking At Winston*, which has been deepened and
lengthened. Part two is all new and is subtitled *Winston
Loses His Head*.

# Foreword

In the UK, suicide is the leading cause of death in those aged thirty-five and under.

I have seen in both my personal and professional life as an NHS Doctor the damage that suicide causes to families and loved ones, but I have also seen how isolated and alone those with suicidal thoughts feel. Barry Stone's novel offers a great account of the impact that sexuality can have on people when society tells them they must live in a certain way; the raw emotion pours out of this book in a way that will touch anyone, not only LGBTQ+ people.

A *Guardian* article in 2021 claimed that LGBTQ+ youths were three times more likely to self-harm and twice as likely to have suicidal thoughts than their heterosexual, cis-gender peers. Bullying, homophobia, transphobia and difficulty 'coming out' are some of the biggest factors that make mental-health problems more common among LGBTQ+ and, although being LGBTQ+ is more accepted in the UK than it was in the 1970s, when this book is set, these problems are still rife, especially against those in the trans community. Although we still have a long way to go as a country, you can support LGBTQ+ people through some small actions:

Talk – Talk to your LGBTQ+ friends and loved ones and even if they are not in the right place to talk, let them know you are there. Let them know they are loved.

Listen – Listen to them. Ask if there is anything you can do to support them. It might be something as simple as going for a walk or watching a film with them. Distraction is a wonderful tool to improve a person's wellbeing.

Signpost – If you are worried about someone, help and enable them to contact their GP, their local crisis team, NHS 111 or Samaritans on 116 123. If they plan to end their life, encourage them to call 999 or go to their local A and E.

Support – There are many great charities that support LGBTQ+ people, such as the Albert Kennedy Trust, Stonewall and Switchboard. You can donate or volunteer for these charities, if you are able.

Remember to let them know they are not alone.

*Jack Mowatt*

# 1

The hottest day of 1972 was 25 August. It was also the date on which I, Brucie-Dog, was meant to be offed by an ill-tempered human known as Psycho Vet. Luck was on my side. Just after midday a red-headed visitor in her fifties came looking for a rescue dog to make her family happy. I feared that the heat of the sun was making me see things.

Rachael and Craig were fifteen, Vanessa and Jack sixteen: two pairs of twins with the same thick black hair, green eyes, big noses, large chins and short legs. On realising they were not imaginary I fell in love with them and their mum.

Already I'd dubbed her Ginger and it was fitting that she was surrounded by a red mist, which any mutt would have seen meant she was big-hearted. That may sound odd, but when it comes to understanding of human behaviour, the starting point for all dogs is the reading of their colours.

The mixed shades of the four twins excited me, too, though within this I saw much whiteness around the junior boy Craig. That was telling and scary.

All young humans are given to moods, which may show as small bits of white, but anything more signals hidden unhappiness that could lead to self-offing.

It would be a little while before I knew that in this case the danger was partly Craig's alcoholic dad, Raymond. In the months before his own recent self-offing he'd attacked his youngest son for being queer, and queerness was despised at the kid's school so Craig had known tough times.

The same was true of me. My first human was a cruel alkie. He'd called me Runt, and when he was drunk he used to set a live electric cable to my spine. That's why the council dog man took me from him. I was twelve months old and my rescuer had to put a net over my head to stop me biting his hands – I'd loved my first human, my saviour, I'd thought.

I was one of five collie-cross pups that were tied into a sack and thrown into a river. Luckily he'd chanced by and fished us out. Unluckily for the others I was the only survivor. For weeks he'd hand-fed me. He couldn't have been more loving. Then his old problem with booze returned and he started to look at me with eyes that were crazy. Soon after that my punishments with the electric cable began.

Each time he got ready to set the exposed inner wires to my spine he made the same remark in the same sad slurred voice: 'This is cos you're a bad dog.'

Contact was made. Words cannot describe how horrible this felt. Afterwards the reek of burnt fur lingered as an accusation directed at me. This felt right. The matter of my badness was something I didn't question.

I'd been dumped into a river within twenty-four hours of birth and now I'd made the only human who'd loved me so miserable that I deserved to be punished.

Sometimes I wanted him to fetch the electric cable. If he doubled the treatment I might become a good dog. As it was, I was worthless and vile.

I accepted this for several reasons: first, because he stressed how bad my nature was; second, because much of my black and tan coat had been destroyed by mange; and third, I had conjunctivitis, which made my eyes run with smelly gunge. The conclusion was obvious. Inside and out I was a rotten mutt, who'd even tried to bite the council dog man.

Then I met the large, proud pedigree I dubbed 'Her Hoityness'.

She was the gleaming black and gold Alsatian in the cage next to mine, and I was fascinated by her tale of how she'd ended up at the kennels. Her humans were well off and had shown her many times. But she was not always well guarded. A door was left open on a bright day when she couldn't resist a romp in a nearby park. Unfortunately a passing mutt took an interest. He would never know the fateful outcome of their brief encounter.

Her Hoityness produced a tiny white pup, stillborn. Had it been alive it would probably have been drowned in a bucket. Her shock delivery occurred on the fireside rug that lay before the armchairs where her humans were sitting. She was amused that as she'd gone into labour they were watching *Coronation Street*.

The next morning she was slung into the kennels and an hour later I was brought in, her new neighbour, making us quite a twosome. The mange-ridden young mutt and the show-winning pedigree, both on Death Row, seven days' grace each.

My confidence was at zero, and for a while I considered eating one of my paws. But I couldn't do it. My eyes were stinging and my red-raw flesh itched. Adding pain to that was beyond me.

Her Hoityness soon turned wolfish and tore at her flanks with claws and teeth. That horrified me. She was on a mission to get offed early by the human known as Psycho Vet. Yet it was this very directness that also helped to save my life.

Her response to my sad tale made my ear flaps point up so sharply that they hurt at the roots. She couldn't have been clearer. Far from being my saviour, my first human had plucked me from the river so that I would become his Runt. A helpless victim to torture with the electric cable, which, she claimed, had caused the mange. Tougher stuff followed.

I'd been an out-and-out coward, staying with a dog-hater when I should have bitten him and fled. On hearing this my ears collapsed into flatness, which made her even angrier. She was done with life, but she saw a future for me. 'Fight!' she snarled, through the hard steel bars that divided us. 'Fight to become a rescue dog!' she added, silencing all the other dogs. Her eyes bored into me. They were deep blue. Just like mine.

Soon after that she was offed by Psycho Vet as a dangerous dog. This was not the last of her. After her corpse was tossed into the incinerator, black smoke drifted over the cages, reminding us all she'd at least died on her own terms. It was too much for me to accept. I needed to believe she was still alive. Her strength was uplifting.

The other mutts yapped that my brain had been fried by rabies. I was, according to them, the biggest no-hoper of all. Perhaps that was true. They didn't have mange, gooey eyes, sticky-out ribs and a notion that a dead dog was somehow still living.

When Ginger and the twins turned up on the morning of day seven I wagged my near-hairless tail, made big blue moons of my eyes, and even rolled onto my infected, scabby back. 'Well, I must say!' cried Ginger. 'Aren't you an artful bugger!' I loved that. It made me even more determined to survive. Exactly as I'd been ordered to do.

Despite the family's laughter at my tricks, the door of my cage remained bolted. I could see why. Ginger was awaiting approval of me from fifteen-year-old Craig. The implication was clear. I was being considered as his dog, meaning that if he'd moved on to the next cage Psycho Vet would have offed me within hours. I knew where to seek help. 'Please,' I prayed to Her Hoityness, 'make him love me.'

To my relief he went down on his right knee and peered through the bars. That got his mum and the others watching us closely, as did the kennel lad. His role was to set me free if I received the thumbs-up. I liked him. He was called Marcus and was also fifteen.

But it was young Craig who held my attention. We had to connect. My life hung in the balance. So, too, with all the whiteness he was showing, did his. No sooner had he set his face nearer to mine than I saw much pain within his big green eyes. That was dodgy. If I was pegged as a fellow loser, I might be rejected after all. Which at least made sense.

Craig needed a lovable mutt and my first human had left me convinced that, as much as I was bad, I was repulsive. That put me on my mettle. Keeping my back straight and my bum to the floor, I wanted him to see that I could at least become worthy of him. This was not easily done.

My ears were back to points and I was making big blue moons out of my eyes but everything about this face-to-face between us felt unsafe. At any second he would move on to a non-scabby mutt, leading the family in his wake. I had to stop that happening. Begging was not beneath me. This time, Her Hoityness would hear my prayer. I willed her to do so.

'Please, please, please,' I implored, 'make the kid love me.'

It was then that I noticed tiny yellow dots within the green bits of his eyes. At the same time I feared I'd angered Her Hoityness, the apparent result of which came fast and was horrible.

Tingles that made me feel faint zipped to my tail and to my neck, just as if my first human had set his special electric cable dead centre to my spine, as was his custom. This almost spelt disaster. Or so I thought.

From the widening of Craig's eyes I knew that just when I'd wanted him to see the handsome collie-cross I had the potential to be, I'd looked as if I was about to collapse. At that moment nothing could have made me angrier with myself. Things felt dire.

I had enough health problems on display and didn't want the kid and his family fearing I was also a weak sort who'd be an embarrassment to them. What happened next was unplanned.

Before I could check my thinking box, I was ranting at Her Hoityness that she was the one who'd instructed me to fight, just as I was doing, eye to eye with the kid, each of us at risk of losing his life: me to the poison needle of Psycho Vet and him by self-offing. 'Make him love me!' I demanded of her.

Three scary seconds passed before I felt I'd won her respect.

A huge grin stretched the kid's lips more than seemed possible. I was a beautiful dog, he told Ginger. Redness showed around each member of the family and Marcus the kennel lad (who, I'd realised, they knew). Big things then occurred.

My denial of Her Hoityness's death became an un-shakeable belief that she would always be there to help me through the years with Ginger, Craig, Jack, Vanessa and Rachael. This was the moment when I changed from a useless mutt into the most admired of all canines everywhere: a rescue dog. Which, of course, has two meanings, each joined to the other. Dog lovers know that they rescue us. We save humans, old and young, when their colours go wrong. We exist to help. Now I know why I had not become my first human's rescue dog: his soul was too corrupted to recover, which put him beyond the reach of any canine help.

That, though, was already in my past. I couldn't wait to start protecting the kid and what happened next took us both by surprise.

## 3

**M**y mind-of-its-own tongue shot between the bars to meet the big straight nose Craig had inherited from Ginger. Hers was badly broken. I'd noticed that straight away and, because it must have hampered her breathing, I'd wanted to lick her face, soothing an old wound as best I could. That had not been possible. From the moment of the family's arrival she was set on giving the four kids room to meet me, so she'd stepped back from my cage, helping me to focus on Craig.

A new problem developed, which I should have anticipated.

As soon as an ordinary mutt changes into a rescue dog, he acquires his second sight, enabling him to explore the lives of his humans and even those who went before them. It gives him a picture of what has caused the most harm and the best way for him to help.

That second sight can be overwhelming.

As I licked his nose, Craig squealed with joy, which made the others laugh, but because Ginger was his mum there was a risk that my second sight might open on her instead of him, speeding me through window after window of her life until I understood what had led to the breaking of her nose. That would have been disastrous. I'd become a full-on rescue dog whose number-one mission was to save the kid. Without me he was doomed, and I was too weak to give half my energy to Ginger. It would have killed me. Besides I knew I'd learn much of her story via my discoveries about him. At least the proof of our bonding was strong.

Craig's joy at having his nose licked by a sorry-looking mutt that other visitors to the kennels had looked away from made me love him more. He was no snob. Maybe he loved me because I was such a mess.

'You're a lovely, beautiful darling!' he cried, making my baldy tail wag so much that it ached.

Ginger's decision on my future – on my life – came, and the news was good. She was satisfied that I was the right mutt for the kid and Marcus the kennel lad got the thumbs-up. I was overwhelmed by gratitude for the help I believed had come from Her Hoityness.

'Thank you! Thank you! Thank you!' I told her, though to the family this burst of yapping must have appeared to be excitement that Marcus was about to release me. Things changed. He stopped in his tracks and my vulnerable doggie-gut clenched.

All young humans bicker, but from the minute

of their arrival I'd seen that when it came to family in-fighting Ginger's lot were world champions. They'd sniped about this, bitched about that, and now young Rachael was objecting to the kid's way of talking to me. 'Blimey, our Craig!' she'd exclaimed, with a mix of anger and embarrassment. 'You can't go around calling dogs lovely beautiful darlings!'

Jack, the older brother, was quick to speak up. 'Craig can say "lovely beautiful darling" if he likes,' he rebuked Rachael.

That got up her nose and soon they were all at it, banging on until big streaks of black showed within Ginger's crimson. It was a signal of fury. The twins were driving her mad.

'If you lot are going to turn this into yet another row we're going home empty-handed – so you'd better stop right now!' she threatened, with a ferocity that set the mutts in the nearby cages shaking more than I'd ever done (except when I was being zapped by the electric cable). The silence that followed was thick with dread.

All of Ginger's kids had fallen for me and they each knew that their mum wasn't bluffing about leaving empty-handed. I was so scared that I almost growled in protest, which might have driven Ginger to the breaking point she was already close to. Instead I seized the chance to take stock of her family.

Rachael, Craig, Jack and Vanessa didn't only share

their mum's lovely green eyes, strong nose and big chin. They also had identical black eyebrows that I thought of as furry caterpillars, and thick mops of black hair. Wild mongrels, whose odd good looks I adored. To see them thunderstruck now made my heart thud so hard it was a wonder my ribs didn't crack. Terrified my rescue was destroyed, I felt a squirt of pee escaping. This was embarrassing and an added reason for alarm.

Even the kindest humans wince at weak dog bladders. It ruins their carpets. This was not a helpful line for me to follow. All I wanted was for them to quit arguing and get me to my new home.

My life stayed in the balance, as did Craig's, and things could have gone either way. Yet again I was surprised by the next development.

# 4

The younger pair started arguing again. Incredibly this was about my new name. Craig had declared I should be called Bruce, Rachael insisted on Blue, and when the older twins tried to help, another full-scale battle kicked off. It seemed that, thanks to Ginger's mad family, I was to have my final meeting with Psycho Vet after all.

Then Marcus stunned everyone: he laughed at them and suggested my new name should be put to the vote. It was Ginger who got her wits back first: 'I say,' she beamed at Marcus, whose silver-blue eyes were twinkling with fun, 'what a simply fabulous idea! Why don't we do exactly that?' she asked.

The scowls on the faces of the twins began to soften. Plus they were now each showing the same dark green, signalling that they were glad their fighting had been checked by Marcus's idea of a vote. Which, as it happened, was not required.

Rachael cleared her throat. 'Okay, our Craig,' she conceded, crouching beside him and facing me. 'Bruce it is. But he'll get Brucie anyway,' she added.

Brucie was not Bruce and I was scared that the kid himself might now throw away my rescue. This was not a hard judgement on him. Young humans who show a lot of whiteness are driven to extremes by the pain that chews at them. Maybe Jack understood this. 'C'mon, our Craig, what's the bloody difference?' he pressed. 'Brucie or Bruce?'

The next bit was confusing for me. Craig's eyes were still a twinkly shade of green and I saw even more bits of yellow in them. If he was feeling attacked I would have expected a single dark shade.

Also, I wasn't the only one who was weighing him up.

Ginger, Marcus, Jack, Vanessa and Rachael were all staring at him warily, which showed that they knew things were critical. That was enough of a warning for me, and I decided to risk an added doggie-trick.

Keeping my ears pricked, I looked deep into the kid and willed him to accept Rachael's concession of Brucie. For a few moments it seemed I was failing but then his face lit up and my long-suffering tail thumped the floor in anticipation of my rescue being completed.

'Brucie-Wucie-Lucie-Darling!' he loudly exclaimed to me.

'Brucie-Wucie-Lucie-Darling!' he repeated, while everyone laughed. There would be no lingering ill-feeling over my name and my bond with Craig had strengthened, just as I'd wanted.

'Brucie-Wucie-Lucie-Darling,' he repeated quietly. 'Brucie-Wucie-Lucie-Darling,' he whispered, while the family looked on. That put the seal on us: Brucie-Dog and the kid.

Things advanced fast.

'You'll love Brucie to bits,' Marcus remarked for the benefit of Craig, who turned red as a beetroot and showed an odd mix of colours, which made me see what I'd missed so far.

There was some sort of history between Craig and the gay-natured kennel lad, which was connected to the kid's showing of too much whiteness. That was odd. Marcus's colours were good. He would not have intentionally harmed anyone. Yet Craig was now on the defensive against him any getting closer.

'We love Brucie already, thanks,' he replied, with a sharpness that put a shadow across Marcus's face. 'Loads and loads,' he added, as he got up and stood aside to give space for my cage to be opened.

By now Vanessa and Jack had their four big eyebrows raised, Ginger was thoughtful, and Rachael as inscrutable as a bulldog. Shoving my right paw through the bars before any of them could get a new fight going, I raised it high for the opening of my cage door. Marcus snapped into action. 'Well,' he declared, slipping the bolt that had kept me imprisoned, 'Brucie's all yours, folks.'

With that he avoided giving the kid a last look and went to muck out the cage opposite mine. Thrilled to have escaped Psycho Vet and in love with my new family, I bounded onto a grassed area and ran in circles, which made them clap and laugh. How things had changed for me that day.

Far from being the Runt, I was now an adored rescue dog. My thanks to Her Hoityness were even stronger than before. If I'd seen what lay ahead I might have been overwhelmed.

5

The 'taxi' waiting outside the kennels was a silver mini-bus with enough dents to suggest that it should have been scrapped. Its driver clearly had a similar thought about me. 'Blimey!' he exclaimed. 'They must be low on dogs!'

That was like throwing a switch. All four of the kids stopped their laughter and scowled so hard at him that he put his hands up in surrender and apologised. Ginger was amused. 'Back to Shangri-La,' she ordered, with a chuckle.

It was a dizzying ten-minute ride that ended outside a big terraced house, which had a double-storey bay window and shiny gold curtains on the ground floor. That pulled me up sharp. And with good reason too. Sometimes a sickly dog's grasp on reality can go haywire, making what's unreal seem real. The pricy-looking gold material was out of place and I became panicked that the other mutts at the kennels were right about my brain: it had been fried by illness. I could no longer tell if my rescue was real or imaginary. Perhaps the great heat of the day had destroyed my thinking box.

There was only one way to find out. I had to get proof that I was not in a dream, which put me at a remove from the murder of Her Hoityness and a coming meeting with Psycho Vet. I was quick to act.

The mini-bus had a side door on runners. Even before Jack had slid it half open I was scrambling to be on the pavement. 'Look at our Brucie!' cried Rachael. 'Look at him go!'

I sniffed the low garden wall for the scents of other mutts. Happily I found more than enough to confirm that my rescue was true and lifted a leg to squirt against the brick post that supported the rusty wrought-iron garden gate. That worked wonders. The cries of mock-protest that came from Ginger and the twins made my tail wag at its fastest.

The air was dense with salt, so I looked down the sloping road to where the sea was. Until then I'd been too busy with survival to notice its huge shimmering blueness yet now it struck me as the brightest sight of my life so far. Blue, blue, incredible blue: for some moments everything around me also went blue, making me feel sure that as soon as my health was on track, I would be the best rescue dog in the world. The blueness of the sea promised this.

But no sooner had the twins finished laughing at the long howl the sudden flood of blue had made me give than my heart skipped several beats and I had to brace my front legs. Which otherwise would have given way.

Waiting for what little strength I had to return, I stayed like that: a brand-new rescue dog carved in stone, ears up, tail raised, staring at the sea and its promise of joy, as if transfixed by phantoms. It was Jack who misjudged this behaviour.

'Ha! Our Brucie doesn't care for Winston Churchill either,' he exclaimed.

Luckily for my already dizzied mind, the cause of this confusion was obvious to me. He thought I'd been gawping at a white marble statue of a little round human, which looked over the sea from a semi-circular promontory, dead-centre to the bottom of Ginger's road. Her response was swift but controlled. This Winston Churchill thing was clearly an on-going battle between them.

'If I've said it once, Jack, I've said it a thousand times,' she retorted, 'I have nothing against Winston Churchill. I merely resent the damn council sticking him there so we no longer get a full sea view.'

By now dark colours were showing around the kid and his sisters, who were giving Jack looks to kill. By goading Ginger into an argument, he was tainting my arrival at the house. Scrubbing his right hand through his hair, he apologised.

This, however, was Ginger's household, and half a minute later she was the one to cause more trouble. We were still on the sloping pavement beside the rusty gate, which had a two and a zero screwed onto it for number twenty.

'Don't be so damn cheeky!' she scolded Rachael, in response to a quip about the brightly painted front door of the house.

Rachael retorted, 'I was not!'

Jack insisted, 'Oh yes you were! You said Brucie will think Mum's painted it like a boiled sweet!'

'Actually,' corrected Vanessa, 'our Rachael said liquorice allsort.'

'Who the heck cares?' Craig was tickling me between my ears where the hair was patchy but not as bad as it was on my back. 'If Brucie can't cope with his first impression he'll be so freaked by the rest of the house that he'll flee back to the kennels anyway.' It wasn't hard to see that he wanted to end the argument, which stopped as fast as it had begun.

Everyone eyed him and me, and I fancied my fur was already coming back under his loving touch. Probably that's exaggeration.

Ginger's front door really did make my blue moons bulge from their sore old sockets as I peered through a gap in the curvy metal of the gate.

It was the work of an artist and, because the doors of the surrounding houses were pastel, it made my new home, number twenty, stand out so much that it might have been a palace. I couldn't tear my gaze away from it. It was mesmerising and suggested an exciting life ahead.

# 6

Four salmon-pink panels were framed by heavy blue-grey mouldings and the rest of the door was black. Bold would have been an understatement. The brass letterbox was wider than usual and, imagining it might break into a big smile of welcome, I leapt the garden gate, drawing gasps from my astonished family. That felt great. Never mind mange, weakened legs and other problems, I was more impressive than Lassie ever was. Within moments I was hit by the scent of flowers, which left me fainter than an exhausted greyhound that had just run his last race.

The short concrete path I'd landed on was beside a little square garden packed with irises, yellow, pale blue and deep purple. Their petals shone like velvet but the mix of shades was almost too much for my eyes. Looking back, now that I'm one of the oldest rescue dogs alive, this should not have been a surprise. The huge blueness of the sea and the rich colours of the liquorice allsort had been enough for my sickly eyes to cope with.

Dizzy and unable to focus, I needed to rest and good old Ginger understood. She opened the squeaky gate and swept past me to where the house key lay under a brick by the bay window.

'Okay, you bloody barmy lot,' she instructed. 'Leave Brucie to settle in. Otherwise,' she set her shoulder to the liquorice allsort, which was stiff where it caught the frame, 'he'll end up as mad as the rest of us … Oh, blast!' The kids laughed as she fell into the porch.

Under her watchful eye I passed through a glass inner door into a passage that, after a short distance, split into two: the stairs went straight up on the left, and to the right the corridor ended at another door with five oblong glass panes. It was here that a step led into a kitchen, where I glimpsed a grey parrot in a rusty domed cage, which sent shivers through me. Following my stay at the kennels I feared all bars.

'Now he's got an eye on our Picasso,' observed Vanessa.

'Never mind that,' retorted Ginger, before anybody else could speak. 'Each of you is to get on with your own thing and leave him to sleep. I'll make sure he doesn't eat the parrot,' she added, which annoyed me as I'd never harmed a fly in my life. Then she gave me a long, warm look. 'Actually, I couldn't imagine Brucie hurting anything,' she remarked, making me happy again.

A bed of old coats was made for me on the kitchen floor. In a sense it was floating: the tatty lino that covered the boards had yellow seahorses on a turquoise background. A glass mixing bowl, filled with water, stood nearby. That was especially good news. The day was getting hotter and I was so dry I feared my throat would close and starve me of air.

Vanessa was the first to obey her mum's order to let me rest. She went into the front room with the bay window and the fancy gold curtains. Rachael slipped into the adjoining back room while Jack shot upstairs. That left Craig, whose whiteness again made me think of Marcus the kennel lad. I wondered what had occurred between them. Still, it was reassuring that the kid had a spring in his step.

Shooting a cheeky look over his shoulder, he went out of the back door to a concrete yard, leaving me with Ginger and Picasso the parrot. Everything now felt so calm that I sensed the century-old bricks of the house moving. That's another thing that all rescue dogs know. Houses are never silent. They speak non-stop.

Ginger took several moments to adjust to the whisperings. I was standing four-square beside the open glass door, on the step from the corridor. She was no more than six feet away. To her left was a chimneypiece where an old mirror hung at a tilt. The side of her head was reflected in it. The sadness that showed in her eyes as she looked at me set off my itching, which got worse when she showed a touch of white. I was not the only one paying such close attention to things.

Beyond her back Picasso's gaze was fixed on me. He was just a parrot – weird creatures – yet because he had a problem akin to my mange, I was starting to like him.

He resembled a pigeon that had been scuffed by the underside of a moving car, leaving half his feathers on the road. What he made of my own baldy bits I couldn't know. Besides, his beady eye was soon cocked at Ginger's reflection. The best view he could get of her. The words she spoke were soft arrows that found my rescue-dog soul.

'Their bloody father jumped into the sea,' she whispered, confirming my sense of grief flowing through the family, like a small river. 'Help me with them,' she added, while Picasso looked at me. 'Help me with him,' she stressed, putting the seal on my love for her. 'Please, before something else terrible occurs,' she concluded.

She was talking about Craig, and all rescue dogs know that generations of misguided people have put self-hate into the hearts of those born to love their own sex. Which to the old rescue dog I now am is one of the biggest human mistakes ever. It leads to all kinds of destructive – even murderous – behaviour. Often on a grand scale too.

In different circumstances I would have padded to

Ginger, gone onto my hind legs and licked her big damaged nose. That was not what she wanted and I knew that I had passed my first test as a rescue dog. At our best we know when to hold back. Ginger busied herself with chores and I took a long drink of water, at the end of which I noted that Picasso was sleeping with his head tucked under his wing. Eager to be a good rescue dog, I hoped I'd met his expectations.

Instead of resting on my life-raft of coats I went to the bottom of the stairs. It was cool and comfy there. Lying on my side I thought about Jack, Vanessa, Rachael and Craig and how I loved them all. The first three would be fine. I was 99 per cent sure of that. Still, I made a big decision.

Despite the risks to my life, I intended to confirm the wellness of the girls and Jack before focusing on the kid. It was my duty to do so. Ginger had made me see that. 'Help me with them,' she'd said. I couldn't let her down. Any delay would have marked me out as ungrateful for my rescue. I had to begin there and then. It heartened me that Her Hoityness would have approved of my determination to do things properly.

After leaving my place at the bottom of the stairs I nosed through the doorway of the room with the gold curtains. That was where I would find Vanessa. My mission was under way.

# 7

She was sitting on an old sofa while half-heartedly sewing the light blue material that was plumped over her lap, but what really got my attention were the paintings on the walls. Their colours were so rich that I knew Ginger had made them. This was a distraction and it took some effort for me to focus on Vanessa.

She was eyeing the gold curtains and I saw that they were made of thickly woven velvet, which, in places, was threadbare. That explained why they were in the house. Ginger had got them second-hand. I liked their tattiness. It underlined that there was nothing flash about my new family. Still, the cloth Vanessa had intended to work with was sad by comparison and I wanted her to use the gold velvet. It suited her nature. Maybe that drove her on. The bond between rescue dogs and humans is extraordinary in many ways. By now I was curled on a squishy cushion at her side and taking in her scent, which had the healthy sweetness I'd hoped for.

'Velvet is nice, isn't it, Brucie?' she responded,

tickling my ear while staring over her shoulder to the bay window, which faced the sea. Like a hound contemplating a butcher's display. 'And gold's such an inviting colour,' she added, her eye remaining on the curtain.

It was now or never: Ginger had nipped to the bank and could have returned at any minute. Very soon Vanessa had decided. That enticing material was hers for the taking. What happened next was so wonderful that I even forgot how itchy I was.

Red showed all around her while she clambered on the furniture to release the many brass hooks, which had tiny wheels that, under the weight of the tumbling velvet, gave off mouse-like squeaks, setting my ears twitching.

'There,' she declared, as she resettled beside me, with a guilty glance at the fully exposed window. 'She'll never notice.' My tail thumped hard. Ginger's eyesight had seemed good to me.

Vanessa was obviously thinking the same thing. Killing the uncertainty that had entered her voice, she repeated, 'Never,' and scissored the velvet before she could change her mind. It was a great thing to witness. She would have faced a hundred deaths before quitting anything her heart was set on.

The moment for which I'd come into the room had arrived.

I sniffed the air and, although I found much pain beneath the sweetness, I confirmed that her insides were not being destroyed by the acid that's brought on by long-term misery. This might have been a moment for me to have a breather. It was not.

Before I knew it my thinking box went from her to the kid, about whom I already understood three things for sure: first, that he was a natural-born queer; second, that he was desperate to be non-queer; and third, that Marcus Wright, the kennel lad, loved him with all his heart.

The sort of stuff rescue dogs just know.

For a few seconds my all-over itching became all-over pain, as if each of my hair follicles was getting its own electric shock. It was the worst I'd felt so far and the thoughts that caused this were grim and simple. I was a rescue dog but a pointless one. Self-offing or gut rot, young Craig was doomed.

It was then that Vanessa brought me back to the moment. I was lucky that she did. Otherwise I might have given up on my mission before it'd really got going.

'Hey, dog!' she cried, in a way that revealed she had spotted my sadness. 'You're with us now. Everything's going to be okay.' It didn't matter that this was a misreading of my thoughts. Her love lessened my painful itching and I was grateful for it.

It touched me that she had raised one of her furry caterpillars on high. I'd never seen that trick before. It amounted to a question mark and, just to let her know I adored her, I answered with a happy-sounding groan. The knock-on effect was good. Her smile indicated that I needed to avoid expecting the worst for the kid. I had to stay positive. It was the only way forward. Otherwise I had no purpose.

Besides, even if Craig's gut contained an inferno I could still do my best to lower its heat. Her Hoityness would have wanted it of me, as would Ginger, who, after all, had mainly saved my life for the kid's benefit.

But first I needed to be doubly sure that my understanding of Vanessa's inside health was right. All rescue dogs need this certainty. Even young humans who show very little whiteness and have a sweet scent may be in hidden trouble. The gold material that lay on her lap was rumpled like a big rose. I snuggled against it, getting as near to her as I could without being in her way while she sewed.

To Vanessa, of course, I simply wanted to sleep at her side. But the time had come for me to trust my second sight, enabling me to visit her past as if it was occurring in the present.

No sooner did my eyes close than I was surrendering to its power, all to be sure that Vanessa's thinking box was in the same good health as her stomach . . .

# 8

It was the previous summer and Raymond was feeding a long, shiny needle through pre-pressed holes on a leather moccasin. His fingers were brown from where he held cigarettes and black from fixing cars. Alcohol oozed out of every pore, but he seemed content. The slipper-making kit had been a present from Ginger. Vanessa was at his side. They were sitting on the rocks below the promontory where the new statue of Sir Winston Churchill was awaiting its civic unveiling beneath a green tarpaulin. I was struck by their closeness. There was no doubting the love between them. While they chatted, their bare feet dangled in the sea. The lower bits of rock to either side were covered with carpet-smooth green weed. It looked beautiful.

Two ships were on the horizon. To Vanessa's surprise, something resembling a scaffolding bar came from the lead vessel towards the one behind. It landed with a splash that carried towards them. Raymond's calm lessened. It was shell practice, he announced. The quiver in his voice revealed that he was reminded of bad days at sea during the war.

Still, he pressed on with the moccasin. That was brave. But it was Vanessa who made me wish I was there for real and could nuzzle her. I was so proud of her care for Raymond, whose fag-stained beard and moustache were the same dull grey as his bushy eyebrows and unkempt hair. What she said next brought the blueness of the sea all around me again, as if I was now sinking within the ocean, yet was still up top too.

'We all love you, Dad – me, Jack, Rachael and Craig. Whatever you think, we all love you.'

The skinny lips of the four twins had not come from him. His plump lower one trembled, as if he was crying inside. 'I'm not sure I'm lovable, our Vanessa,' he explained, working the needle through the next pair of holes in the sable-coloured leather. 'Not for some time,' he added, mindful not to embarrass her by looking at her – her eyes had filled with tears. They did not spill. In common with her dad she was showing green, and I saw from this that they each understood where Raymond had got to with his life.

Whatever reassurance Vanessa offered, he would never accept he was worthy of his family's love. That put me on the spot. I suspected what had happened between his fist and Ginger's broken nose but felt his loneliness as if it were my own. That was hard to take. I was in sympathy with Raymond, which felt like I cared for the devil. For Venessa it was different.

She could draw on the natural love of a child for her father and it was her big heart that was making her try to reach him. By now I knew she was the kindest of young humans.

When the tide was in, the limpet-encrusted rocks they were sitting on would be covered, as was the case when Raymond later jumped to his death from the promontory. My second sight wanted to take me there but I resisted. There was no point in using part of my precious energy in that way: Raymond was already gone. It was hardly as if his future depended on me. For now I became content to know that, however sad things had got for Vanessa, her alkie dad did not vent his anger on her. The blueness I had been floating in became dark, making me blind. Into this eeriness came voices.

'Make me a promise, Daddy.'

That was Vanessa again.

'Depends what it is, Vee.'

'Give up drinking. For all of us. For the family. Give up drinking. Please?' she asked, as my sight returned. They were now at the top of the beach steps where Sir Winston Churchill was beneath his green shroud.

'I'll make you a promise,' Raymond replied, after a while, his blue eyes flitting to where the sea's sparkles were being killed by a fast-approaching black cloud, 'and that promise,' he continued, touching her chin with the side of his finger, 'is that I'll never again make my family a promise I cannot keep.'

That was even harder for me. I was starting to love him. With some effort I kept Vanessa as my focus. Her brow was creased with thought, but whatever she might have said next did not come.

The cloud from over the sea was on them, with all the chaos to be expected from millions of tiny bodies, with twice as many fast-beating wings. I wondered if what I was seeing was real or if I'd entered the confusion of Vanessa's head. Human nightmares offer up the strangest things.

'Good God!' exclaimed Raymond, spitting one of the creatures from his mouth as he got down low and clasped her to him. 'Good God!' The air was now as black and dense as if it was alive. 'Amazing! Extraordinary!' he continued.

After releasing Vanessa he remained crouched in front of her and watched the swarm as it crossed the promenade, making for the air above a heavily sloped red-topped road that led to the town centre.

'Ladybirds, Vanessa!' He laughed, his hands framing her face as he planted a kiss of reassurance in the middle of her forehead. Seeing him reborn by a freak event of nature she, too, became joyful, her wide green eyes as beautiful to me as anything on earth.

'Ladybirds, Daddy!' She threw out her arms and

looked to where the statue's face was hidden from view. 'Ladybirds, Sir Winston, you old bugger!' she sang, as if the great man was hearing and watching her.

'Ladybirds, Sir Winston, you old bugger!' they crooned, as Raymond led her in a foot-stomping dance around the promontory, an escapade that climaxed with a joint salute at where Sir Winston faced out to sea.

Vanessa's achievement in helping to lift her dad's spirits had been great. What I did not know was just how great. I was yet to discover that Raymond was an embittered boozer because of the war. The placing of the statue at the bottom of the road to mark nearly thirty years since victory over Hitler had driven him into a series of benders that would end in his self-offing.

Yet, hard on the heels of the shell practice, Vanessa had had him laughing at Sir Winston, as if they'd been old pals all along. Today I'm no longer surprised by this.

Many men go in for self-offing, and while in the weeks beforehand their mood may seem upbeat, that which drives them comes from deep within. There, the barbs that tear at souls, hearts and minds do their worst out of sight of others. Destroying happiness. Destroying hope. Making everything too dark for life to continue. My conclusion about Vanessa's wellness, though, was correct. Not only was her mind in good shape, it was also in harmony with her gut: grief at Raymond's death, yes, but minus the long-term pain that was destroying the kid from within.

Vanessa had loved her dad. Her dad had loved her. But he was gone and she was dealing with it. I wished Her Hoityness had witnessed what I'd seen. She would have admired Vanessa's gutsiness. Especially the gold velvet curtain bit.

It was time for me to move on to Rachael.

# 9

I nosed into the back room where Rachael had gone. It was her bedroom-cum-gym and she was counting towards press-up number two hundred. Her power was incredible and her scent even sweeter than Vanessa's. That was good news. If the strength of character I'd seen so far was a front, her tang would have stung my nostrils.

The blue rubber exercise-mat she was using was near a divan, which had a cover showing athletes of every kind. Looking about the rest of the room, I became quite the police dog, seeking hard proof that, as well as being a keep-fit fanatic, she was a team player. The evidence was everywhere.

I saw tennis racquets, hockey sticks, a rounders bat and more, which signalled that she knew how to connect with others. That made me even happier about her. Lone wolves often become lost and no rescue dog wants that for a young human he loves. Plus, a development in her colours since we'd arrived at the house now made me even surer about her future.

Red had become her primary shade, revealing that,

as well as having the grit of a pit bull, she was passionate and loyal. The irony attached to this made my tail do another of its craziest wags. Rachael was full-on when fighting with her twin brother Craig. They were true to each other, though. I felt this as firmly as Sir Winston's marble feet were fixed to his stone pedestal.

'Hello, Mr Big Dog!' she cried, on noticing I was there. 'Watch me do another fifty!' she added, meaning the press-ups, which got faster as I paced around the mat.

Maybe what happened next came about because this energy was so exciting. Or perhaps it was a sign that, despite the problems I faced, I really was going to become a good rescue dog. Either way this time my second sight started up without me trying to bring it on. One second I was pacing the floor, and the next I became young Rachael from some months before. She was reclined in a black chair that was surrounded by all the clobber of a dental surgery. A truly startling transition of scene.

The pig-like eyes of an ageing dentist were close to, and I noted that he was wearing a thick brown wig, which – even though I was now three-quarters Rachael – I would have enjoyed tearing to bits. Just for the fun of it.

Very soon, though, that man made me feel so wolfish I wanted to bite him to the bone, which was no more doable than my instinct to destroy the wig.

Still, I was frightened by my attack of wolfishness and prayed to Her Hoityness for the last bit of my second sight to open. I soon had reason to believe that she'd helped me yet again.

On becoming Rachael, I saw from the dark blue veins that snaked across the dentist's purple skin how he'd been rotted by time. Also his breath was so bad that I imagined his stomach was a mass of ulcers surrounded by trapped food. There was no misunderstanding what this signalled. His was a mean spirit, and because Rachael now had something urgent to say to him, I had to let it come out pronto. Of course the voice I used was hers.

'Absolutely not!' she spat into his face. That shocked him. She was just a young girl trapped in the dental chair where he was bent over her, razor-sharp drill ready for an attack on her mouth. 'Last week you said I needed two fillings!' she continued. 'This week when I've come for those two fillings, you say I need four! You're a conman,' she added, tearing off the thick cloth bib as she got clear of him and his apparatus. 'A Mr No-good who bodges perfectly good teeth for money!'

I saw that when she was fired up, she was a young version of Ginger.

The dentist didn't know how to respond. I doubted he'd ever had a patient stand up to him like that before. My respect for my brave young human grew by the moment. Life wouldn't overwhelm her, as it was doing to her twin brother. The powerful bark that came out of her next would have set Her Hoityness four-square in admiration.

'You ought to be ashamed,' she raged, giving the dentist – whose name was actually Mr Nosgood – a glare to kill, then striding out. It was all I'd needed to see. The feistiest member of Ginger's family was in tip-top shape and I loved her. Her final press-up count was like the bell at the end of a boxing round: 'Two hundred and fifty, Brucie!' she declared, as my second sight closed, bringing her gym-cum-bedroom back into focus.

She flopped to the mat and rolled onto her spine with her eyes shut. Several seconds passed while I waited for her to speak again. 'Two hundred and fifty, Brucie,' she repeated, on opening her peepers to find me standing over her. Our bond was deepening fast, yet these moments were gentle.

Mindful of my sorest areas she reached to the side of my neck and tickled me. This was so lovely that I wanted to curl up on the blue exercise mat and sleep at her side, just as I'd done with Vanessa. Had that happened, I would have flaked out for hours. Or – and especially given what was coming – forever. Dead as a dodo on my first day as a rescue dog.

Instead I stood looking down at her and felt my tail

slow to its mildest wag. I was charmed. She was a wonder to me. Not many young humans would have had the nerve to challenge a dodgy dentist, whose face was just inches from their own.

She was strong. She was gentle. She was a miracle, and before I knew it, my mind-of-its-own tongue was shooting out to lick her nose, which, of all the kids', was most like that of beautiful young Ginger, whom I'd earlier seen with handsome young Raymond in a wartime photograph in the front room. 'Pooh, Brucie! Stinky breath!' She laughed.

Under different circumstances I might have wondered what that signalled about my own insides. Rachael didn't seem concerned. She laughed, kissed my nose and began what I knew were going to be many sit-ups. I padded happily out of her room.

I nearly skipped my visit to Jack. It seemed obvious that, with the exception of Craig, Ginger's family was doing well. This line of thought didn't last long and horrible shivers went through me. My inexperience as a rescue dog had nearly led me into making a big mistake.

It was crucial that I confirmed Jack was also in good health. My sense of urgency renewed, I trotted upstairs.

# 10

He was working at an easel that was dead centre of his room. Apart from an unmade three-quarter bed, and an old dark brown chest with clothes bulging out of its drawers, the rest of the floor was largely taken up by canvases resting at least five deep against the walls.

My discovery that he was such a productive painter might have made me dizzy again but his concentration was so strong that I felt calm. Plus it touched me that he was following in the artist-footsteps of Ginger. Sadly, my relaxed mood didn't last long.

When I saw what the painting was about, the chain of my old life yanked so hard that I almost barked. It was of Elvis Presley, whom my first human used to listen to while smoking home-rolled cigarettes that were thick with something extra. Those were the times when his violence was stilled and his eyes became so soft that I wanted to curl up and sleep within them. Sometimes his on-off friend Pauline shared the smoking with him but never got the same dreaminess in her own eyes, which were an unusual shade of honey-brown and full of the strength his nature lacked.

Still, the cigarettes had an effect of sorts on her, and there was a day when she suddenly faced him and mused that he needed the soulful voice of his hero Elvis because his own soul was like a grape withering on a vine. Then she'd laughed and added that, of all the unhappy men on earth, Elvis Presley was quite obviously the most lonesome one of all. Today that makes me wonder if she could read colours in the same way as all dogs do. Some humans can, and in 1972, Elvis Presley still appeared to be Superman.

Pauline saw the sickness that was already destroying him, and perhaps even admired my first human for feeling the mournfulness in his songs long before most had awoken to the sadness of his life.

'Davey,' she told him, as whiteness and smoke swirled around them, 'you should've been a poet.'

Even now I cannot decide if this was meant to be kind or cruel, and after she left he gave me an extra bit of punishment with the electric cable. That was no surprise, and neither was I taken aback that, on this occasion of my punishment, he sobbed afterwards. I shall never forget the smell of his acid-wrecked gut.

Pauline never visited him again, and while Elvis's early discs gathered dust, my first human constantly played songs like 'Crying In The Chapel'. I felt for him. Did it make me weak? Did it make me gullible? Did it make me his victim? At least after Pauline's attack on him I knew what was going on around me. It was personal and epic.

My first human was all alone with only Elvis's feel for the pain of lost men everywhere to keep him going. If young Jack only half understood this wider context of soulfulness, his portrait was nonetheless unforgiving of poor Elvis Presley. The reds, yellows, blues and golds of the famous jumpsuits dissolved into sickly swirls of white, black and pink. All in all it gave an impression of bloat in which the only precise detail was a bright blue eye that, for reasons I didn't immediately grasp, made me look harder at what he'd painted. Then I realised what I was seeing. Not only was this eye as lonely as my first human's had ever been, it was unquestionably that of Jack's dead father, Raymond, not Elvis.

Maybe Jack knew this. Possibly he did not. Either way my concern was for him, not the two destroyed men depicted on the canvas. Young, naive and inexperienced as a rescue dog, I shook away the unease the painting had brought on and took comfort from knowing that Ginger's elder son was channelling his grief at Raymond's death into his art. That had to be healthy. I also noted his scent was good and decided his gut was not fizzing. That, too, was reassuring.

After thickly loading the palette knife, he added a

slash of crimson to the top right corner of the painting. As if the canvas bled.

'Lie down,' he said, glancing at me with eyes of such intelligence that I wondered if licking his hand would make me as brainy as Her Hoityness.

'Rest, Brucie-Dog, rest,' he added, as I settled on the floor where many splodges of paint had landed that were as much a record of his early work as his finished paintings.

On placing my chin between my outstretched front legs, I allowed my second sight to conjure the bright day of twelve months before, when the statue of Sir Winston Churchill was unveiled by the mayor. Twenty-six years since Raymond had shared in the triumph of VE Day.

# 11

He was very drunk, unclothed and outside the house, where young Jack was encouraging him to come inside. That was when Ginger came storming out and set her outstretched hands to the frame of the liquorice allsort, blocking their way. Black, red and other powerful colours exploded around her. She was in a rage because the housekeeping money had been spent on booze again.

The kid and Rachael were leaning out of the upper bay window and their sister Vanessa was at the opening directly below. They wanted Raymond out of public sight but their mum was having none of it. It was as if she couldn't hear them. They were desperate and their cries overlapped.

'Mum! Mum!'

'Mum!'

'Please! Let him inside, Mum!'

'He'll get arrested for flipping streaking!'

Sensing something terrible to come, I itched so much that it was as if lit matches were being flicked at my body, setting what was left of my coat alight. Just as my first human had twice done to me before I was taken from him. Even that was not as bad as what I was now seeing and, more than anything, I wanted to close my eyes. That was not an option.

Rescue dogs never shy away from what needs to be witnessed. Our job is to understand the very worst that our humans do to each other and to themselves. Ginger was heedless of her own safety. Suddenly the three kids at the windows stopped protesting, and I realised, from their big sad eyes, that they knew what was coming next. Jack appeared helpless to prevent it too. He sagged beside his father, as if his strength had drained away, leaving him weak as a kitten.

'Oh, no, you don't!' his purple-faced mum cried, a blob of spit landing on Raymond, who developed a knocked-sideways expression. 'You don't! You don't come into this house in that state! Pathetic sozzled spendthrift!' she added, and went on with more of the same, drowning out Jack's sad, last-ditch cry for her to let things go, just this once.

Or, at least, that was how it was until she did the opposite of what her son was begging for and came off the high stone step, driving a befuddled Raymond back towards the rusty garden gate.

'Worthless excuse for a man!' she screeched, making me hopeful that they might play growls over serious violence – a notion destroyed by the crunch of bone and gristle, which rattled me from head to tail. Aside from its brutality the blow had precision, which meant it wasn't the first. My suspicion about Raymond's fist and Ginger's nose was confirmed, and it was as well I was there only via my second sight.

Even the calmest of rescue dogs can be taken by extreme wolfishness, and I would have sunk my fangs into Raymond's flesh and gone the same way as Her Hoityness. As it was my gut felt like it had erupted into flame, making me far too hot inside as well as out. That was dangerous. Overheated dogs die.

'Bitch!' Raymond snarled, eyes bulging, mouth and cheeks drawn tight. I glimpsed a terrifyingly black soul. 'Vile, vile bitch!'

All four kids pleaded for him to leave their mum's face alone. The next bit was a minor miracle. For all his drunkenness he heeded them. The second punch was to the side of Ginger's head. She reeled back towards the gaping liquorice allsort, giving me hope that, in swallowing her, the house might save her from Raymond. I suppose I was becoming part of the family insanity. What was done was done, and nothing could change it.

A copper sent from the unveiling ceremony got my attention next. Tall and broad, he had kind brown eyes and, though he was a second too late to have seen the blows Ginger had taken, the blood that was dripping from her nose made the situation obvious.

'Oh, my God!' exclaimed Vanessa. 'Daddy's going to jail!'

'Serve him right!' spat Rachael, who was giving off so much blackness that for a little while I couldn't see the kid at all. That left Jack, who to my alarm was now showing a fair bit of white.

'Mum?' he asked Ginger, whose fingers were cupped over her nose, 'Are you okay?' Rachael cried something about idiots asking daft questions, but I was too intrigued by the copper to take in Jack's reaction.

A different policeman might have torn into the garden and grabbed Raymond, but I judged from the green that showed around him that he was not about to make an arrest. I was right. After a few moments' thought, he rested his right hand on the brick gate post. Despite his continuing befuddlement Raymond clearly took this gesture as an order for calm. For one thing he wanted to avoid being handcuffed.

All eyes then settled on him as he looked at his fist as if he wanted to bite it off. Her Hoityness would have done it for him, and in her own way, Ginger was now equally fearless. Raymond could crush her nose but not her spirit. The stormy movement of the colours around her told me that. She was not going to be his victim.

'Carry on,' she ordered, moving forward again and offering him her bloodied face. 'Do it,' she insisted, to the dismay of Jack, whose hands went over his eyes – he couldn't bear violence. 'Do it, and see how good you feel afterwards.'

There was no doubt about who was in charge now. Her boldness put shivers along my spine, making me cold, when five seconds before I'd been boiling. I wondered how many times Raymond had broken her nose. Had I been able to flee I would have done so. Even the best rescue dogs can take only so much. But my second sight was strong, tethering me to my purpose while the green around the copper darkened.

It struck me then that his gaze was mostly on young Jack. Maybe Ginger saw this. Maybe not. Either way she had a point to make. Raymond could punch her face and head all he liked but she would not be cowed.

'Do it! Weak, weak man!' she cried.

I thought that was it. He'd clout her with all his strength. Perhaps I would have died. Possibly she would have had a haemorrhage. Suddenly I experienced the sensation of being drunk, as Raymond was. It took me a moment to realise why. The hand of the copper was no longer on the gate post.

Jack had found his strength. Jack was wiry. Jack was powerful. Jack was driven to protect his mum. Now everything made sense. The removal of the copper's hand was the signal for him to bring an end to Raymond's violence against Ginger.

After seizing Raymond's clumpy mass of grey hair Jack spun him away from her and tripped him face down into the garden, crushing many irises and releasing the juices that had made me dizzy. A huge moment.

The younger twins and Vanessa were shocked. Their brother had never done anything like that before. His knee was pressed hard into the spine of his naked dad and, as fast as I'd become drunk, I was sober again.

Raymond the wife beater was getting his comeuppance. Ginger was astonished. Things were changing for them all and Jack was the force behind it. It even seemed that the gathering on the promontory for Sir Winston's unveiling had been a part of everything. The copper stayed quiet.

'If you ever,' said Jack, through gritted teeth, as he pulled Raymond's head back so hard that I feared the click of a breaking neck, 'hit Mum again, you'll answer to me, Dad. D'you get that?' he added, giving the hair in his fingers an even stronger pull. 'You'll answer to me. You never,' he hissed, right into Raymond's lughole, 'hit Mum again.'

I wondered if, when he was on the edge of becoming a man, the copper had done something similar to his own dad. He weighed things up while Jack released Raymond and switched his attention to Ginger. 'And you,' he scolded her, 'you just don't have to go at him when he's drunk. You just don't have to,' he added, with an unhappy stamp of his foot, which reminded me that he was still a boy.

Everybody knew what he'd said was true. Ginger looked contrite. Nothing could excuse Raymond's violence, but I'd seen enough to know that theirs was a strange game. It can get that way with humans. Rescue dogs see it all the time. My concern had to be for Jack. That was what Ginger wanted.

Help me with them, Brucie, she'd whispered.

It was essential that I saw how the day ended for him.

Things with Sir Winston's statue were moving on too.

Those who'd watched the removal of the green shroud were clapping, and as far as the drama in Ginger's garden went, that felt right. Raymond would never punch her again.

The show between them, however, was not quite over.

# 12

After patting his bare hips and left breast as if looking for a hanky, Raymond took the head of a maroon-coloured iris and pretend-dabbed Ginger's bloodied nostrils with it. Irritated, she jerked away and turned on her heel. It looked as if she was going to allow the house to swallow her, after all, leaving him to the mercy – or otherwise – of the watchful copper. That was not how things went.

On reaching the high stone step at the liquorice allsort, she paused and set her gaze to where the hallway ended at the glass door to the kitchen off-shoot, through which I guessed that Picasso – whose cage was atop the fridge against the far wall – was staring right back at her. Maybe it was this that made her think again about going inside alone. The old parrot saw into the heart of everything. He could probably have spooked Her Hoityness and even the likes of Sir Winston Churchill.

Or perhaps Ginger was checked by the unusual silence of the twins, each of whom now showed the same shade of yellow, proving to me that they were united in wanting her to lead Raymond inside. Probably she heard those feelings. A mother's intuition.

First, she sighed and turned away from the liquorice allsort. Then she stepped to where Raymond was watching her with the maroon iris head hanging limp in his right fingers. Surprisingly Rachael began to cry. 'Please don't let him get arrested, Mum,' she said.

Ginger looked aside to the copper, who trailed his gaze from her to Raymond, then to the kid and Rachael, who were still side by side at the upper window. It touched me that Craig now put an arm across the shoulders of his twin. On noting this, the copper winked at them.

'Your call, love,' he said, facing Ginger again.

He didn't deserve it but Raymond was about to become the focus of her loving heart. On moving to his side she made a fan of her hand over the wrinkled stump that his dangly bit had become. I couldn't stop myself pitying him, and the thought of what Her Hoityness would have made of me for that still causes me to shudder. My defence is that I was not being disloyal to Ginger. It was her nose that had been broken yet she was now protecting the culprit.

Many humans would have wanted Raymond arrested, and today I accept that within this number there would be those who felt Ginger's reaction was wrong, making her even more of a victim. But I, Brucie-Dog, saw love and a need within her not to destroy Raymond. Especially in front of the twins. Judge me as wrong. Judge me as underrating Raymond's brutality, but don't think I didn't feel for Ginger. Was I right? Uncertainty is an old rescue dog's lot, and on tying things up at the end of our lives – as we're compelled by our natures to do – we cannot alter that. Nothing is black or white. Accepting this is one of the biggest steps we have to take when setting out.

The garden where Jack had brought his dad down had many flattened stalks and crushed flower heads. A right old mess that pathetic pot-bellied Raymond was moving across with rubber ankles. Dismissive of her own injury, Ginger was mindful that he didn't fall and hurt himself. I ached to my core with love for her. 'Come on, Ray,' she said wearily, guiding him towards the liquorice allsort. 'We'll clean up together.'

It was then that my second sight yanked hard on me, as if to tell me I'd seen enough of what had happened that day. It was a risky thing to do but I resisted. Only when I was certain of Jack's well-being would I move on to young Craig. I had to be thorough. Otherwise there was no point in my being a rescue dog.

# 13

It alarmed me that Jack had shown whiteness and was a hero who deserved all I had to give. I already feared that my goal of understanding the kid by the end of the day would exhaust me. Doubly determined to make a success of things, I sought yet more help from a familiar source. 'Please make Jack be okay,' I prayed to Her Hoityness. 'Please,' I begged. 'Please.'

To my relief, all I saw around him next was green, from which it seemed there was no doubting his resilience. Or that, in contrast to the kid, he was well on the way to becoming a strong adult, stomach and head working as one, though right then his face was ashen. I liked that. It implied that, rather taking a thrill from using violence against Raymond, he was stunned by his own actions and what came next confirmed this.

'Stone me,' he remarked, gawping to where the liquorice allsort had been left wide for him to follow his parents into the house. 'Did you see that?' he asked, turning to where Vanessa, Rachael and the kid had watched everything, pug-eyed, from the open bay windows. 'I mean,' he continued, 'did you bloody well see that coming? I didn't,' he confessed.

By now Rachael's tears had stopped, Vanessa was making a question mark out of her right furry caterpillar and Craig appeared awestruck. The impossible had happened. Raymond the tyrant was toppled.

But, far from feeling excited for them, I itched as if I were being eaten alive by maggots. That was because I knew Raymond's days were numbered and the family was soon to suffer hard. The copper's friendly gaze had stayed on Jack.

'Everything under control here?' he asked, with care that made me love him as an added member of the household.

Jack avoided his eye and the silence that came from the others thickened until I could have bitten into it. It screamed at their brother to answer the question. He seemed not to hear. Or want to hear.

Shoving his right hand backwards through his unruly hair, he looked again to the gaping doorway, as if he might obey its lure without saying a word to the copper. The anguish this caused in the eyes of Vanessa and the younger pair made my insides reach their hottest so far. At least I understood why this was so.

Jack was playing with fire that could have burnt the whole family. All the copper needed to hear was that both sets of twins were confident the crisis was over.

It was Vanessa who barked loud and clear: 'Hoi, you!'

she cried at her twin brother. 'The policeman's asking if everything's okay,' she continued, while a mix of bright colours went off fireworks-style around her.

That shook Jack to his core, and as he jiggled his spine, some pink returned to his cheeks.

Rachael grabbed her chance to back up Vanessa. 'Talk to the flipping policeman!' she scolded Jack. 'Tell him, our Craig,' she urged her twin, though rather than doing so he looked warily at his older brother and chewed a fingernail.

Vanessa soon spoke from below again. 'Answer the policeman, Jack! Speak to him, dolt-head!' she insisted.

An unpleasant smile broke on his face. That was not good news. Young Jack had had enough of father figures for one day. Being polite was seemingly beyond him. 'Yeah,' he replied to the copper, without making eye contact. 'We're doing fine,' he added, stepping from the wrecked garden to the concrete path before the liquorice allsort.

'Jack!' Vanessa protested, shooting a pleading look at the copper, who had slapped the top of the gatepost. 'Jack!' she repeated. 'You're being bloody rude, you are!'

After which, her furry caterpillars dropped low. That was upsetting to see and, to my alarm, she now showed a touch of white. The younger twins were so pale that they could have been carved from the same white marble as Sir Winston Churchill.

It seemed that Vanessa's attempt at bossing Jack into being polite to the copper had backfired. Hope was gone from Ginger's family, and without their cooperation, the chances were that he would go official on them. My mood sank in time to the latest silence skewering into my thinking box. I was not the only one under pressure. Vanessa waited. Rachael waited. Craig waited. The copper waited. Eight eyes riveted on Jack, whom I'd come to see was a young human with a streak of honesty so strong he would always have trouble controlling it. Even when the stakes were high for those he loved. Finally, though, he took a deep breath and shaped his skinny lips to speak.

All I needed to hear was confirmation of what the green around him had been suggesting. That despite his insolence towards the copper he was in good emotional shape.

# 14

Jack explained that he felt in charge of the situation
and apologised for being disrespectful. This did not
mean that the twins were out of the woods yet, and
by way of reply the copper kept his gaze on him. This
was not hard for me to understand. I smelt the conflict
he was in. A brutal assault had been committed against
Ginger and his duty as a policeman was to take action.
Or he could trust that the four young people who faced
him had seen the end of the violence against their
mum. A point Jack had already pressed hard.

If you ever hit Mum again, you'll answer to me, Dad.

Taking this at face value was risky and Ginger might
have paid the price with further beatings. Suddenly it
was clear to me why the copper was showing no
colours. He was incapable of making a decision. Clever
Jack had seen this and done his best to be reassuring.

The look he was now giving the copper was intended
to prove he was old enough to be leader of them all. At
that moment I wanted to lick his big beautiful nose. He
was standing up for the family as best he could.

I saw traces of red around the copper. After he'd

unglued his coffee-coloured eyes from Jack, he looked at Vanessa, then to where Rachael and Craig were staring slack-mouthed at him. Maybe it was their openness – they were only fourteen and desperate for the family to avoid humiliation – which helped him to find his voice.

'Well,' he said, shifting his gaze back to Jack, 'they call me Robson. Or Bill, if it suits,' he added, showing more of the redness, which confirmed he felt deeply for them all.

Vanessa's furry caterpillars rose while those of Jack and the younger pair came down from on high. Nobody could have missed the shared hope that their dad was unlikely to be called outside and handcuffed. I was so impressed by the copper's sensitivity that a twitch in my second sight made my tail feel as if it was being tugged inwards at its root. That was dangerous.

Rescue dogs are open to tales that are not ours to follow and something about the copper had got to me. Luckily he stressed where my weakened energies had to stay: helping Ginger's family and protecting the kid from self-offing.

'Any problems in this house you can't manage, you bring them to me. Deal?' He had put extra force into his voice.

Rachael and Craig reacted with greyhound speed. 'Yes!' they cried.

Vanessa was calm: 'Thank you.' She smiled.

And – overlapping his twin – Jack was decisive. 'We'll do exactly that,' he promised.

I loved him even more for that, and the colours that showed around all of the humans were so good that, for five or six seconds, my skin and eyes felt fine. Jack, though, had not quite finished.

'I promise you, Officer,' he continued, giving off so much green that I knew my earlier judgement on his wellness was safe, 'everything will be fine. Won't it?' he asked the others, whose cries of agreement made the copper laugh.

'Everything under control, then,' he concluded, giving Jack a nod and starting the downhill stroll to where those who had attended the unveiling were chatting. Sir Winston Churchill had become the official resident of the promontory and I was at last free to make Craig my sole focus.

# 15

Ginger's cries exploded through the house and into my sleep: 'I'm back! I've been to the bank! I've shopped! I've even booked Brucie for the vet tomorrow! Come on, Artful Bugger, wherever you are!' she added.

Before I knew it I was fully awake, and Jack was grinning down at me from where he was still working on the strange painting of Elvis Presley. 'Hey up, Brucie! Mother Goose is back all right!'

By then I'd lifted my chin from where my front legs were outstretched on the paint-splattered floorboards. This was the best awakening ever and I loved that Ginger was again calling me Artful Bugger.

Plus it did not matter that as I padded from Jack's room my pricked ears were hurting at the roots. Ginger was calling me, and the only thing I cared about was finding her. Two hours at the most had passed since my rescue from Psycho Vet but it seemed like a year.

'Come on, Artful Bugger!' she repeated. Bark after bark escaping me, I cleared the stairs to where she was waiting by the newel post, which marked the halfway point of the ground-floor corridor. No sooner did she get down to my height than I was licking her laughing face like crazy. I wished I could make her bent nose straight.

'He really loves you, Mum,' called Jack, from the top of the stairs.

'Actually,' added Vanessa, 'he really loves us all.'

That was a surprise. I hadn't seen Jack's twin poking her head out of the front room in response to Ginger's shouts (she didn't want to show yet that she was wearing her mum's much-altered gold velvet curtain).

'Of course he does,' agreed Rachael, who had come into the space that ended at the glazed door into the kitchen off-shoot. Red-faced and soaked with sweat, she had an even sweeter tang than when she'd been doing her press-ups.

'You look like you've been exercising hard,' remarked her mum, with pride, which made me even happier to be a part of the family.

By now Ginger had straightened and rested her right hand on the end of the wooden banister rail. I guessed that was because being low down with me had made her legs go stiff. Before I knew it, I'd yapped twice and was offering my right paw. Just to let her know that I truly did love them all. It was a message she understood.

'Well,' she remarked, as shades that brightened the middle of the house came about her, 'it seems we've chosen a wonderfully affectionate dog. In fact,' she concluded, 'he's beautiful.'

For a moment I thought of my scabby skin and feared she was teasing: my first human had taught me I would always be ugly. It was time to put his influence out of my life and I acted fast.

Standing four-square I shook myself from end to end and almost leapt up to lick Ginger's face some more, especially her battered nose. It was as well I decided against doing so.

While Jack, Vanessa and Rachael shared a happy moment of quiet, her eyes did not leave me and I became ten times more determined to save Craig. Looking out for him would be a measure of my loyalty towards them all. Thanks to Ginger, my mission to protect the kid had now become a full-on family thing. I was an all-legit rescue mutt ready for action.

# 16

Twenty minutes later she'd finished rubbing into my skin the pink lotion she'd got from the vet. A temporary measure until I was seen the next day. Despite her light touch it hurt, and only Picasso's watchful eye stopped me whimpering. No rescue dog would show weakness before a parrot unless it was unavoidable. Still, I welcomed the cooling after-effect of the lotion as the first step in my healing.

She left me where I curled up tight on my life-raft and I watched her wash her hands, then put fruit and sugar into a heavy saucepan. After adding water she transferred it to the cooker and turned her gaze back to me. The moment I'd been praying for had come. She was deciding whether or not to send me outside to where the kid had gone earlier.

I wagged my tail, sharpened my ears and set my biggest blue moons towards the rear door of the house. She understood what I wanted and opened the door to a long yard packed with metal dustbins planted with big ferns. Ginger's magic forest of sorts.

Coming on top of what I'd already seen since my rescue from Psycho Vet, this surprise made me dizzy and I was worried she would remember that I needed to rest. What I saw next confirmed the wisdom of this. My sore eyes all but left their sockets.

The faded yellow seahorses on the old blue kitchen lino began to swim around me. Picasso looked harder at me then and I realised he knew what this was about. The risk I was running with my second sight was testing me to the limit, and the immediate results were almost as bad as being zapped with that electric cable.

My aim to press on with helping Craig wavered and I became boiling hot and freezing cold at the same time. For this I blamed the seahorses, believing they had pushed me to the edge of what I could take. It was Ginger who – far from wanting me to rest – now urged me to keep going.

'Go on, Bruce!' she said, in the manner of one who was speaking before she could change her mind. 'Keep my younger boy company!'

It was impossible for her to know how intimidating this was.

To reach the step from the kitchen into the yard I had to pass over the swimming seahorses. That was unsettling enough, but Picasso's fixation on me was becoming even stronger. I couldn't escape his eye. It was more powerful than that of a hawk. Though angered by this I understood it. If I failed the seahorse test the outcome would be severe for Craig. Fatal even.

After all, with the amount of white he'd been show-ing, there was no saying when he might try to off him-self.

Yellow showed around Ginger, and I knew her worry about the kid was severe. I stood up in readiness for ac-tion. As I did so the seahorses stilled. On seeing me peer closer at them, Ginger laughed. 'Brucie love! The seahorses aren't real!'

I felt my tail wagging and looked to where Picasso's cage stood atop the fridge to her left. Humans, we knew, did not always see what was going on. With a swift movement of his head he plucked a feather from the underside of his wing and dropped it to the cage floor, challenging me to be bold. 'The seahorses aren't real!' he mimicked.

'Hurry now, Brucie,' Ginger said, through a burst of laughter at the cheeky parrot. 'Find my Craig!' she in-sisted.

It was impossible to resist her and, having padded over the lino, I was soon standing where the sun shone hard on the concrete outside.

'Keep going, Brucie,' called Ginger, as I peered through the ferns. I saw that the back door to an old brick workshop was done the same black, grey and pink as the fantastic liquorice allsort. That was reassuring, and her next words made me glow with pride. 'Keep

Craig happy! Be his dog! And don't pee on my ferns!' she added, making the temptation for me to do so irresistible. Exactly as she'd intended.

I cocked my leg where the largest fern-tree grew in a bin with '20 Sea View' painted on its side, my new home, where everything between me and the kid was set to begin. It was so big a moment that I was extra grateful for Ginger's sense of fun.

'Oh, you artful bugger!' She laughed as I headed towards the colourful door with my raggy tail up like a half-moon. Craig. The kid. My kid. The sooner I reached him the better. There was no time to waste. And no turning back.

Her Hoityness would have been impressed.

# 17

I was struck by the heat of the workshop. Mainly this was because its flat top was made of clear plastic sheeting – a big window through which the sun poured in. Plus the kid was on his right knee, welding a strip of steel into the side of a big red car, with the blue oxy-flame making the air so dry my nostrils felt as if they were stuffed with wire wool.

On becoming dizzy, I made myself concentrate on Craig, who was still wearing the black T-shirt, blue jeans and scuffed brogues he'd come to the kennels in. I soon realised that, if I was going to avoid collapsing, I had to lie down, weakness that was not only because of the hot, dry air. Now that my mission was at last focused on the kid, I was about to learn something basic to his make-up. I had no choice. Very soon my second sight excelled itself.

I found myself in a grey-painted ship where handsome wartime-Raymond was spewing into a galvanised bucket. I saw blood. Despair rots humans from within.

Another sailor looked on. Like Raymond, he was in his early twenties. They were in a small windowless area with cold steel walls, cold steel decking and a cold steel roof. I guessed it was a nook to which those who felt done in by the war escaped. The only light came from a weak overhead bulb, which was protected by a thick glass cover secured with a wire cage. It was all very hard, and as the sea pounded the hull, I felt its cruelty.

Raymond looked up from the bucket. His eyes were strikingly blue and I realised that he was crying. His jet black beard and moustache were messy. My heart went out to him. The gaze he fixed on the other sailor was sad. He was at the end of his tether.

'Jesus Christ, Oliver,' he said. 'Endless, endless bloody slaughter.'

That got my ears up. Oliver came forward. Where black had been showing around Raymond, Oliver's shade was red. As the gap between them closed, each colour cancelled out the other, a sure sign of those in love. Whatever had happened to make Raymond into a queer-hater, Oliver was involved: bone knowledge, carried by Craig since before his birth. The engine room thrummed beneath my paws. It didn't miss a beat.

Oliver crouched. He and Raymond were now face to face over the bucket. For some moments I was terrified of where my second sight might go next. Then I remembered that this was all about helping the kid. I, Brucie-Dog, now became young Raymond. 'Movie-star looks' understates the handsome face I was peering into.

Oliver had hazel eyes, plump lips and a medium-sized nose with a slight curve. He placed his hand on my right shoulder and gripped me hard. 'It's just war,' he argued. 'War,' he repeated, with an emphasis that cut clean through me. This was ironic. His voice had an Irish edge, which was normally like a warm liqueur. I remembered in *All Quiet on the Western Front* where the infantryman reaches for the butterfly and is killed. That was the First World War. Our war was the same. All beauty was being destroyed. Even the gentleness of Oliver's voice.

For three years I'd got by, a reluctant participant in what I considered to be madness, and I knew Oliver felt the same. At least the ship on which we served was not an outright killing machine, such as the big destroyers were. She was one of the smaller vessels that protected the North Atlantic convoys. I was an able seaman assigned to radar, Oliver a petty officer cook. Before the war he'd been a ballet dancer. Since 1939 we'd seen and been through the most appalling things. Ships that were literally blown apart, and always there was the fear of U-boats. I lived every second of every minute in terror.

The fear was a cage whose bars I could rattle but not break. In a way that, too, was ironic. Most parts of the ship were so damn cold you'd have thought my grip might shatter anything, the bits falling away like broken glass.

Then in February 1942 we were torpedoed.

Nothing can prepare you for that. The noise was incredible, the vibration through the decks as violent as an earthquake, then the sinking. Another maritime grave in the making.

Many were killed outright. Those trapped below were even worse off. They drowned in waters as dark as they were cold. Young men. Death. Death. Death. Again. Again. Again. Things up top were no picnic for the blast survivors either.

If the waves are high they smash your limbs, or they're so icy that, within ten minutes, you're done for anyway. And that's without taking into account the oddity of a sea that is ablaze. Get too close and your skin melts, like wax. Our lives meant nothing. I lived in terror and I lived in anger. Hating the war. Hating myself. Hating life. Then Oliver saved me from what I feared most of all: dying.

# 18

The torpedo had destroyed the hull below the rear deck. Within a minute the bow was lifting hard. Two lifeboats were launched. They were full when they reached the water. The options for others such as me were stark. Stay aboard with the men trapped below or go into the sea and die anyway. I chose the latter. The cold made it feel as if I were swimming through wet concrete that thickened by the moment.

Burning fuel floated in crackling islands of red, yellow, orange and blue. A gunner who'd been beside me was sucked into one. His face melted while he screamed for his mother. When he stopped I lay on my back, letting the current take me where it liked.

Death from cold, death by drowning, death by fire, death by breathing in the foul black smoke that obscured much of the sky, my exact end made no difference. My number was up. I was convinced of that. The nearest flames seemed to understand. They roared higher as if angered by my calm. It struck me that perhaps this was the devil. Maybe I'd gone crazy. Extreme fear gets you like that.

It was then that I was gripped as if in a vice. It took me a moment to realise what was happening. I was locked in the rescue position. Oliver was swimming us clear. After a short distance he let go and I swam with him. He'd given me back my fight. I wanted to live. He looked aside and, despite our fast movements, his eyes stayed on me. I knew then that I loved him.

'Come on, Ray!' he cried, putting in even greater effort. 'Come on, Ray!' He was taking the lead and I saw that he'd dived from one of the lifeboats to get me. We had thirty yards to go. The dozen or so men who were aboard were hollering like mad. If we didn't speed up one of the fires might change direction and consume them. Several stood up and wielded their arms as if drawing us forward.

'Swim! Swim! Swim!' they cried, again and again.

We were passing the destroyed ship, a hundred yards to our right. Groaning like a sick old monster that knew its time had come, it was upended, pointy bow to the sky, big anchor hanging at a funny angle.

Several men clung to the rail of the forward deck. They faced the seaward drop as if readying to do press-ups. They were doomed. I swam harder, making my limbs work when giving up would have been easier. Oliver sensed this increased determination. When he shouted next, his voice had hope in it. I could make it to the waiting lifeboat. He knew that. 'Faster, Ray!' he urged. 'Faster!'

He'd stopped just short of the lifeboat. 'I won't go without you!' he threatened, making me responsible for his survival. 'Quicker! Quicker! Quicker!' I heard from the other men.

I was close now and got carried forward by the surge as the ship began her slide. That was lucky. It might have driven me sideways, away from rescue to more fires on the sea. Oliver shouted again. 'Please, Raymond, please!'

His right hand was now on the white-painted rim near one of the rowlocks. Pulling him aboard would have been easy. Deliberately he held himself at an arm's length. Had those in the boat begun to row away they'd have had to hit him with an oar. It was a heroic gamble. I wasn't surprised. I'd always known he was strong at heart.

'I'm not going without you!' he shouted again. 'You have to swim harder,' he insisted. Again the flames were listening. Or, at least, that was how it seemed. A tongue of orange came from the biggest mass, licking over the grey water to my left. That sent an added bolt of fear through everybody.

'Harder!' Oliver screamed, as if I was not putting in enough effort. It was unnecessary. Thanks to him, I'd got this far and I wasn't slacking off now. Besides, there was another terror to overcome.

I tasted oil. I'd missed that out of the equation: death by swallowing oil. Clenching my lips and hardly daring to breathe, I entered a tarry slick. It was hell to get through. Ten seconds that felt like an hour.

Once clear I became faster, not with the sole purpose of surviving but also of reaching Oliver who, still holding onto the lifeboat, was beckoning me forward with his left hand. Drawing me forward with his left hand.

'Swim, Raymond!' he hollered, as a lick of flame came close.

'Swim!' he roared, as I heard the ship's final groan and her bow went under.

I had to be with Oliver. There was no time to worry about what that meant, or how my life was changing. I swam like fury.

# 19

We headed for a patrol boat, which had thrown a scrambling net over its side. It waited while the convoy moved on from where a U-boat had also been sunk. A big man was standing at the side rail. I guessed he was the captain. For some moments he held binoculars to his eyes. Then he shouted. We were not near enough to make out his words, but his message was obvious.

Vessels that paused in those waters were sitting ducks. The captain shouted again. Pretty soon we were close enough for me to see that he had a large grey beard. We all knew that if we took too long he would leave us behind. Those who were at the oars redoubled their effort. Though the swell wasn't bad, we rose and fell hard. Everything was precarious. Our lives were in the balance.

My eyes met Oliver's. Since I'd been hauled aboard I'd avoided this. It was wrong. Real men did not crave other men. That was a basic fact. He was sitting directly opposite me. We both shook with cold. Miraculously neither of us had been burnt. Some of the others were not so lucky. I looked away from him.

One sailor was cupping skin that had melted from his lower face within his hand. He must have sensed me staring. When his gaze shifted to mine I was struck by the hopelessness in his eyes. There was nothing I could do or say to help. The state he was in made me sick at heart. It was a reminder – as if I'd needed it – of just how greatly I hated the war.

I could not resist facing Oliver again. It was no surprise that he was still staring at me. He'd been doing so ever since we'd taken our seats, no more than two feet between us. What happened next took me by surprise. He leant forward and put his mouth to mine. Under different circumstances I might have pushed him away. I wasn't queer.

My lips parted and for five seconds it felt as if the sun shone where my heart was. It was the most beautiful thing I'd ever experienced. When he stopped kissing me, I opened my eyes. The side of our rescue ship loomed over us. It was a wall of grey steel. Men were already climbing the scrambling net. Above them, the captain was looking directly down at me and Oliver. Too scared to contemplate what this meant, I returned my gaze to the sailor with the burnt face.

He, too, was in his early twenties. This time I did not break eye contact. To do so would have been cowardly. I knew what he was thinking. There was no way he could make the climb. It was vertical. The ship was heaving up and down. He would have got so far up and fallen back, like a shot seagull. If ever a death warrant had been signed it was his. It felt wrong to leave him. I glanced at Oliver. We stood up and spread our feet for balance. Within moments we'd nearly tumbled.

'Put your arms out,' advised Oliver. I did as he'd suggested. A moment of clumsiness could have spelt death for us both. We looked to where the burnt sailor had remained seated. He seemed to have shrunk. My sadness for him made me feel leaden. Again, I didn't know what to say.

It was like we were his brothers seeing him off on a long journey. He kept the molten part of his face within his hand. We all knew what was coming for him. The captain shouted, 'Come on, pansy-boys! No time for cuddles.'

I felt Oliver flinch. Our kiss had been seen. It had been impossible to miss. Lifting his head as best he could, the burnt sailor smiled up at us with his eyes. He was about to die but wanted us to know that the captain's words sickened him. I wish I'd learnt from him. The engines that thrummed below the water line got louder. The captain roared, 'Come along, daisies!'

He had a point. A torpedo could have destroyed the ship at any second. Oliver's kindness got the better of him. 'You'll be all right, mate,' he reassured our companion. We all knew it was a ridiculous lie.

The captain roared again and the burnt sailor struggled to clear his throat, which must have been scalded inside. It was then I realised his job had been to keep the decks clear of ice. His lower teeth showed where his lip used to be. He was trying to speak. I willed him to find the words. They came as a broken croak: 'They called me Derek.'

By now he'd taken his bum from the plank that served as a seat and shifted it to a space between two of the rowlocks. Pushing with his feet he made himself go backwards to where he sank like a stone. Oliver put one hand to the scrambling net. The engines were vibrating hard. The patrol boat was about to go. 'You three pansies!' thundered the captain. 'Get a move on!' he ordered.

That confused me. I wondered if he'd missed Derek going over the side. Then Oliver said something, which made me to look to the rear of the lifeboat. We were being observed by a man called Heston, who, like Oliver, was a petty officer cook. He was known as 'The Watcher'. My suspicion over what this meant had prevented me from asking why. I'd sought to avoid him.

He was well built yet able to move without making a sound, and I'd always found him unnerving. Occasionally it had been disturbing to find him eyeing me as if he knew something I didn't. Despite the tar-thick oil clinging to my skin, I felt as if the hairs on my neck were rising. The glint in his eye was that of one with two rodents cornered.

The captain screamed more abuse but the Watcher was unfazed. On getting up from where he'd been on the end bench, he, too, spread his limbs for balance and tugged at his crotch. We knew what that meant.

It was the 1940s. Queerness was illegal and blackmailers had ways of tormenting their victims. The smirk on his face made me want to smash his head. That was new. I'd never hit anyone before. Violence repulsed me and I considered myself a pacifist. Oliver calmly suggested that we should begin climbing. It went through my mind that he'd already dealt with homo-haters. The Watcher shrugged and laughed. His left hand was now gripping the scrambling net. Every second was vital but his priority was to make clear the ground between us.

'So …?' he asked, with a wink, as if we were his oldest friends. 'Who's the bitch?' That shocked me. Like a hand grenade going off within my heart. Precisely as the Watcher intended. His work done for now, he began his climb to safety.

He was strong, I'll give him that. Soon he was halfway up the scrambling net. Oliver touched my shoulder. It was like an electric shock. I turned to him. Our eyes locked. 'Take no heed, Raymond, mate. Men like him are all bluff,' he said. Giving an upward tilt of his head he added, 'Captain Big Mouth, too, for that matter.'

That was easy for Oliver to say. He wasn't married like me. He wasn't normal. The grenade within my chest had done its job. I felt empty and wondered if I truly had gone insane while I was in the water.

Briefly I envied Derek, who'd gone over the side and drowned. He was out of it. I'd allowed myself to do something disgusting and lost my right to call myself a man.

I was college-educated. I knew the implications of queerness. It was only forty years since Oscar Wilde had been sent to jail. Men like Oliver were criminals. I almost believed he'd saved my life to queer me. The patrol boat was beginning to move. Any second and it would surge away, leaving us in its wake.

Peering upwards I saw the Watcher clear the rail and speak with the captain, who shook his hand. That didn't surprise me. I'd already decided he was a man who could talk his way out of any situation. They looked down on us. That really put fear through me. I sensed they were pausing to see if we would climb or take our chances. The sight of two queers adrift on one of the cruellest seas in the world would probably have given the Watcher his best kick ever.

I turned back to Oliver. His were the most beautiful eyes I'd ever seen on a man. I'd noticed that at the beginning of our friendship. They hid nothing of his nature. Right then, they were bleaker than Derek's when he'd realised he couldn't climb to safety. The engines got louder and vibrated even more. Our lifeboat could have been tipped over.

It was time to move or die. Throwing up my right hand, I set a foot on the net and began to go up. No wall of steel could have beaten me. Each heave was proof of my masculinity. Oliver was the queer. I would trust the captain to see that.

I felt movements from behind. Oliver, too, was climbing. The patrol boat surged. We had made our escape from death.

# 20

I cleared the rail five seconds ahead of Oliver. The captain was waiting for me. I saw that his grey beard had lingering traces of rich ginger and noted that his eyes had lost something. Though still dark blue the impression they gave was of grey. These thoughts were fleeting. There was nothing unusual about the war leaving its mark on those tasked with leading young men into death. The only thing anybody could do was keep going, and the captain was no exception.

By the time Oliver was also on deck we were doing a semi-circular manoeuvre, back to where the U-boat had been blown up. The Watcher was seated at a Vickers machine-gun. It struck me that he looked at home. Horribly so.

Most of the smaller protection vessels had these weapons. They had a steel shield to the front and could be spun from side to side. No sooner did I realise what was going on, than my heart froze. So did Oliver's, I'm sure. We were heading for thirty or so Germans in the sea. They were in two groups, treading water, forty yards apart. The Watcher did not look aside. His finger was ready on the trigger. The captain's gaze stayed firmly on us.

We stopped near the first group of Germans. I could see their eyes. The Watcher's face was impassive. For a moment I felt pity for him. He was as queer as they came. The depth of loathing he felt for himself must have been deeper than the ocean below our feet.

Oliver threw up. The acid churning of my own gut made me feel weak. I was in a nightmare I could not escape. Nobody disobeyed a captain. A bit of Oliver's puke had splashed his well-polished black boots. He looked down at it, then back to Oliver, who kept glancing beyond the Vickers gun to where the U-boat survivors were. The horror on his face was absolute. The captain scowled at Oliver as if he were the vilest creature on earth.

Beyond him some of the Germans, who had been alive a minute before, were face down in the sea, dead from the cold. Others tried swimming for the scrambling net but an order had been given for it to be pulled aboard. That has always been in my worst nightmares. Their only hope snatched away at the last second. The captain spoke to Oliver. He was like a judge delivering a sentence.

'War is no place for pansies,' he said.

Two sailors came close and stood to attention. They were given an order for Oliver to be taken below. As he was led away he looked over his shoulder at my face. I'd like to say that his sadness disturbed me. That would be untrue. It was the pity in his eyes that got to me. I was about to become a lost cause and he knew it. The captain's gaze rested on me. It softened as compassion entering his voice. 'You, laddie,' he said, 'we can fix. Do it,' he ordered the Watcher.

The firing began. None of the other sailors on board watched. By now the scrambling net was fully up. I saw a shoe within it. That gave me something to concentrate on. I couldn't look at the men who were dying. It was soon over. The worst was yet to occur.

The Watcher swung sideways on the movable gunner's seat. That meant he was now facing me and the captain. Using the strength of his arms to propel himself forward, he sprang off, and landed on his feet. It was an impressive move. Neither excited nor distressed, he stepped aside to give me clear access to the Vickers gun. The meaning of this was clear. My turn to do the killing. Seeking distraction, I wanted to untangle the shoe from within the squares of rope. The captain barked so hard I felt as if I'd taken a torpedo to my midriff.

'Look him in the eye, laddie!'

I had no choice but to stand fully upright. My head wanted to rebel but my guts made me obey. It was a point of family disgrace that an uncle in the First World

War had been shot for deserting. Obedience was hard wired into me. The Watcher's eyes were blue, like mine. There was no feeling in them. They were like the cold flames of burning oxygen. He had advice to give. It changed my soul.

'Way to do it,' he said matter-of-factly, 'is to think of them as queers.'

The captain gave a grunt of approval. Killings like this were explained as acts of mercy. Some whispered that they were murder. I couldn't help looking beyond the Watcher's shoulder. The redness where the shot men floated was already going and soon would be no more. Their lives had counted for nothing. The captain's gloved hands were behind his back. Without stepping nearer he leant forward and put his mouth to my ear. 'War is for men, laddie,' he whispered. 'Men.'

The other sailors were watching now. It was obvious that I was a virgin at 'mercy-killing'. The Watcher stood with the captain as I got seated at the gun. Setting my finger to the trigger, as I had seen done a minute before, I knew I was entering a place from which I could never return.

The second group of U-boat survivors was to my right. Several of them, too, had now died from the cold. I was grateful for that. Their deaths would not be my doing. Bracing my feet, I swung the gun into position. Again I could see the eyes of the Germans. Rising and falling with the swell, those men were deadly silent. I felt accused.

It crossed my mind that killing the captain and the Watcher would have been easier. Within a trice I realised that the gun could not be turned far enough to get them. I think I laughed. I think I cried. I know I shat myself. The stink made me ashamed.

'Queers,' urged the Watcher. 'Just think of them as queers and it's fun.'

The captain cleared his throat. There was no choice. I squeezed the trigger and swung the gun wildly. Several of the Germans flipped upwards. Like big fish that had become electrified. I roared over the phat-phat-phat of the bullets. 'Queers! Queers! Queers! Queers!'

I'd never known ecstasy before. Every bit of me became hard. Even when they were dead I kept going until the bullets ran out. Then it was silence. I was spent, used up, mercifully purged of my love for Oliver. Or so the captain seemed to believe.

'There now,' he concluded. 'A real man for a real war.'

His confidence reassured me. I had an official seal on my normality. I'd done what was necessary. War. Fought like a man. The captain turned on his heel and left me to the care of others. Already our nifty patrol boat was doing another U-turn and would soon rejoin the convoy. A tiny incident was over. In the big picture it was nothing and all eyes avoided mine.

I leapt from the gun to the deck. The Watcher lit two cigarettes. He handed one to me and I drew hard on it. Tobacco had never tasted so good. We smoked in silence. The grey sea passed to either side as we cut through the waves.

The scrambling net was stored. One of the men threw the stray shoe overboard. Neither he nor his companions looked at us. We were in a bubble, a glory bubble, such as it was. Flicking his cigarette butt aside, the Watcher picked his moment to speak: 'So now you're an internationalist,' he declared, with a sly smile.

That foxed me. I didn't have a clue what he meant. Stringing my puzzlement out, he lit more cigarettes and handed me a second. I took a couple of drags before admitting my confusion. It irked me that he'd waited for this. I was being teased. He put his mouth close to my ear. Like the captain had done. Cigarette smoke was breathed over me.

'Russia, Germany, Japan, Australia – Jews, Christians, Arabs, Eskimos: the entire fucking planet,' he whispered. 'What unites us all?' he asked.

I knew the answer. Knew it in my bones. But waited for him to say it anyway.

'Queers,' he confided. 'Queers.'

I wondered if he was proud of his knowledge of the world's workings or simply laying it on thick for effect.

Either way it made no difference. He'd a point to make and nothing would stop it coming.

'We all, every last man of us, we all hate queers,' he concluded.

I shuddered. The truth of what he'd said was undeniable. Maybe it was why men needed to kill each other. Maybe it was why the war had occurred, men needing to be men, to be normal. Something like the Lloyds Bell sounded inside me. Very nearly I'd become wrecked on the rocks of homosexuality. Oliver had been to blame for that.

The Watcher was still bent forward with his mouth near my ear. He blew more smoke against me. Flicking his cigarette in the same direction that he'd sent the first butt, he laughed, straightened his back and strode off. I felt as if my feet were bolted down. I stayed there for a long time. Even the cold and the rain that came didn't get to me. Three hours later a torpedo sank us.

# 21

The captain was grey now all right. His body floated with others on the oily swell. I was one of the luckier men, treading water in the hope that one of the remaining patrol boats would come back. It didn't always work like that. Survivors might be left to die or the enemy commit a mercy killing.

The Watcher was alive, too. One of the lifeboats had been blown to bits. He was clutching a piece of keel with planking attached to it. It shocked me that, amid the life or death aftermath of the sinking, he was staring at me alone.

'I know you, Watcher,' I called, as a wave lifted me high and lowered me again. 'I know you're queer.'

I hadn't pre-thought this. The words simply came. He went on staring while black smoke drifted between us. It was like he was a silent demon. Unseen one moment, visible the next, watching, watching, until I had to look away from him.

The coldness of the sea was making my bottom half feel like lead. Three more minutes and I knew I'd be dead. I would have preferred the company of Satan to that of the Watcher. I didn't have to look at him again to know that his eyes hadn't left me.

Suddenly there was shouting. Half a dozen men who'd been in a nearby cluster were swimming like fury. They were escaping a fast-moving island of orange flame. Crackling and spitting, it threw off tremendous heat. I looked back to the Watcher. Not even the threat of being cooked alive seemed to affect him. It was then that I heard Oliver. He was yelling from behind me.

'Raymond! I need help! Raymond!' he pleaded.

The Watcher heaved more of his torso onto the planking. He was intrigued to see what I'd do next. Oliver was close to the flames, which the others had only just escaped. His big hope of rescue was me. From my very gut I wanted to go to him. Making my arms and legs do the required swimming was impossible. I could not move them.

Somebody to my right called out. A patrol boat was coming, scrambling net lowered. Assuming that a torpedo wasn't fired at it, we might all be safely aboard within two minutes. Most of the men in the sea were shouting and waving their arms. One or two reached out to exhausted crewmates and tried to keep them afloat. Oliver got louder: 'Raymond! I need help! Raymond! Raymond!' Words that would never leave me.

Thirty feet at the most separated us. His eyes were wide with disbelief that I hadn't started to swim his way.

There was still time for me to save him. I saw then that his arm was broken. The arrival of the patrol boat was a distraction. Men began to climb the scrambling net. If I wasn't quick I'd be left behind. Oliver became hysterical.

'Help me!' he screamed. 'For the love of God, Raymond, help me!'

The fire took him. Those who were aboard were bellowing for me and the Watcher to swim for it. They'd written off Oliver but I'd known men to come out of those fires alive. Suddenly I had a plan.

I was going to dive under and pull him clear. I knew it could work. I'd done it when saving others earlier in the war. On those occasions it hadn't been our ship that was torpedoed but I'd always volunteered, though of course I was not in love with the men I'd fought to save. The difference was critical.

For the second time my limbs refused to work. I simply couldn't make myself go to Oliver. In desperation I looked to the Watcher. More black smoke drifted between us. Still his gaze was fixed and I knew that there was no hope of him swimming in place of me. To be fair it was too late anyway. Seconds were critical in such situations. There would be no grabbing Oliver from below now. That left just me and the Watcher, to whom, suddenly, I was very close.

The last of the others had cleared the scrambling net

when, as if by godly power, I'd been carried to the bit of keel he was clinging to. My hands locked on it. Making us eye to eye. His calm was remarkable.

'All of this,' he remarked, in a spooky echo of Oliver's earlier statement, 'is just war.'

We both knew otherwise. I'd allowed Oliver to be taken into the fire because he was queer. I tried to let go of the wood that was keeping me afloat but my fingers wouldn't uncurl. Fate was making sure I would live in guilt for what I'd done. The pleasure this gave the Watcher showed as cruelty in his eye, and a gut need to be rid of him gave me the strength to swim for the patrol boat.

The Watcher did likewise. I was certain that, had I stayed to die like Oliver, he would have done the same thing. My treachery had become the bar of a career blackmailer's survival. We were soon safely aboard. A wash broke in our wake as the dead were left behind.

We rejoined the convoy and I was pronounced fit for service. Little did they care that a sane young artist, who'd married his childhood sweetheart, died that day. I'd become me, one of the many thousands the war left walking yet destroyed within.

# 22

Three seconds had passed. That's how it can be with our second sight, big chunks of human life explored in canine-time, often revealing tough experiences at great risk to rescue dogs. What I'd discovered about Raymond and Oliver in the 1940s had left me even weaker than before and the words of the Watcher echoed in my thinking box: We all, every last one of us, we all hate queers.

That was more profound than he'd known. Since the start of time humans have made a problem of men loving men, their shared bone knowledge becoming so dark that self-offing for queerness has long been an everyday event. Older rescue dogs see best why this rabies of the human spirit continues to thrive far and wide.

For one man to allow another to be within his body is seen as an act of submission. Men allowing themselves to be bitched. Or – just as bad – men bitching other men, all done in the light of fear that adds to the hatred against and within queers. At least the sly Watcher would have understood this better than most.

Brown-hatters, pâté-prodders, shirt-lifters or bum-chums, the abuse against queers has always been lurid but the biggest terror of homo-haters everywhere is of men such as themselves being seen as womanly. Or at least unmanly – a perception that any rescue dog may well become wolfish at.

To us, love is love, and what pains us most is that many young queers have to suffer life-threatening loneliness before they learn that sharing is trust, with the coupling of male bodies as natural as the love between men and women. Or by females who are also natural-born queers. Why else would humans be driven to make love if it was otherwise?

Still, after what I'd seen of Raymond and the betrayal of young Oliver, who'd loved him, I now knew for sure what I was up against when it came to saving the kid from his own bad bone knowledge and high likelihood of self-offing.

Self-loathing at what Raymond had done to Oliver was the poison Craig had inherited from his dad, and I had to hope that this would not destroy him before he'd discovered that being queer was something he might even celebrate. Especially with happy-natured young Marcus in his life.

As things stood, though, his situation couldn't have been worse. From the moment he was conceived, his lousy bone knowledge was set for conflict with his natural-born queerness. Hatred, treachery and killing: the odds against him becoming at ease with himself were so low that my mind whirled with a twin mystery.

Why wasn't the kid permanently shrouded in white? And what had stopped him self-offing before I was around? There was only one word to describe these thoughts. Terrifying. They took me near to accepting that, no matter what I did, Craig was doomed to a brief, miserable existence in which his gut would be burnt, twisted and otherwise tortured by stresses he could not escape. I itched, shivered and shook as if I was about to be consumed by the enormity of everything.

'Help me,' I prayed to Her Hoityness, who must have been listening, as very soon I saw that fighting for my own life – as she had growled for me to do – also meant fighting for the kid's. That pulled me sharp.

Breaking my bond with Craig because of his bad bone knowledge would have been disloyal to the four twins, their mum and even Raymond, whom, despite his violence against Ginger, I couldn't bring myself to hate. Maybe this touches on why rescue dogs are so important. We accept that bad deeds flag up a sad personal history. After all, ill-treatment leads to ill-treatment and a dog that's been kicked about when young will bite first. Likewise human behaviour everywhere.

With what hope I could muster I looked to Craig,

99

while he calmly continued with his welding, and read his colours.

To my relief I found several bold shades, including much crimson, which proved that he loved what he was doing with the big red car. This fitted well with my discoveries about Rachael, Vanessa and Jack. On the plus side, life at number twenty was rich with creativity, which fed the souls of both sets of twins, making them stronger than they otherwise would have been.

Vanessa had her dressmaking, Rachael her sport, Jack his art and Craig his workshop, all of which was so exciting that I now contemplated exploring Ginger's past after all. Another potential mistake.

I had to stick with Raymond and the kid, whose own creative streak signalled that I'd underrated his strength. That put his bone knowledge in a new light. It was bad but not impossible for him to overcome it. I was determined to know everything about him. 'Thank you,' I told Her Hoityness, for making me feel brave again. 'Thank you,' I repeated, sure she could hear my thoughts.

# 23

I saw how things had gone at home for Craig. The bullying would have begun years before he knew that, in the eyes of his queer-hating, queer-fearing dad, he was not manly enough. 'Brucie-Wucie-Lucie-Darling!' he'd cried at the kennels. That was a sign of his innocence, and I could identify with his old hurt at Raymond's disapproval. I, too, had been there. Not understanding why my first human had made me into his Runt had been the hardest thing of all to deal with. But at least I'd learnt something from it, and Ginger's wish for me to be with Craig now made even more sense than it had earlier that day.

For all that he was part of a big family, Raymond's attitude had left Craig in an isolated place. He was going to get all the companionship I could give him. That was what Ginger wanted from me. To help with his healing.

Shaking myself from end to end, I defied my legs to buckle. I was a rescue dog with a duty to be strong, though before I allowed my second sight to whisk me into his past, I wanted more details about his life with cars, making me quite the detective dog.

Peering beyond the spot where he was at work I saw a second reason why the clear-topped workshop was so light. The double-width up-and-over door at the front of the building was fully raised, revealing the small terraced hotel across the lane.

That was reassuring. It offered an escape route if there was a leak in either of the rubber welding tubes that were red for the acetylene and black for the oxygen. They were taped together at six-inch intervals and snaked over the floor from the bomb-shaped gas cylinders to the aluminium welding torch, which the kid was handling so well.

It struck me that while in most ways he was still a pup, he was also clever beyond his years. Not many fifteen-year-olds could fix cars like he was doing. From this I understood better why he hadn't already offed himself.

His love of cars had been his saviour. So far.

After all, rescue dogs everywhere know that if young humans suffer too many hard times their brains become riven with paths of hurt that never heal. The risk to Craig glared. Even when he was showing crimson, bits of white were still around him.

Raymond was many months dead, but where the kid's wounds were concerned, nothing had changed. Self-offing, madness, alcoholism or plain old gut-rot: the ways in which the denial of his nature could destroy him were so upsetting that I pushed them aside. Otherwise I might have cracked before him.

Still, my precise role was clear now. I was there to help him embrace Love. Like Raymond should have done with Oliver, who, because of his own queerness, had been left to die in the burning sea.

I knew exactly where to start.

The affection between the kid and Marcus Wright, the kennel lad, had been obvious to the family. I needed to discover what had driven them apart and lost no time in seeking yet more help from Her Hoityness.

'Please,' I implored, 'please send young Marcus to be with the kid.'

Within moments, it seemed, she was winding me up. A different visitor came to the workshop.

# 24

The click of a door catch made my ear flaps lift, and a man beyond the high wall of the little hotel that stood opposite number twenty began to sing. The song was 'Are You Lonesome Tonight?' and it continued until he opened the dark green back gate, which led into the lane. What I saw next became scored on my mind.

His jet-black hair had the same crash-helmet style that my first human had grumbled about in Elvis Presley. He'd wanted Elvis to go back to the quiff of earlier days. I could see why. This shape looked heavy and, in order not to wreck it on the stone lintel, the man ducked. That was quite funny. For a second it appeared he was being weighed down by his hair.

I soon saw that he was over six feet tall, with a broad frame that carried a lot of muscle and fat. As he approached the kid's workshop his belly wobbled in his shiny turquoise shirt and the gold medallion dangling from his neck was as bright as the E-shaped brass buckle of his belt.

Kitsch might have been the word but, from the redness that showed around him, I knew that he was as true in his feelings as Ginger was. Real people with hearts that pounded with love for others.

When he bent over the kid to see how the welding repair was going, the big brass E of the belt was pulled into his gut. He appeared not to notice. 'Brilliant!' he boomed to Craig, who now showed his best mix of colours so far. 'A brilliant job by a brilliant laddie!'

For the second time that day my itching stopped and my eyes lost their soreness. Though taken aback, I was thrilled. It seemed that the kid had a dad-like friend, who was determined to make him feel good about being himself. It didn't mean that the high praise for Craig's work was over the top. The kid's hands were rock-steady and the new patch of metal so neatly done that, if it wasn't for the danger of making him drop the welding torch, I would have charged forward and licked the side of his face. At least my restraint enabled me to savour his pride in what he was doing.

On completing the last inch of welding, he nipped the valves on the torch and put it aside to cool. After getting to his feet, he raised the dark green goggles that were protecting his eyes to where they stayed within his clumped-up hair. Like bumps on a frog's head.

'Thanks, Big Eddie!' he exclaimed, returning the broad smile of his visitor. It was a name that almost made me bark with joy.

Big Eddie! Already I loved him and was further buoyed up by the enthusiasm with which Craig remarked that, once the car's restoration was complete, he would look amazing in it. I wondered to what extent Big Eddie's influence could help make the kid's life come right.

'Why Mustang?' Craig asked, trailing his fingers over the seven chromed letters at the front of the bonnet. That made Big Eddie chuckle.

'It's a wild American horse,' he replied, with a shrug, before adding that Ford also made a smaller car called a Pony.

For some moments after that, the redness of the pointy-fronted Mustang filled the workshop, and I could see Big Eddie cruising in it, like Elvis himself might have done. This vision was short-lived. Until then I had been an unseen observer but things were about to change.

## 25

Everything went black and, beneath me, I felt movements from the other pups in the sack: the litter I was part of, which had been thrown into the river. Three bitches and three dogs, one of which struggled to be where I'd chanced on a pocket of air. I pushed down as hard as I could and he became still.

The blackness was replaced by a cold grey, which tasted of salt, and not far off the Watcher clung to the bit of lifeboat from which he'd earlier observed Raymond let Oliver die. His cruel yet sad eyes were on me and I knew that I, Brucie-Dog, was being judged a poor protector of the kid. Something he was keen to spell out.

'You think you can rescue that boy?' he asked, as the swell took him. 'Good luck,' he sneered, coming down again.

From this I understood that he believed Craig was a born loser, beyond the help of the rescue dog I had become that day.

Though angered on behalf of the kid, I felt pity for the Watcher, whose thinning hair was flattened by the water, making him appear even baldier than me.

I know you, Watcher, Raymond had cried, when they were in the burning sea together. I know you're queer.

Remembering that, and the Watcher's advice to Raymond to think of the Germans as queers, made me so extra-cold I feared I wouldn't rise above the hate that my mission to help Craig was thick with. At least it was not a surprise.

Self-loathing had turned the Watcher into a black-mailer of his own type. I wondered if I was strong enough to cope, and somehow Her Hoityness now became the leaden sea and sky.

'Ignore Raymond's wretched Watcher!' she ordered. 'Ignore him!' she persisted, snarling that he was a rotten-at-heart human whom – given the chance – she would have bitten to the bone. This was not a comforting thought. Her anger scared me, and later I saw a similarity between her and Jack, who, in being a determined young man, was often close to a bully.

This time I was lifted by the swell and, on coming down, I looked harder at the Watcher, whose eyes were so dark that I finally understood the extent of his malice. Not only did he want the kid destroyed by his queerness, he needed it to be so, vindicating his own sad queer-hating life. For which Her Hoityness had no mercy.

'Get rid of him, Bruce!' she barked, though it now seemed that she was at the very bottom of the ocean. Where all the dead had gone.

'Get rid of him!' she repeated.

'Get rid of him now!'

## 27

The salt-laden greyness went and I could breathe more easily. Under the circumstances, this was a miracle. I was being zapped by a high-pitched whistle, which reverberated against the walls and the plastic roof of the kid's workshop. It was no wonder that this racket had sent my thinking box haywire, placing me in the sea with the Watcher decades after the war had ended.

'Blowback!' thundered Big Eddie, who moved fast to wrap his hands over the top of the acetylene cylinder as it erupted into flame around the brass valve where the red tube was connected. It broke free of its frame, turned in the air beside the cherry-coloured Ford Mustang and whooshed, rocket-style, through the plastic roof overhead.

'Shit! Shit! Shit!' yelped the kid, whose fear made me focus on what was actually happening. 'Shit! Shit! Shit!'

I grasped that if it didn't launch itself the steel cylinder might have blown into shrapnel and killed us all. What happened next was dreamlike for me.

Craig took the welding torch from where he'd earlier

put it to cool and a flame bloomed where the red tube fed the gas through the handle to an angled copper tip. This fire was beautiful. A bright yellow rose. Keeping his hands on the cylinder, Big Eddie watched the kid, and from his smell, I knew that he, too, was terrified. 'Open the red valve, Craig lad!' he ordered.

I saw the sense in that. The acetylene was burning within the hollow torch. Opening the valve, which was a couple of inches down from the handgrip, would propel the fire out of the tip, ending the danger. When Craig did not respond to Big Eddie I knew why. He was entranced by the lively yellow rose, making me so extra-scared that I even became snappy with Her Hoityness.

'Make the kid do as he's told!' I ordered her.

My next impression was particularly vivid.

Holding the torch out as far as possible in his left hand, Craig still did not touch the valve. A few more seconds and we could have all been goners. Big Eddie's eyes bulged and shone like blue marbles.

'Open the red valve, Craig lad!' he roared, while I itched so badly that it was as if my maggots of earlier had grown needle teeth.

Worse than this, I splashed beside the kid's compressor and made it smell like a fox had been there. It was a shaming thing for me: collie-crosses are clean and proud.

Still, Big Eddie's shout had at least got Craig facing

him, and his blank expression showed he knew the fire could speed backwards up the rubber tube. It was self-disappointment in his eyes that made Big Eddie change tack. 'The red knob,' he advised, loudly enough to be heard over the whistle but kindly too. 'Open it, please, son. Now, if you will.'

It worked like magic. Using his free hand Craig tore off the welding goggles and threw them aside. Arching his spine so that his head and upper torso were well away from the yellow rose, he closed his eyes and turned the valve. The result was hard for me to take.

The whistle became a howl that skewered past my ear flaps to where my thinking box was already at its limit of suffering. Two seconds longer and I would have been a goner after all.

As things went we all got lucky. The yellow rose was dead. We were safe without a moment to spare and a sudden silence crashed into me. This did not last long. Big Eddie was quick to reassure the kid.

'Well done, Craig laddie!' he boomed, while my tail wagged. He picked up the welding torch and felt the rubber tube for any fire that might have lingered within. The moment ought to have been happy. Disaster had been avoided. This was not reflected in Craig's pale face.

His normally wide and bright eyes were small and dull, with the yellow bits I'd seen showing as grey flecks.

This was not only because of the shock he'd had. He hated himself for letting the blowback occur. It confirmed his worthlessness.

I stood beside the Mustang and watched the humans. It was vital for Craig to get over his mistake. Otherwise I might soon have been a redundant rescue dog.

For the time being success in the workshop kept him from self-offing. Everything now hung on Big Eddie. His next move would decide Craig's fate.

# 28

His snazzy blue shirt was darkened by sweat that smelt of the fear that was still with him, yet the calm he affected would have impressed Her Hoityness no end.

'Dead, dead lucky,' he advised, showing where the screw-connector from the red tube to the torch had been left loose, allowing acetylene to leak.

There was no doubting the obvious. In failing to nip the thread, Craig had made a dangerous error and, despite Big Eddie's kindly tone, his eyes went even smaller and duller than before. 'People are right,' he mumbled. 'I am the retard.'

That was when my ear flaps began to hurt at their roots.

Rachael had caused extra trouble at the kennels by calling him a retard and in a flash I realised it was the label Raymond had favoured until he'd turned openly hostile because of his son's camp manner. The Watcher would have approved. The kid had been under attack by his queer-hating dad for years.

On seeing my ears sticking up, Big Eddie chuckled.

Already it seemed that we were working in cahoots to save Craig from destruction.

'Don't be sad,' he told him. 'Your welding's the best ever. Just remember to tighten the connections. Otherwise,' he gestured around the workshop, 'whoof!' I thought of the cylinder, which my second sight had shown me launching through the workshop roof, and feared the onset of a new round of severe itching. As things stood I was far from at ease anyway.

What might have resulted from the blowback still terrified me as much as it did Big Eddie who, after tightening the acetylene connector, showed his faith in the kid by hooking the welding torch onto the metal frame that held the cylinders. Ready for work to start again, once things had settled.

'Go on, Dog-Dog,' he boomed, suggesting the time was right for me to go the short distance to Craig, who crouched down to face me with his furry caterpillars arching high above his green eyes.

'Bloody hell, Brucie!' he cried, near to tears. 'It's your first day and I nearly blew you up!' That was typical of him in those early times, on top one moment, crashing low the next, a way of being that, after my first human, I understood.

Pressing the flat of my head against his chest I sought a connection to touch his heart, exactly as we both needed. Proof that I was succeeding came fast.

'You're a darling and I'm glad you're our dog,' he declared, while redness filled the air and Big Eddie chuckled.

Craig kissed the bit between my ears, and I loved it that he'd said I was for the family, not just him. It showed that meanness of spirit was one thing that had not been inflicted on him at birth. Or by Raymond. 'Hey!' he cried, as I put what added strength I could into my push against him. 'You'll have me shoved over!'

Which, because I loved him dearly, was exactly what I did, much to the added amusement of Big Eddie. Who, in case I became exhausted before I'd found out all I could about Craig and Marcus, I dared not explore with my second sight. It was enough to know that he was looking out for the kid.

This easier mood did not last long.

When the sneck on the green back gate of the hotel – which was called the Heartbreak – clicked again I became nervy as a whippet. Who was Her Hoityness sending to see Craig now?

# 29

A small human with a big black beehive hairdo padded across the lane in white rabbit slippers, which contrasted with her blood-red trouser suit. Though this was another big test for my sore eyes I saw that she was married to Big Eddie. The first clue was her extra-wide gold wedding ring. It flashed in the sun. It glared in the sun. It was identical to the one her husband wore.

Neither greeted the other. As she entered the workshop and stopped by the kid, Big Eddie became surrounded by a glittering mix of shades. What had been his number-one saviour in life?

The answer was no surprise.

He enjoyed such love that I knew Craig's future would be assured, and wonderful, if he could make the same connection with Marcus. Exactly as my mission was meant to bring about.

Rescue dogs believe in the power of love, and that Big Eddie's kitsch Elvis-thing was shared by his wife made me adore her as much as I did him. Impersonators on the outside, they were their own people at heart.

'Hello, lovely,' she said to Craig, in a firm yet tactful way – just as Her Hoityness would have been if carrying her little white pup by the scruff of its neck. Within half a second the kid was showing the same redness that came when Big Eddie had praised his welding on the Mustang. From that I knew the kid loved her and she loved him. The Heartbreak Hotel was nothing but good news. So far.

'Hiya, Viv,' the kid replied, his cheeks pinking in the way of an easily embarrassed young human whose soul had been touched. Again I saw her tact in action: having lifted her shoulders, she held a shrug of amusement that allowed Craig time to master his bashfulness.

It was then that I noticed her eyes were dark violet, making them even rarer than a collie's silver ones.

After turning away from Craig a little and relaxing her shoulders, she took from her hip pocket a pack of king-sized cigarettes and lit up using a gold lighter that had a flame worthy of a dragon. If, like me, Big Eddie feared that this might ignite her eyelashes, he didn't show it. A game was getting under way between them and he was waiting for her to go first. At last she did.

'So?' she asked him, while keeping an eye on Craig, who shrugged as if their antics were not his concern.

'So?' Big Eddie calmly replied, as she drew on the king-sized cigarette. (If she wanted the banter that she'd come outside for, she had to get to the point.)

'So?' he repeated. 'So?' he tried again, making her laugh and flash her gorgeous eyes at him and the kid, who could not help grinning. 'So?' Big Eddie boomed, as she picked something from her front teeth with a long red fingernail.

'So…' she responded at last, giving me a warm look that was clearly intended to reassure Craig that she was aware of the new dog he must have been eager to show off. 'So,' she said again, on returning Big Eddie's brazen gaze, 'what on earth was all that noise? And no lies,' she warned, offering the kid another shrug, as if she knew Big Eddie was going to fib.

'What ya on about now, woman?' he asked, with a cheeky note of offence that made the kid's furry caterpillars do a dance of sorts.

'I mean, Edwin,' she retorted, then taking yet another drag and exhaling, 'the whine from this workshop that nearly had the hotel windows blown in. The most terrible screaming noise,' she added, putting him exactly where she wanted him. On the defensive: a role he played well.

First he shook his head at Craig and then – to my amazement – at me.

'No whine that I heard,' he said amiably. A breathtaking lie.

No sooner was this said than a violet mist that matched Viv's eyes blended with the colours around Big

119

Eddie. Who – incredibly – got even cockier.

'You must be hearing things, love,' he deadpanned.

This time she had to bite her lip against laughing, giving me space to note that where Big Eddie had a small straight nose, his cheeks were rounded and he had a double chin. One tiny word brought me back to Viv.

'Ah,' she responded, in a way that said much.

That tickled Big Eddie, who winked at the kid and waited for what was coming next. Viv was in no hurry. She'd already demonstrated that she could light up with style, and now the life of her king-sized cigarette ended with equal flair.

Though it was only half smoked, she dropped it to the ground, where I saw that its gold-ringed filter was smeared with the red lipstick that matched her trouser suit. Three seconds later she ground it out beneath her left rabbit slipper. 'Whatever you say, Eddie, love,' she said, and repeated her special shrug for the kid.

By now Big Eddie had the look of one who accepted he was never going to win, but wouldn't have changed it for the world. Their four eyes rested my way and I knew that another crucial moment had arrived for me and Craig, whose features were sharpened by his need for Viv's approval of me. Offering my best blue moons I remained stock still, waiting for her verdict.

# 30

'And this,' she remarked, with a grin, 'must be the lucky new dog.' At last I could relax my eyes, which had been stinging even more than earlier. The kid, too, was glad to loosen up. Getting down beside me again, he placed an arm about my neck and confirmed that I was the mutt the family had rescued that day.

'Brucie-Brucie!' Big Eddie sang, clapping his hands at the bond that, second by second, was strengthening between Craig and me. This did not distract Viv from observing things for herself.

After repeating her risky ritual with the flame-throwing gold cigarette lighter, she squinted at me. I wondered what she was seeing and soon had an answer. I was an observant dog, she decided, which delighted the kid and made my tail wag. Yet another quick turnabout of the mood within the workshop then occurred.

Viv took a second drag on her gold-tipped cigarette and coughed hard. That was telling. But not as much as the bitterness of the smoke she exhaled. Her lungs were being eaten by tumours and I smelt that they were advanced. I also sensed better than to yelp. It was not what she would have wanted. Especially where Craig was concerned. Already his brow was crinkled with anxiety for her.

She glared at Big Eddie, took a drag and ordered him to clean the Heartbreak Hotel cooker. I imagined something very different from the single burner on which my first human had heated baked beans. Big Eddie nodded. Viv's coughing fit was past, and it was time for him to leave her and Craig to talk between themselves.

'See ya later, bonny lad!' he boomed, ducking beneath the stone lintel of the green gate across the lane. 'See you later, Brucie-Bruce!' he added, from behind the high boundary wall of the hotel. Viv's eye returned to me and everything again became shaded with violet. An eerie quiet that did not last.

'Wait for it, Brucie-Darling,' advised Craig, as my pricked ears became painful again.

The violet was replaced by redness: Viv smiled as if I was a dog she'd always loved. 'Ah!' she exclaimed, as Big Eddie struck up with 'Are You Lonesome Tonight?'. This time I heard what I'd earlier missed in his singing. Big Eddie didn't only dress like Elvis Presley: he sang like him too.

The insides of my ears became warm and I now realised the irony young Jack had poured into his disturbing image of Elvis. Nobody sang about love like Elvis

Presley, yet the swirls of sickly pink within the portrait suggested that, in common with my first human's girl-friend Pauline, Jack saw that Elvis would never find the enduring love that might redeem him.

In the early 1970s Elvis still appeared to be Super-man-like, but no rescue dog anywhere would have believed him to be invincible. All humans are vulner-able. It's how they're born and how they die. Maybe that's why so many men need superheroes to help them outface days and years that otherwise make them feel small. Insignificant.

Tingles to rival those caused by my first human's electric cable zipped along my back, making me refocus on the kid. He was my purpose, not the colourful pro-prietors of the Heartbreak Hotel. I had to stick with Craig. That was why Ginger had chosen me.

At the end of the song Big Eddie laughed and I saw the kid shiver, telling me that his spine had also tingled. There was a distant thud of the Heartbreak Hotel door as it was closed. Like a full stop behind the sparring that had taken place between Viv and her husband.

'A good-looking dog for a good-looking laddie,' he'd said.

'Are you sure everything's okay, lovely?' Viv asked of Craig. 'That nothing went wrong with that awful noise?'

I realised that, despite the love Big Eddie's singing

had embodied for her, she was determined to stay focused on the kid. If she could have seen the amount of whiteness her questions threw around him it would have scared her. I was scared for him. He was still unnerved after the blowback and I itched like mad to hear his reply. We were in everything together. Just like Ginger had wanted.

# 31

'Everything's fine,' he replied, with a tremor that showed Viv he knew just how dangerous things had been. Drawing on her cigarette, she squinted again, signalling, of course, that she was not fooled by what he'd said.

That made Craig ashamed, and as his eyes slid away from hers, the heat haze over the ruby panels of the Mustang became brighter, making mine feel as if they were being burnt away to nothing.

No rescue dog could have ignored this and a growl that I just managed to hold down hurt my barking box. If I'd turned wolfish on the kid it might have spelt disaster for us both, though the Watcher and his queer-hating type would have been smug. Itchy, light-headed and shaky, I was back to my worst and it was down to luck that Craig spoke before I became wolfish after all.

'I mean,' he admitted, 'there was a problem but Big Eddie sorted it. Thanks, Viv,' he added, going even redder than the car he was standing beside.

Yet again her kindness showed. She took another drag and spoke with affection, which made me feel better. 'This is how it is, lovely,' she explained, with a smile that brought dimples to her cheeks. 'I'll ask no more about the whine I heard on condition that you promise always to be safe when working. So,' she continued, looking harder at him, 'don't go promising if you're doing anything careless.'

A guided missile could not have hit the mark better.

I saw that Craig had been scared she might ban Big Eddie from letting him use the oxyacetylene gear until he was older, and his relief was thrilling to see. Red, orange and gold flared around him. Colours of hope. Colours of joy. Colours of elation.

'I promise,' he exclaimed, with conviction that would have melted any but the iciest heart, 'that I'll always keep everything safe in this workshop. And,' he continued, 'that I'll always tighten the connections properly. Always!'

Viv chuckled.

His furry caterpillars went right up and his eyes shone with the innocence that brought a return of their spiky yellow bits.

Pressing him for the details of any loose connections would have been unkind. The kid's promise to be vigilant was enough. Though what neither of them knew was that, from that day on, I would always sniff for leaking acetylene. Just as everybody who loved Craig would have wanted me to do. Especially Ginger.

Viv became so relaxed she was almost floppy.

After stepping closer to the Mustang she peered through a side window at the silver vinyl interior, aware that, like me, Craig was watching every move she made.

'You'll have my Edwin more flash than ever,' she announced, with a fond sigh.

The kid was quick to deny the suggestion that her end was near. 'You'll both be flash!' he cried. 'You'll see! The flashest couple in the whole wide world!' he insisted.

On lightly touching his cheek she remarked that if she and Big Eddie were to be Mr and Mrs Flash in the Mustang, they ought to be quick about it. It was then that the kid's mixed colours gave way to a rich green – meaning his life really could come right. Craig loved Viv but his acceptance that she was dying suggested he was even stronger than I'd realised.

Still, I was careful not to lose perspective. His bad bone knowledge and all that Raymond had done to him dwarfed everything.

After taking a final draw, Viv crushed the king-sized cigarette, half finished, beneath her left rabbit slipper. The kid didn't comment. He snuffled, nodded and got a hug, like she was his second mum. If only she could have read my mind. Thanks to her, I understood things better now.

It was true that my second sight was going haywire

when the Watcher had pegged me as a failed protector for Craig but the accusation had stuck. Armed with all that I'd discovered about the kid's inner resilience, I was going to prove the cynical old Watcher wrong. Or die trying.

## 32

The concrete top of the lane was smooth with a drainage dip at its centre. Viv turned to face the workshop at this point. Craig had been watching her go. On seeing that she had the look of one who needed to add something, he leaned on the front of the Mustang, folded his arms and tried to hide the unease I smelt on him. 'Nothing up, is there, Viv?' he asked.

'Does he never come visiting?' she probed. Oddly, an ear on one of her rabbit slippers fell flat. Craig appeared not to notice and I understood why. It was clear that she was talking about Marcus and the kid was determined not to bite.

Now he used the flats of his hands to push his backside clear of the bonnet lip. As he did so the big Mustang rocked on its springs, making me shiver, as if many electric cables had been set to my mangy skin. At least this gave Viv the chance to let her unanswered question pass by.

Redness showed around her as she watched me shake my body from end to end. I had become her excuse to change the subject. 'Your Brucie's going to be such a handsome dog,' she announced, with a big smile, which Craig returned.

'Thanks, Viv,' he said. 'That means a lot.'

Neither of them knew that, on top of banishing my shivers, her prediction had made me see my role in the kid's life even more positively. If I could recover from my bad start, it was likely Craig could repair from being his dad's retard. Especially with me at his side. Maybe Viv sensed this. Either way she'd clearly achieved what she'd come outside for.

'See you later, Craig lovely,' she called, closing the green gate of the Heartbreak Hotel behind her, leaving a new silence that brought me back to reality.

Just because Ginger had got him a rescue dog the kid was no safer from self-offing. The sea where Raymond had died at the foot of Churchill's promontory was just down the lane from the workshop, and something that Pauline had once said about my first human – whose dad was also an alcoholic – spooked me: Like father like son.

Even more scarily, as soon as I'd had this thought, my second sight placed me on the promontory, where Craig was now surrounded by so much white that I knew self-offing was back in the air.

Very quickly, though, the kid changed into old Raymond, who arched his back to the sea rail, lit a cigarette and looked up to where Sir Winston's marble face reflected the pink of the evening sun on the sea, which was as flat as the seahorse lino in Ginger's kitchen.

'You!' he barked. 'You sent me to that damnably cold Atlantic where we were sunk. Ha! But I found a handsome fair-haired lad. The same age as me. Twenty-one! Twenty-two! Thereabouts. Boys – boys, Winston! Scared for our lives and needing comfort. Needing love!' he bellowed, his blue eyes flashing as he crushed his cigarette beneath his boot.

'But, Confusion,' he resumed, 'with a capital C was mine! To be young and full of love for your bride. To be away at a brutal war and find another love, the kind that creeps up on a man unexpectedly. The kind you don't dare call love when queers are hated – blackmailed! And,' he roared, swaying as he ripped off his upper clothes, 'plain illegal!

'So,' he continued, calming a little as he fumbled out of his trousers and underpants, 'you just feel it. The comfort. The companionship. The unspoken beauty,' he added softly, making me wish I could have turned the clock back for real and helped Ginger and the four twins as Raymond's rescue dog before he was a father. Absorbing his pain and guilt as my own. If that had been possible.

Just as quickly he was barking again, his dangly bit whipping from side to side as he staggered this way and that. A passing motorist beeped, enraging him even more.

'Beauty,' he went on, 'that left me squirming with damn guilt. For my marriage . . . for what I was turning into! And so, dear Winston,' he became very still with his arms out at his sides and his bearded face set right back, 'damn me to Hell for all eternity, I let him go! Into the sea that was on fire when I could have got him to safety.'

And even though he saluted Sir Winston and climbed the sea rail for the jump that I knew would kill him, I was mostly dizzied by the connection between the kid and his dad's wartime story.

It was a lot for me to take, and as my thinking box whirled with images of Oliver and the murderous war scenes I'd earlier witnessed, I heard Raymond's cry as he fell to his death. And the plea Oliver had made as the fire at sea had consumed him came to me loud and clear.

'For the love of God, Raymond, help me!'

The next bit was even worse. Craig was back on the promontory and, in a foreshadowing of what would happen if I failed in my mission, he glanced up at Sir Winston and began to climb the sea rail at the spot his dad had used. Nightmares did not get worse than this.

'Like father like son,' Pauline had said.

The pink blush of the sea became so dense that, for the

first time, redness alarmed me. I knew that when my second sight took me backwards in time it was accurate. That's how it always works. Equally, I understood that what I was seeing now was just a possibility, but I couldn't bear it.

And yet there was hope for the kid's survival too.

Big Eddie's crimson Ford Mustang represented all that I wanted Craig to feel about creativity as a boost to salvation. Rescue dogs see that if humans can find it within themselves they may turn rough experiences – and even bad bone knowledge – into beauty. It's the very thing we do for ourselves and was what Her Hoityness had demanded of me at the kennels.

Fight! Fight to become a rescue dog!

The thick redness made it hard for me to breathe and I realised that maybe Raymond had known that in encouraging Craig's love for cars he had compensated in part for the harm he'd done to him. Human behaviour is rarely one-sided and the kid's dad loved him. Of that there was no doubt.

It was clear, too, that Big Eddie and Viv understood the restoration of the Mustang meant much more than fixing up a snazzy car. It was about using creativity to save Craig's life. Mine, too, come to that.

Had he gone over the sea rail I know I would have died. Luckily for us both my front legs gave way, my chin hit concrete, and everything went from red to a blackness so heavy it might have been made of tar.

133

## 33

I was being shaken and the kid was crying for me to open my eyes. That was easier said than done. The lids did not want to separate, and when I forced them, it seemed as if the rims were being torn apart.

The discomfort was worth it: I found that Craig was crouched by my side at the front of the workshop. The spot where I'd collapsed. For a moment I thought things were about to get easier. I was wrong. Very wrong.

Reds, greys, greens, black and other conflicting shades swirled around him. I took it as a rebuke for letting my legs give way. The strangeness of his eyes added to the punishment. They were so wide, dark and deep that I knew he'd feared me dead, and the thought of how this made him feel was grim to contemplate. Also it was no surprise.

Everything seemed real but I half believed I had passed over. It was my doggie-snout that saved the day. The smell of life on the kid was powerful, and from this I accepted that we were both still living, albeit in pain.

'Drinkies, Brucie-Darling,' he said, on offering a

hub cap he'd filled with water at a metal sink in a far corner of the workshop.

'Drinkies,' he repeated, while, to his amazement, I got back on my paws without too much difficulty. A recovery of sorts driven by my determination to beat my fever, tingling, itching, aching, dizziness, infected eyes and other symptoms.

Plus, and almost without my seeing it, my mission had gained an added purpose. Getting Craig to accept the love of Marcus was still the priority, but a close second was my fight against all queer-hating humans. Or against all queer-hating behaviour.

The Watcher, the captain and Raymond had taught me much.

The more that men like them saw natural-born queers happily sharing love, the less misery, self-offing and ill-health they would cause. Becoming Craig's protector had connected me to a fight that rescue dogs the world over understood. I, Brucie-Dog, was now part of a struggle for the wellness of young humans everywhere.

Half a minute passed while I lapped from the hub cap, which the kid had balanced between two bricks. He stayed on one knee at my side, his colours settling as he got over his alarm that, after the blowback, he'd yet again put me at risk.

'Sorry for letting ya get so hot, Brucie,' he said, as I finished the water. 'I promise I do love you,' he continued, looping his right arm about me and pressing the side of his face to my neck. That was wonderful. Rescue dogs need all the contact they can get, especially from their number-one humans. The following moments, though, were not straightforward.

My sore old eyes bulged at what I was now seeing. Maybe Her Hoityness was behind this. Maybe not. But one thing was sure. The Watcher would have been vexed. Young Marcus was directly in my line of sight.

# 34

He was coming down the lane on a yellow Raleigh Chopper that sparkled where the sun touched its chrome, making it impossible for me not to bark. Unfortunately for Craig this might have burst his eardrum. 'What the heck?' he protested, standing up from my side.

By now my tail and bum were wiggling so fast you might have thought they were competing. No rescue dog would have reacted differently. Marcus's huge grin, windswept blond hair and tanned face conveyed his hunger for Life.

I loved him and for now everything seemed simple. As soon as the kid got over the shock of his visit he would be happier than ever and their love would thrive. Clearly I'd exaggerated the bad stuff.

'Yahoo, Craig!' Marcus called, as I noted his kennel overalls had been replaced by a sleeveless mustard T-shirt and dark blue denim shorts, showing off legs that were as strong as the powerful arms that braced him where he stood tall on the pedals. Had I been told that things were about to get even more exciting I wouldn't have believed it possible. But they did.

Just as he became surrounded by crimson Marcus sang: 'Yahoo, Brucie-Wucie-Lucie-Darling!' The words the kid had used at the time of my rescue! It seemed I was already bringing Marcus and Craig together.

On locking the rear brake, Marcus laid down a long tyre mark that ended outside the workshop. He was eye to eye with the kid, who stayed next to the red Mustang.

'Marcus Wright!' he cried.

It had been impossible for him to keep the delight out of his voice, and I saw that Marcus knew he should now hold back a little. Too much enthusiasm too soon and any fledgling chance of their rift being closed would be lost.

After parking his bum well back on the long, thin saddle he kept a plimsoll-clad foot to the ground and chuckled at the use of his full name: Marcus Wright. Things then roughened up fast for me.

Streaks of black came within the redness, which had spread around them both, and the details of a short exchange between Rachael and Vanessa as we'd left the kennels returned, like the booted foot of my first human to my rear. Because of the abuse he'd suffered at school for being queer, Marcus had recently taken his mum's happy pills. I worried my legs would give way again. Plus I imagined the Watcher sniggering at my failings and thought it an apt judgement.

Wisdom is supposed to be the marker of all rescue dogs but I had been so carried away by my hopes of an easy fix between Marcus and Craig that I'd overlooked Marcus's own attempted self-offing. Shame might have made my tail drop but it stayed up. At least the reason was a good one.

The scene before my eyes suggested that Marcus was now happy with his natural-born queerness, the proof of which was easily found. Because he was sweating hard after cycling, it only took a sniff for me to confirm that his gut was free of the acid rotting the kid's stomach. That and a new burst of fun from him made me feel less inadequate.

'That's me!' he responded to Craig, sticking his right arm out and dropping his wrist in mock-camp. 'The most infamous Marcus Wright!'

It was quite a show and, for a little while, my all-over itching stopped again. Something similar appeared to happen to the kid. Despite his terror of queers he smiled at Marcus and all traces of white left his work-shop, where the heat-haze over the Mustang shimmered as if it was caressing the red panels.

Excited by what might come next, I couldn't stop myself splashing the same bit of ground as before. At this point Marcus made my eyes bulge again.

After setting his left foot to the pedals he levered the

front wheel of the Raleigh Chopper high off the ground, swept his right hand through his hair, and laughed as more bright shades joined the crimson that still showed.

Craig was laughing, too, and I almost lay on my back to kick the air. That would have hurt my raw skin but I was distracted from doing so. Twisting one of the luminous green handlebar grips, as if it was a motorbike accelerator, Marcus made engine sounds that had the kid rolling his eyes. That did it for me, and before I knew it, I was running circles in the lane, chasing my tail in celebration of their love for each other.

'Look at ya brilliant new dog go, Craigie!' cried Marcus, who drove me on by continuing to 'rev' the raised Raleigh Chopper.

They fell quiet and eyeballed each other with a hardness that thickened the air until I could have gnawed it. Marcus lowered the front of the Raleigh Chopper to the ground and kept a foot to its chrome pedals. The meaning was clear. If Craig refused to talk he would cycle away. I couldn't blame him. Surviving his mum's sleeping pills must have taught him that life was not to be wasted on self-hate. The kid was being given a last chance and, to my surprise, the abrupt change of the red, which had been between them, to white was not all bad. It enabled me to feel what lay at the heart of their broken, hopefully repairable, friendship.

Above all else, Craig was terrified of contagion by Marcus's acceptance of his queerness and was thereby advancing his own destruction. I knew what this meant for me. There were no easy fixes.

The damage his rotten bone knowledge and Raymond had done could not be overestimated. It had to be faced. For one thing, Her Hoityness would have demanded this of me. My starting point was stark.

The kid himself was the ultimate queer-hater.

Love had become his enemy and it was no wonder to me that I was now fixated on the Watcher and his queer-hating type.

Things were trickier than I'd understood and I itched as if somebody had doused me with petrol and flicked a match. Worse was to come.

The whiteness I'd sort of welcomed became so thick that my throat twitched hard several times. That was serious. An agitated mutt at the kennels had died after his barking box had gone into a spasm. Instinctively I swallowed to ease my breathing and braced myself for what would happen next between Marcus and the kid. It was going to be tough. I smelt that all right.

# 35

Craig was standing behind the front wheel of Big Eddie's car, close to where he'd welded the lower part of the door. Marcus was sitting on the Raleigh Chopper, just outside the entrance to the workshop. They'd been eyeball to eyeball for some time when the kid smiled at me, proving that, even when things were tricky, my doggie ways still worked. Plus I'd yet again had help from Her Hoityness. Or so I believed.

After pleading with her to make things less tense I'd parked my rump mid-way between the kid and Marcus and lifted a paw for them to be kind to each other. That was part of my mission, and because I sensed her approval, I even felt that Her Hoityness had made the gesture with me.

But it was clear that Marcus was not going to be distracted from his aim in visiting number twenty. He, too, was on a mission.

'Well?' he pressed Craig, who, instead of replying, took several backward steps deeper into the workshop, thwarting, as best he might, this challenge to his buried feelings. Marcus was having none of it and twice repeated his question before rocking the Chopper's set-to-go pedal. The threat almost made me turn wolfish on him.

Above all I feared that, with nothing more to be said, the kid would be left to the self-hate that was now turning the white bits nearest to him to the same sickly pink I'd seen on Jack's painting of Elvis Presley. What happened next was the oddest thing of all.

It was as if I was within the painting. Just by looking at them, I turned some of Elvis's sequins into the eyes of Raymond, Oliver and the Watcher. Each was scrutinising me to see if I could cope with the growing complications of being the kid's rescue dog. They were right to have doubts. I was not in control of what was happening.

Compelled to look harder at the remaining sequins, I conjured the eyes of the young German sailors who were machine-gunned by the patrol ship, whose captain was the big, bearded queer-hater. That was freaky.

'Queers,' the Watcher had advised Raymond, as he took his seat at the Vickers gun to do some killing. 'Just think of them as queers and it's fun,' he'd added.

That had not shocked me.

Even as a very young rescue dog I knew that those humans who live in fear of their own desires are the ones who hate queers most. It's called queer-bashing and it often leads to murder in every part of the world.

Still, the past: it seemed I would suffocate within it, a feeble mutt who'd barely lasted an afternoon with his new family. Perhaps this would have been easier than what did occur.

Caught within the sickliness of Jack's canvas, I now became young Marcus Wright the kennel lad, the memory of which is his tale, his voice.

## 36

Infants, juniors and high school, I'd been in the same form as Craig since I was five. So had a boy called Trevor Carlton and, time was, we were all close friends. It would have taken a lot for things to remain that way. Even when very young I was teased for being a cissy, and over the years this had darkened. I was shoved about, spat at or worse, but I took it in my stride. School wouldn't last forever. That was what I told myself and Craig. For Trevor things were different.

School was his stage and he created laughter at my expense. Even some of the teachers went along with it or, at least, did nothing to stop it. Finally this led to a crisis involving him, me and Craig, who was terrified of being seen as gay. Which I suppose was a tribute to Trevor's powers of mockery against any boy suspected of it. A role that, with his good looks and flirty manner, he was born to play. A queer-punisher general. Sort of.

Shiny black hair tumbled down each side of his young-Elvis face to where his loosely knotted dark blue school tie made a buckled Y. That was his style. Cocky as they came. I couldn't help it: I liked him. He made his mark every week and got away with it. Including the day when a teenager from another part of town hanged himself and Trevor declared to our class what I knew to be true.

'He was a willy-woofter! Took his life cos he couldn't cope!' While saying this he'd tugged on his crotch, and most of those nearby – including Craig – had laughed. The phrase 'willy-woofter' spread like wildfire. It made people gleeful.

That was how it was. Teenagers who feared they were gay often took their lives. A week later I even heard our caretaker, Mr Blewitt, tell a dinner-nanny it was the same as sick dogs being put out of their misery.

Alarmingly she'd then caught my eye, set a hand to my face, and said not to worry, I'd be fine. That wasn't how it felt. Only later did I see this 'kindness' in context. The crisis involving me, Trevor and Craig had begun and would gather pace the next day.

We'd lingered in a maths room while the rest of the form went for dinner. That was not unusual. Much of the banter with Trevor was fun and even worth waiting for. I was hungry yet unconcerned about being at the end of the food queue. In a sense I was under Trevor's spell that day.

His eyes were greeny-blue, and the way he'd flash them had long ago lulled me into accepting his cruelty as harmless. In fact he now had an evil little plan in mind. The memorable tug on his crotch in front of our classmates had not only been theatrical. Suicide number one had juiced him up and – perhaps without realising the implications of his game – he now wanted a second queer suicide. Mine. I would later marvel at my blindness in not seeing this straight away.

Trevor might as well have been carrying a baseball bat with which to smash my skull and Craig's. My lack of awareness made me easy prey. As was Craig.

The exaggerated manner in which Trevor was chomping on a big wad of bubblegum while facing us in the maths room should have set off an alarm in us. But we failed to sense that our lives were about to change. Every second of what occurred next became scored onto my mind. It was more than unforgettable. It did something that altered my brain and the telling of it is not easy.

# 37

We were near the wide-open door to the corridor where stragglers for dinner passed by. Trevor had placed himself so that Craig couldn't leave the classroom without a squeeze. He took the bubblegum from his mouth and held it up in his right hand, as if examining an uncut diamond. With the back of my neck prickling, I realised that, since the start of his willy-woofter campaign, things had darkened between us.

No longer greeny-blue, his eyes were slate grey and dull. The bubblegum was a threat, summoning up all the queer-hating I'd blanked out at school. Concern made me look into Craig's eyes. They were like frozen peas and I shuddered on his behalf. Trevor didn't know that the boy who'd taken his life was once our friend, and as he tugged a few times at his crotch with his left hand, I wanted to punch him. I couldn't make myself do it. Also, it was unnecessary.

There was a time when I was young and had put salt on slugs that came from a rotten skirting board at home. After a few moments they'd burst open from end to end and I'd been thrilled. Later I'd regretted this. When I imagined the guilt that Trevor's delight in that first suicide would one day cause him, I felt like puking.

Queers were queers and no 'normal' boy could sympathise with them, alive or dead. Remorse was a luxury queer-hating Trevor would not be able to permit himself, and it seemed to me that he was set for self-destruction.

There was no doubt that Craig saw all of this too. The next bit was surreal.

After again tugging on his crotch Trevor passed the shiny pink gum to where Craig accepted it between his right thumb and first finger. It was clear that this repulsed him, but all power was on Trevor's side and I braced myself by holding the strap of my haversack tighter.

Maybe I was wrong not to shove between them and into the corridor but more than anything I wanted to see if Craig would find the will to resist what was expected of him. At the same time I knew that what was coming my way was unstoppable.

It was within the strawberry stress-blotch on Craig's neck. It was within the buzz from an over-head strip light. It was Fate. Sorting the non-queer from the queers, pre-determined since we were in the same reception class. It was as well that I braced myself harder. Pointing his finger at the gum, which

Craig held at a space from his chest, Trevor had laughed and spoken boldly.

'Slap it in his blond puffter hair, Craig. Otherwise,' he continued, 'I'll know you're as queer as Marcus is. Won't I?' he added, skewering Craig, who now made a defence that I never would have expected.

'But I can't just put bubblegum in somebody's hair!' he protested. Panic caused him to bite his bottom lip, which showed a dark bruise at its left side.

Smirking, Trevor did not appear to notice, leaving me so angry that I gripped my haversack even tighter. Otherwise I might have lashed out at him after all. Still, I knew that the growing pressure in the room was on Craig more than me.

It was barely three months since his dad had gone over the seafront rail at the bottom of their road. I was then about to turn fifteen and Craig a month younger. For years we'd gone everywhere with our arms linked across our shoulders and our hearts beating as one. The closeness had felt so natural and right that I slept well and had sweet dreams about a future world in which queerness was embraced as normal. Now, though, it was as if Craig was accusing me of infecting him with a disease and Trevor was clearly in tune with this sad change between us.

High on his willy-woofter glory, he'd cornered us each in more ways than one. Especially Craig, who, I accepted, had to put the bubblegum in my hair. I waited for it to come. The noisy strip light flickered, about to die.

## 38

Craig closed his eyes and I looked at Trevor, who also avoided my gaze. This was not what I expected of him, though the gum was enough for me to cope with.

Its stickiness was predictable but my hair felt grainy where the strands were caught, making the attack on me even uglier. Almost like I'd been branded. And yet compared to Craig – who'd now gone so small it was as if his bones had shrunk – I was in fair shape.

Wiping his sticky fingers on the side of his grey school trousers, he peered down at his brown brogues, which had scuff marks showing the paleness below their surface. That said it all. His terror of being thought gay was exposed by what he'd been made to do with the bubblegum. Rather than swaggering at this success, though, Trevor was lost in gloom, which drew my eyes back to him. He shifted from foot to foot and suddenly boiled up in my face.

'Do not be giving me the evil eye!' he shrieked. Desperate not to appear panicked, he tugged twice at his trousers. Maybe he would have shrieked again but we now had added company.

Several girls who were late for the canteen had paused by the open doorway and were staring wide-eyed at what was going on. To my amazement, Trevor also went small, like Craig, and, still bracing myself with the haversack, I set my back against looking equally pathetic. After peering hard at Trevor and my hair, one of the girls spoke for her group.

'You don't half pick some crappy mates, Marcus,' she said drily.

The girls had turned away and were leaving for the canteen, when Trevor at last reacted to them. 'It was only a joke!' he screeched in their wake. 'Only a joke!' he added to me and Craig, breaking into hysterical giggles, which had us watching him in awe. It was a loud pop and a final flicker of the strip light that spurred me to break the silence I'd held since he'd taken the gum out of his mouth and given it to Craig.

'Well, thanks very much for everything, mate,' I said, doing my best to be cool. 'You too,' I told Craig, whose eyes were back to their normal size.

I stepped between him and Trevor into the corridor, where a little way off – and much to my surprise – the girl who'd spoken up was waiting to one side for me.

After reaching into her bag she smiled and showed me a pair of nail scissors to cut the bubblegum out of my hair with. Trevor was furious.

'Fag-hag!' he screamed, from where he was watching at the classroom door. I wondered then if I should have punched him but it didn't matter. It was obvious that I'd come out of the attack better than he or Craig had done. Maybe that left me complacent.

I was an idiot not to see that, of all people, queer-hating Trevor Carlton would get his own back at the first chance. If the danger I was now in had had a smell, it would have choked me.

# 39

The girl with the scissors was called Susan Terry. Her dad was a vicar so the family was well known about town. After snipping the gum out of my hair, she wrapped it in a tissue, then binned it in the empty classroom we'd ducked into. I appreciated why she was so thorough. With the evidence of Craig's betrayal towards me now gone, I was no longer a target for those who would be encouraged by a homo who had been queer-bashed with bubblegum. A topic on which Susan was blunt.

'That flipping Craig Harrison is not fit to be a friend of yours anymore,' she insisted, while cleaning the scissors on a second tissue. Little did she know that this echoed recent advice from my mum.

It was just after breakfast the Saturday before and I'd told her I was going to visit Craig, who for weeks had been fixing up an American car owned by his friend Big Eddie. I knew I'd sounded nervous and part of me wanted to be talked out of going. My reason for this was strong. When I'd called to see him the previous weekend Craig had kept the garage door at the back of his house shut and pretended not to be inside. That had hurt. I'd gone down the lane to where the statue of Sir Winston Churchill faced the waves.

Most times this was a happy spot for me, especially when I was with Craig and the sea was at its bluest. We'd grown up on that seafront together, sharing its colours and moods. It was part of what bonded us, and being there by myself still put me in touch with him.

This time the water was choppy, and when some gulls that were floating a little way out took flight I guessed they were off to seek a calmer place, such as the grass-topped cliffs a mile along the road to my right. Later I wished I, too, had found somewhere more restful to be.

Instead I returned to the garage door and called for Craig, who again did not respond. I knew for sure he was inside and became so sad that my gut felt as if it was being twisted. The build-up to this had begun a year before when I'd realised that Craig needed to placate his homophobe dad, who had recently taken to calling me Mandy instead of Marcus.

Then Mr Harrison had killed himself, and my heart had leapt with hope that Craig would want our closeness back. It all seemed so simple but the reality was harsh. It was at Craig's wish that the garage door now stayed lowered against me. My gut hurt more at the irony of the situation, it was almost unbearable.

I knew that Craig treasured me. Just as I treasured him. We loved each other. Fact. I dreaded that we would never again stroll on the beach, arms across shoulders, sides touching, hearts beating in sync. It was as if Craig had died and my feelings had to spill.

On getting home from my failed visit to his garage I couldn't help crying. When my parents asked, I'd replied that I was upset about the boy from the other school, who'd taken his life. That did not mislead them and what came next was carefully done.

# 40

My dad moved aside to wash some dishes but kept an ear cocked to what my mum had to say next. It soon came. Craig, she advised me, was in grief and should be left alone for a time.

That made sense but I also heard a tougher meaning to her words. In the wake of Mr Harrison's suicide, Craig had turned mean towards me and it was best to let the friendship go. The added hurt this caused must have shown in my face, and on taking my hand in both of hers, she picked up on my thoughts exactly.

'Sometimes we have to leave behind those who've been most special to us,' she explained, with a look at my dad, who nodded in agreement. It underlined that on top of knowing how much I'd loved Craig they'd also been fine with it. Even if, without my knowledge, they'd recently been fixing it for me to move on with my life and leave him where he was.

My mum produced a letter from an old family contact who was the managing director of an American-owned sewing-machine company in London. Before my dad had married her and moved north, he'd been one of the firemen who'd put out a blaze at the factory where the machines were built. In response to an approach by my parents, the grateful MD had written to the parent company, requesting to enrol me early for a coveted apprenticeship in the design and development of new sewing machines.

'If they say yes,' enthused my mum, who knew I loved the intricate workings of all machinery, 'you'll even spend two days a week at art college. It'll be a unique chance,' she continued, while I took in what she'd said. By now my dad was drying the dishes and took his turn to speak up.

'If America says yes, son,' he remarked, with a wink, 'make the most of it. There's a great new life for you out there.' He turned his attention to the cutlery that was yet to be washed.

'There now,' concluded my mum, who kissed my forehead and got up to help him.

Somehow, and without a fuss, the prospect of a different world had opened up before me, though for now it was almost too much to take in. Still, this off-the-wall talk with my parents had at least clinched my decision against making further visits to Craig's house. In common with the seagulls that had fled the choppy sea, I needed somewhere less unsettling to be. What a difference a day then made.

The more I thought about the apprenticeship, the less

sad I was about losing Craig. All I needed was a second letter confirming that it was all systems go with the sewing machine company. A challenge I wanted with all my heart to meet.

# 41

Susan Terry's widened eyes were dark green, like Craig's, and I stressed that the apprenticeship was to be kept secret because if I wasn't accepted, I'd be a laughing stock. Dimples came to her cheeks, as I added, 'Please, Susan, say nothing about it for now.'

Leaning closer to the chair I was sitting on, she double-checked my hair for neatness where she had cut out the bubblegum. 'Not too bad,' she mused, then remarked that my mum was right about me staying away from Craig: he'd got his own life to sort out.

That hurt but she was the best person I'd ever known at school and, left alone in the classroom, I wanted to call after her that I loved Craig. It was as well I didn't. Several boys who must have wolfed their dinner came from the opposite direction, and if they'd heard that, Craig's life would have been hell.

Besides, what would be would be. That was what my dad often said, even when it didn't apply. This time it was apt. What I didn't know was that the worst few days of my life were about to begin.

# 42

The first class of the next day was PE and our games master, Mr Heston, decided that we would play five-a-side in the open air. Following overnight rain, the pitch was bad and Craig – who disliked football at the best of times – cheekily called for a vote: inside or outside for our hour-long session. That didn't happen.

A tough old type from the Second World War, Mr Heston dismissed all objections and barked that the mud would make us work harder, which it did.

Aside from wanting to win for the sake of winning, each team threw itself into the match to outface the mud and him. For me, though, there was an added incentive to play well. At breakfast that morning my mum had asked why part of my hair had been cut out. Panicked, I'd replied that after a seagull had dive-bombed me on Churchill's point, it'd gone frizzy. A lie, which drew a piercing look that touched a nerve.

I couldn't stand it if anybody, least of all her, suspected I was a victim of bullying. The queer who was too soft to stand up for himself. And the nagging possibility that my parents would not have forgiven Craig for the attack disturbed me so much that, walking to school, I could smell the bubblegum as if it was still there, defiling me and marking me out as queer.

At first the sickly-sweet scent was on-off. Then it became constant and was stronger at the school gates. It was impossible to ignore and twice I had to swallow bile. I wondered if I was going mad and realised that I was feeling some of what Craig lived with, so determined to be normal that anxiety gnawed at his insides non-stop. Saddened, I also knew that in the long term it would destroy me. Surviving the day without cracking up already felt impossible.

Luckily Mr Heston's game of five-a-side was my answer. I would prove my strength with my best football ever. Even the mud couldn't have put me off.

Craig in goal at our end, Trevor as goalie at the other, I scored a hat-trick, which did away with the bubblegum reek and made me feel myself again. The game had gone fast, and as soon as Mr Heston blew the whistle, I wanted to dive into the showers, which were always lovely and hot.

Craig, I knew, hated them, and though we'd never discussed his terror of getting turned on, I'd always nodded at him across the locker room. Easing his stress without getting close enough to make things worse.

Later I would see that I should have been looking after number one. Throughout the twenty hours since the bubblegum attack had backfired on Trevor, I'd been on a cliff with a leg over the edge and now my hat-trick against Trevor's goalie skills had upped the danger. There was a sound reason why I stayed blind to this. My mind was fixed on a coming performance from Mr Heston. It never failed to impress. He was quite a preacher-man.

# 43

Fat, bald and in his mid-fifties, he wore a red tracksuit, which made him look as if he was made of rubber. 'Beware public lavatories!' he began, on taking up his regular place at the entrance to the showers where all ten of us were. 'Beware bushes! Beware homos!' he continued, getting louder and louder. 'Beware, boys! Beware!' he roared, stepping backwards to where our towels were exactly folded on the low benches set before the lockers. Things with Mr Heston had to be just so. No variations permitted. Not on his watch.

Some boys took his anti-queer ranting seriously. Others thought him scary, nuts or both. To me, he was so odd that to avoid being punished for laughing I kept my gaze on the white tiles that were six inches before my nose. Craig, I knew, would be doing the same thing where he was beneath a shower head that was directly opposite mine, but for a different reason.

Fighting his queerness day by day made him more susceptible than I was and there would be no mercy if the thing he feared his body might do, in the school showers of all places, got the better of him now.

Mr Heston liked to use violence and because, on top of his suspected queerness, Craig was a sports-duffer, he lacked the protection my footie skills sometimes gave me. Even if I was called Pele the Puff.

Plus, there was the lingering mystery of a scuffle between Craig's dad and our games master, which had occurred the year before. They were having a Saturday lunchtime drink at a seafront pub called the Gay Hussar and Trevor's dad, who owned one of the nearby hotels, saw them exchange blows, which left Mr Heston with an eye the size and colour of a plum. That created some fun at school.

Even those boys who were full-on bullies saw that a master-thug had had the tables turned on him and, for a little while, Craig's alkie dad was hero-worshipped. Wary of Mr Heston and his strong dislike of queers, Craig played down this episode to me and others. His dad, he claimed, had flogged a Ford Escort with a dodgy clutch to Mr Heston's daughter and things had got out of control between them. An explanation I would have accepted if Craig's eyes hadn't slid to the left as he spoke. It confirmed that, like me, he was bad at lying.

Still, his fib about the Escort was now old and I understood that, with his dad long gone, he felt at added risk from Mr Heston, who in recent months was ever more strident when preaching to us while we showered. To nail Craig as a queer would have made his day, especially if the hard proof was there for all to see and laugh at. Craig's body betraying him.

Instead of worrying about things I couldn't change, I put these thoughts aside, closed my eyes, and lifted my face to the shower head square-on. I'd scored a hat-trick that morning and wanted to savour the moment. If only I'd glanced to my left, where, unnoticed, Trevor had swapped places with the boy who'd been there first. It was warm. It was steamy. The scent of soap was lovely. I felt smooth. I felt great. I felt invincible. I was wrong.

# 44

The tips of Trevor's fingers came to rest just below the back of my neck. I should have taken control, but my loneliness at no longer being Craig's friend meant I wanted Trevor to touch me more. There was no doubt that he understood the power this gave him.

'Queers never win,' he confided, drawing his hand down my back to set a finger within the crease of my bum.

Shocked at being caught out like that, I looked around and saw that Craig and the rest had gone to the locker room, leaving just the two of us beneath the showers.

'Get lost,' I told him.

Instead of backing away, he came even closer and popped a kiss on my ear, making my body do the very thing I'd been so worried about for Craig. After tugging twice at his crotch he drew his finger upwards from my bum to my lower back and traced circles that, because of my helplessness, I was incapable of resisting. Worse was on its way. Reaching aside with his left hand he turned our showers off so that the silence from the locker room became clear. That was terrifying. I imagined that every ear of every boy and Mr Heston was tuned in for the next bit and Trevor delivered well.

'Oh, Mandy darling,' he said in a loud, camp voice. 'Oh, Mandy, you're so beautiful.'

He gave a bark of laughter that accompanied a jab of his palm to the side of my head. Putting the queer in his place. No more hat-tricks or other cleverness, thank you.

Then he was gone from the showers and, in a rush, I saw that Craig must have told him about Mr Harrison – his queer-hating dad – calling me Mandy, and that probably he and Trevor had even laughed together over the name.

Worst of all, I thought about an older boy from two years before, who everybody knew had attempted to hide what happened to him in the showers, bending it between his thighs and taking penguin-steps, only for it to spring back, sealing his humiliation. Luckily he'd found a girlfriend soon after, and people stopped calling him a homo. I was different. I was Mandy. I was Pele the Puff. I was gay and no pretending otherwise.

Lamb to the slaughter was an understatement for what I now expected and the more I willed my body to behave the harder it got. Leaving me fully exposed but not pathetic. Teeth gritted, I hid nothing with my hands and made for the silent locker room.

# 45

I was struck by the control of the group, which was in a semi-circle with Craig at the far end to my right and Trevor in the same position to my left. All eyes stayed on me as I noted that those who were not yet dressed had covered themselves with their towels, leaving me, the prey, as the single naked boy. At this time queers such as me were targeted so that everybody else could be reassured about themselves. That much was clear from Saturday-night telly. Viewers applauded camp showmen while those in the know felt the violence behind the joke. I now committed the blunder of looking to Craig for support. He avoided my eye and left me scared of breaking into tears. As luck had it, however, the courage of another boy soon distracted us all.

On giving me a double thumbs-up, he quipped that he wouldn't mind having the same oats as me for breakfast. A few others laughed and, out of care for Craig's hidden terror of being unmasked, I didn't look at him again.

Besides, nothing could have prevented the queer-bashing that was coming my way. The air felt so thick that I had to inhale more deeply – I wasn't the only one having trouble breathing. To the surprise of all his pupils, Mr Heston spluttered and coughed as if the locker room was polluted by mustard gas.

Ten seconds at the most had passed. I saw that he'd been watching me and the others from where he stood several feet to my left. After coming forward he halted beside Craig and struggled so desperately to breathe that the thumbs-up boy even risked asking if he was okay. This was not done out of cheek. Our sports master was pillar-box red from the neck up and it seemed a wonder that he could breathe at all. Quick as lightning I understood why this was. Out of everybody there, he was the one most out of his depth.

Somehow everything was upside-down and a bark of contempt from Trevor made me look to where he'd quit the semi-circle and was eyeballing Mr Heston in preparation for what he intended to do next.

Brazen. Outlandish. Shocking. Trevor Carlton delivered again.

Reaching to where his towel was wrapped about his middle he gave a single tug on his crotch, the effect of which was to make Mr Heston snap his head back so fast it was as if a rock had hit his forehead dead centre.

'Punish the queer!' Trevor demanded, before our teacher had had time to recover. 'Punish the queer!' he repeated, as I looked to Craig and saw that, terrified of being seen as reluctant, he was joining in with the chant.

'Punish the queer!' most of the boys repeated in unison.

'Punish the queer!' parroted the thumbs-up boy, who until then had been unafraid of smiling at me.

'Punish the queer! Punish the queer!' all nine chanted, while I looked to Mr Heston and saw that he was incapable of reacting. A bully snared by his own hatefulness and vulnerable with it. It was time to give him a jolt or two. I wanted things over with quickly.

'Punish the queer!' I taunted him, more loudly than any of them.

'Punish the queer!' I repeated, thrilling most of my classmates, who laughed as if I was a good sport, going along with harmless fun. This was not how Trevor Carlton reacted. He needed his revenge on me.

Clenching his fists at his hips, he craned his head forward at Mr Heston and shrieked in desperation, 'Punish the hard-on queer! Punish him!' he added, even louder.

At that Craig could not stop his eye hooking mine, and I saw that the stress marks that often came to the side of his neck were rawer than I'd ever seen them. All of this, and the bubblegum attack, was harming him as much as it was me. I wondered what Mr Heston would do next. I soon found out.

## 46

His roar for me to put my trousers on now scared some of the other boys so much that they looked as if they might wet themselves. They had good reason. Our enraged games master wielded a football boot in his right hand.

My eye met Trevor's and I recalled my dad saying recently that he was a young man who'd never find satisfaction in life. This had been another warning to me against Trevor, and it was a big relief that, unable to look me in the eye, he now turned aside.

This was all linked to my wrongdoing. About to be thrashed by Mr Heston for my queerness I was shocked to realise that, since the start of Trevor's willy-woofter campaign, I'd wiped from my mind the name of the suicide boy – whose death was a joke to almost everyone I knew. Worse, I'd joined in with their laughter while denying that my gut burnt in disgust at what Trevor was doing. Perhaps it was shame that made my cock soften. That was fitting: I'd had enough of Trevor Carlton for a lifetime. We would never be friends again.

By now Craig was hiding behind the thumbs-up

boy, who was tall and broad. That was a stab to the heart but his reason for doing so made sense to me. It had to. It went back to our pre-teen years. The treatment I endured was a reminder that if he dropped his guard at school he, too, would be destroyed. I couldn't blame him for fighting to survive, and on being scolded by Mr Heston for being slow at getting dressed, I zipped up my trousers and reached for my shirt.

That was when my head was shoved downwards from behind until I was bent over one of the wooden changing benches. 'No boy,' bellowed Mr Heston to the rest while keeping me where I was, 'no boy stoops to queerness on my watch!'

I imagined his hand was right back in preparation for the first blow but, to my surprise, Trevor put the brakes on him, curbing the violence I was about to receive. 'Not the footie boot, sir!' he protested loudly. 'It's got studs!' he added, sliding his leather belt free of his trousers.

A long second passed before Mr Heston accepted it with his free hand and simultaneously threw aside the boot. It hit the metal door of a locker. Eight of the group gasped and Trevor jerked back as if he'd been hit on the forehead with a rock.

Mr Heston did not care. There was a thrashing to be given and he was on the case like never before. Meting out justice to a little queer who'd got turned on in the showers. Not on his watch. Not without punishment.

The pressure was taken from my neck and the belt folded for good hitting power. I kept my hands to my knees, faced the scuffed wood that was before my nose, and waited for what was to come. It was lucky that Mr Heston had changed weapons. The first lash across my bum made me squeal like a pig. As more followed I cursed that I was queer and cursed being born.

The follow-on was simple as ABC.

My mum had a bottle of happy pills, which my dad was encouraging her to wean herself off. Nobody would get the chance to put bubblegum in my hair or beat me for being queer ever again. I would take my revenge. Trevor would suffer. Craig would suffer. The others would suffer. Even Mr Heston might suffer. Suicide was a sure-fire way of escaping a cruel world and hitting back at those queer-haters who, because of their close involvement, would not be able to laugh over my death. It was my lowest point ever. The next few days of my life became a void from which I was lucky to return.

# 47

It was painful for me to breathe and I found out later that this was because my lungs were badly bruised by the spasms the overdose had caused. Also, it seemed that the bubblegum Susan Terry had thrown away two days before had returned as a sloth-like creature, which, resting on my chest, made my fight for air even harder. At last, though, I could remember the name of the other boy.

'Hugo!' I called, as I saw him skimming stones for his big black dog on the beach near Churchill's promontory. 'Hugo Moncrieff!' I added, coming out of the dream-laden stupor in which I'd almost died and finding myself eye to eye with my dad. He looked twenty years older and was sitting at the other side of the hospital bed from my mum, who'd also aged. That I had caused them such distress hit me hard and I spoke from my heart: 'I'm sorry for hurting you both.'

It was the loneliest thing I'd ever said, and because it left me in a place where my family was close yet distant, I had to rise above the physical pain of talking and say more to them. 'I mean it!' I blurted, while my mum burst into tears and my dad looked deep into me, as if to discover who I really was. 'I'm sorry, sorry, sorry!'

When he spoke next, it was to her, not me. 'Tell him, Isla!' he urged. 'Tell him to keep saying the boy's name!'

That seemed odd. Everybody knew about Hugo who, after being in the news, was gossiped about far beyond our two schools, the Oxbridge-destined brain-box who'd hanged himself in the loft of his home while his shopkeeper parents slept below. Scandal was not a big enough term for it.

Then I realised that, partly because I'd not said Hugo's name for weeks, my parents had understood how much his suicide had disturbed me. Out of tact they'd kept quiet on the matter. That was typical of them, never making a fuss if it could be avoided.

Dimly I recalled that, after a fat breathing tube had been removed from my mouth, I'd been shouting for Hugo and his dog, which was called Robespierre. There was no doubt that my cries had been heard by the nurses, doctors and others who were nearby. It helped to explain why my throat was almost as sore as my lungs, while the added stress of reflecting on this was making my breathing even trickier. My mum, a big reader, would have called it a Catch-22 situation. It was my dad who tried to shove things on.

'Isla,' he pleaded, while she took hold of my left

hand and held it to her cheek, 'please get Marcus to speak the boy's name again.'

That made me look harder at his eyes, which, instead of being the same blue as mine, had turned grey, making me wonder if we were both dead and my mum a ghost too. If that was insane what I saw next was even crazier.

The bubblegum-sloth was in a corner by the door and, though it had no eyes, it was watching me. That was creepy, and in dread of being accused of wickedness for trying to kill myself, I shut my eyes against it. It was my mum who nailed what was happening. 'He's still drugged up to the ruddy nines,' she told my dad, who asked her to pull the cord for the doctor to come.

That got me going again. 'I'm not saying any bloody name!' I heard myself insist, opening my eyes in anticipation of the quack's arrival. Though the sloth and its sickly smell were gone, I had the oddest sensation that the hideous creature was now living in my gut, with the revulsion that I knew was connected to Hugo Moncrieff. It made me so ashamed that I almost wanted my lungs to pack up altogether and my days to end.

# 48

The doctor who stood at the end of the bed and had huge brown eyes of a type my art teacher once showed my class in some odd 1950s American portraits. Even weirder, while still in my hospital bed I was also on the beach with Hugo, whose eyes, too, were huge, though not for long. He came closer to where I was standing just above the shoreline, smiled as they returned to normal and took the big boxy glasses I'd often seen him wearing from inside his jacket. That tickled me. Their frames were bright pink, and because of the openness this implied, I wanted to kiss him on the lips. That was not how it had been when he was alive. When I remembered that something about him had always repelled me, I felt as if the sloth within my gut was laughing at me. If Hugo sensed any of this as I faced him beside the sea he clearly didn't care a jot.

'They're right, your parents, you know, Marcus,' he began, speaking over the sound of the shingle being moved back and forth by each wave. 'You really should say my name.' He winked, touching my heart and making me shiver in disgust. That caused the cork to fly from the bottle.

'Hugo Moncrieff!' I cried, into my dad's craggy face. 'Hugo Moncrieff!' I turned to my mum, who was again holding my left hand. 'The boy who killed himself because he was gay was called Hugo Moncrieff!' I explained, causing my dad to nod in satisfaction at getting the bigger answer he had been after. The quack, too, was on the ball.

'Tell your parents all about him, Marcus,' she instructed, as Hugo and the beach scene faded away. The three of them stared at me in expectation of a lot more on the boy who, by taking his life, had become the star of Trevor's willy-woofter campaign. For a moment I feared I was going to be sick and would be unable to hide how much I'd come to dislike Hugo when he was alive. But, to my relief, warm feelings for him, which I'd not acknowledged before, were now ready to spill.

Maybe this was grief: everything about Hugo and what Trevor had done after his death had left me more confused than I'd known, and my dad appeared to sense this. 'Whatever you need to explore, Marcus,' he advised, looking to my mum and back to me, 'just begin where it feels right for you, son.'

Using the flats of my hands I pushed down on the mattress to get higher against the pillows and readied myself to unpick the emotions that had been trapping me like a fly in a web.

'Exactly as your father says,' encouraged the quack. 'Tell your parents all about it,' she added.

I saw my mum weighing up my dad in a way I'd never witnessed before. As if he, too, had something big to share and from which it appeared that our family talk might become epic. Or I was still high and exaggerating. Either way I needed to talk.

# 49

The quack listened as I told them about how I'd first met Hugo on the beach the summer before and that, though he was two years older, he'd always stopped to talk. 'He had a massive black rescue-mutt called Robespierre that Craig loved to skim stones for,' I revealed, making my mum and dad smile. That was satisfying. After being unable to say or even think Hugo's name for weeks, I needed to sum up exactly what he'd meant to me. Doing so was hard.

I wanted to report that he'd been like a big brother, but that was untrue. I held the eye of the quack and searched for the words, which eventually came. 'I suppose he was a sort of pointer to the future,' I explained, looking at my mum, who nodded.

They were all thoughtful, and as I tried to get even higher up against the pillows my mind took a turn that left me feeling sick. The quack read this in my face from her position at the foot of the bed and raised an eyebrow, which, because it was boldly done, stopped me clamming up in shame.

'Thing is,' I confessed, looking to my dad for support,

'because Hugo was ultra-camp, neither me nor Craig could let on that we knew him. And if we had been open,' I insisted, as he frowned, 'we would've been slaughtered by lads from both schools.'

Taken aback by the force with which I'd made this case, they waited while the bubblegum-sloth got so big inside me that my belly might have burst open. Unsurprisingly it was the quack who saw me set my hand to the worst of the pain, right over my liver, which I guessed had also taken a beating from the pills I'd swallowed.

'Marcus will have bloating for several days,' she advised my mum, who was alarmed at how bad I looked. 'But we do expect a quick recovery,' she stressed to my dad, who, in his typically gritted-teeth way, had stayed calm.

Little did any of them know that this latest discomfort was also down to my realisation that, in being guarded about Hugo at school and elsewhere, I'd been as bad as the queer-haters. Including Trevor Carlton, who'd unforgettably maligned Hugo as a woolly-woofter.

This was confusing. I was supposed to be a victim, not the culprit I now felt myself to be. The faces of my mum, dad and the quack had become quizzical, and before they pressed for more answers I was not quite ready to give, I claimed I'd been too young to understand an older boy who was wide open about being queer.

'Plus,' I said, with honesty, 'Craig was even more frightened than me. We had to keep quiet about things.'

The silence that followed was soon broken.

'Did your friend Hugo say he was often attacked for being effeminate?' the quack enquired, and because it was daft to think he wouldn't have been a target, I replied that he didn't give a toss about anyone judging him.

'And in fact,' I went, on in a burst of pride that caught me unawares, 'Robespierre's lead and collar were the same bright pink as the frames of Hugo's specs!'

It was my dad who remarked that Hugo was obviously a brave young man who'd wanted to live each day on his terms and not those he would otherwise have been bullied into accepting. That was food for thought but already my feelings were darkening again. After all, it was easy to forget that Hugo had killed himself and I almost asked my mum if this, too, was a Catch-22 situation.

That would have been cruel. Instead I surprised myself by disclosing that when some of the plastic covering on Robespierre's pink collar was lost as he swam for a skimmed stone, Craig was gleeful about the damage.

'And why on earth does that matter?' asked my mum,

while for the first time ever I saw that, despite his love for Robespierre, Craig had always undermined Hugo, who had probably also been sneered about in the garage where Mr Harrison called me Mandy. The queer. The joke. The suicide boys. As we all were.

'Penny for them, love,' my mum said, while I wondered why I'd been loyal to Craig yet wary at best with Hugo. The bubblegum-sloth, however, felt lighter in my gut and breathing was getting easier.

'Time I left you three to talk between yourselves,' the quack decided, after a glance at the screen that showed my stats. 'A nurse will be along to check Marcus's lung function shortly,' she promised, smiling at us, and left.

'You must keep talking, Marcus love,' urged my mum, when the door had closed. 'We want to understand everything,' she said, with a firm look at my dad, who nodded several times in agreement with her.

'Talk to us, Marcus,' they said as one.

'Talk to us,' they insisted.

# 50

I told them that after Mr Harrison's suicide I'd got into a routine of walking the tide line alone. Partly this was to fill the empty hours now on my hands. Otherwise it was the best way to be near Craig, if only via memory.

The long shore from Churchill's promontory to the lighthouse at the far end of the sands was where we'd strolled together: the closeness I would have done anything to get back. Then one Saturday morning I'd happened across Hugo, who was also walking alone beside the waves.

'So where's the mad stone-chasing hound?' I asked. Robespierre had hurt a back leg on the beach some weeks before and I thought the semi-healed wound must be playing up.

The reply was blunt. His beloved dog was dead.

That pulled me up sharp and I saw that behind his outsized pink specs the middle of his face was puffy from what would have been hours of crying. Plus something in his eye suggested a lot more might be said about Robespierre's end, but rather than wanting to hear about it, I wished I hadn't come across Hugo.

After being pushed out of Craig's life, the last thing I wanted was to take on Hugo's problems. Still, it would have been wrong not to ask more about what had happened to Robespierre.

'So how did he die?' I asked, while he took off his glasses and began to polish them on the lower front bit of his dark green jersey.

Instead of replying, he finished his task, looked to the perfectly flat horizon and sobbed as if I'd ripped his heart out.

'I'm sorry, Hugo,' I told him. Perhaps for young men such as we were becoming, life would always be sad. Yet help for us both came from an unexpected quarter.

A seal broke the surface not far off and its face as it stared our way was so funny that we broke into laughter. Hugo quipped that, because of its likeness to a black Labrador, Robespierre had returned to protect us.

After drying his face on his woollen cuffs and refitting his glasses he cleared his throat and faced me square-on. He was ready to share the tale, which, for my benefit as much as his, I needed to hear.

# 51

An evening came when three lads Hugo didn't know watched from the promenade as Hugo skimmed stones for Robespierre. That made him wary. The week before two younger boys had said that unless he gave them a fiver they would tell the police he'd tried to feel them up. On this occasion, however, he'd decided that the onlookers meant well and one even joined in with the stone skimming.

What seemed like fun turned ugly.

The stone flicking was supposed to happen with Robespierre out of the water, yet after a few goes the stranger sent a big stone close to where the dog was swimming. For a moment Hugo thought this was a mistake, but from the jeering of the others he realised it had been deliberate. Words were said and a final stone hit Robespierre's hindquarter, which had only just recovered from being injured.

Hugo turned away and looked again at the seal, whose face appeared to have become more serious. Probably I'd imagined that bit.

Either way, we didn't laugh like before and when

Hugo faced me again he confessed that, before he could stop himself, he'd punched the stranger to the sand and threatened to break his leg. 'His two mates,' he added, 'whooped with laughter at him for getting bashed by a homo with a camped-up dog.'

This was the first time I'd heard of a queer retaliating against those who hated us, but Hugo's eyes were still sad.

'A week later,' he went on, 'I was here on the sand with Robespierre as usual and the one I'd punched turned up – no sign of the others. I thought it odd that he was wearing an anorak because it was sunny. Just like now,' he added, holding up his cupped hands as if weighing the sun, which hit every part of the promenade, sand and sea around us, creating a glare. It made me so woozy just to think of it that I seemed to be in three distinct places at once: the beach where the seal kept its inquisitive gaze on me and Hugo; the patch of sand where the boy in the anorak was; and my hospital bed. My dad asked if a machete was hidden in the anorak. For a moment that was funny. He had a love of bloodthirsty old films.

'No. Dad,' I replied. 'The boy didn't have a machete. He didn't even have a knife. In fact,' I faced my mum whose eyebrows were right up in anticipation, 'he had a gun.'

'A gun?' my parents cried. 'A gun?' they repeated, aghast.

# 52

'To be precise,' Hugo had said, 'it was an air-gun.' Then he'd said, 'And as the boy came forward his eyes turned black with fury. Obviously he'd spent the week in a stew because he'd been sorted out by a flipping queer,' he added. Without a word spoken between them, the weapon was aimed at his face from two feet away.

'Luckily for me,' he continued, 'the bloody thing jammed.'

For some moments I was so disturbed I couldn't speak. It took a sudden bark from the seal to get me going again.

'Jesus Christ, Hugo!' I wailed. 'You could've been blinded! He must've been high as a bloody kite!'

He gave a tight little smile. Neither of us believed that any queer-basher would need drugs for such an attack. Then he revealed that, because the boy didn't have the guts to fire at him, he'd shot his dog instead. 'And guess what? Robespierre was only giving his paw as if to a friend.'

This time it was me who looked aside at the seal, as

Hugo reported that the pellet had entered Robespierre's brain via his eye.

By contrast, my mum's next statement came at me as if she was emptying a bin onto my hospital bed. It was physical. 'But the police, Marcus,' she objected. 'Surely the police . . . And why, Leon, why wasn't any of this in the paper?' she demanded of my dad, who closed his eyes and sighed. I knew what he was thinking. It was exactly what Hugo had argued with me. Some coppers were fair-minded but police forces in general hunted down queers. Of all people, my mum knew this.

Her nephew – my older cousin – was rising up the ranks in another part of the county and, on a visit to us, had boasted about keeping tallies of how many homos he nailed each year. Men whom officers had propositioned and then charged, ruining careers, reputations and families. And this without taking into account those who were left so broken that they killed themselves. Yet Hugo did not show anger at the police treatment of Robespierre's death.

'A friendly young cop came to the house, but in the view of his superiors I'd landed a punch, an airgun toy was fired, and what happened to Robespierre was accidental. Case solved,' he said, as I turned back from the seal and saw the anger I now felt caught in my twin-reflection on his glasses. It left me bitter.

'Want to know the truth behind all of this?' I

challenged my dad, who glanced across the bed to my mum and nodded for me to tell all.

'The boy with the airgun was the son of a magistrate who knew the cops. What was Hugo but a homo flaunting himself on the beach? Join the dots,' I urged.

Despite my mum's tears I had to keep going.

'Listen, nobody cared about Robespierre because of what Hugo was. Especially his mum and dad, who didn't want a fuss. Most parents would have behaved in the same way,' I added.

My mum reacted fast. 'But how can he say that?' she protested to my dad. 'How?' she repeated, while tummy acid rose to my throat and made me splutter, like an old man, scaring us in case my lungs were wrecked after all. Especially my mum, who was horrified at my latest struggle for air.

'Don't pull the cord,' I croaked, when she wanted to bring the quack. 'Please, Mum.' My dad poured a glass of water that I sipped to ease my throat. Perhaps a minute passed, which enabled me to gather my thoughts, though we each knew that we had to press on while the family mood for truth was solid. Otherwise the status quo of knowing but not knowing would have remained as it was, like poison vapour, contaminating not just me, but also them.

# 53

There was a splash and we saw that the young seal had gone under the water. 'Ah,' Hugo drily remarked, 'goodbye to our friend.'

For some reason this made me even sadder than the death of Robespierre had, and after following him to a set of concrete stairs that rose steeply to the promenade, I remained on the sand-covered bottom step. Looming over me, Hugo looked to the line where the sea met the sky, and the loss of the sparkle that had made him defiantly queer cut me like a razor blade slowly drawn across my skin.

'We're unnecessary to normal life, you and I, Craig,' he said. 'Unwanted, unloved, including by those who oppose hands-on queer-bashing.' He laughed, but without humour, and on hearing this reported my mum looked so sad that, to avoid faltering, I pressed on with a firmness that, even to my ears, made me sound older than before I'd tried to kill myself. Like I'd done a whole chunk of growing up in one go.

'It's the avoidance of queerness as a topic that drives boys like me, Hugo and Craig into a place where suicide is the only way out,' I argued, struck by how solidly I felt the truth of what I was saying. They couldn't disagree. I'd become an expert who knew beyond question what he was talking about. My defeated-looking mum sighed and nodded in acceptance.

After all, it was down to luck that I wasn't dead, and she and my dad knew it. Five more pills and my lungs would have been ruined for sure, leaving my heart to flap like a butterfly with nowhere to go.

'You see how deep this stuff is?' I asked, thinking about Craig, his homo-hater dad, Mr Heston and all the rest of it. 'It's every-bloody-where,' I concluded, realising that because most people did not even acknowledge the queer-bashing which occurred somewhere every day, they probably would not have reacted to boys like me being quietly gassed either.

Just a year before, our local news had reported on a man who was left brain-damaged after being kicked in the head by teenagers who claimed he was coming on to them. Plus Hugo was lucky that the airgun aimed at his eyes had jammed. I didn't need to think more about any of this. The full picture glared in its awfulness for us all. When it came to hatred towards queers, exaggeration of what went on was impossible. That was the truth reflected by Hugo's change of character and suicide.

My dad cleared his throat. 'Don't forget, son,' he said, looking across the bed to where my mum seemed to know what was about to come, 'I grew up in an era when to be different was still illegal.' That was a shocker. I'd never thought of him in any context that might have been queer. Yet at the same time I believed the mystery that had been lurking throughout our talk was now to be revealed.

My mum's reaction was even more astute. She nailed what my dad was getting at. 'Ah,' she declared, 'finally, Leon, we're back to him.'

'Who?' I asked, puzzled, wary, fascinated.

'To poor Tony Ridge,' she answered, keeping her eyes fixed on my dad.

'Aye,' he agreed, 'poor Tony Ridge,' but more to himself as the blue of his eyes went grey again.

# 54

He faced me while explaining that Tony Ridge was a clever boy who was in his class at school. Choosing his next words as if picking his way through a minefield, he added that Tony was also a loving young chap. My mum chipped in that the girls had adored him and I got one thing for sure. Tony Ridge was gay. The next bit I was wrong about.

'You, Dad?' I asked, in astonishment. 'You were in love with Tony Ridge?' I went on, amazed at the boldness that had overwhelmed me. After all, he was a tough fireman and until then I'd believed queers were always camp. Like Hugo. And even Craig, when he was feeling more at ease with himself.

For a moment or two my dad smiled sadly, which made my mum cluck her tongue in sympathy. But at the same time the colour began returning to his eyes and I felt sure he was going to speak from the deepest bit of himself, like I'd never heard him before. It was no surprise that this time I was correct.

'I ridiculed the boy,' he admitted, looking down at where his hands were joined on his lap, then back to my eye, which was now held as if his life depended on me hearing his confession. 'Mocked his wide-open heart until the whole damn year of boys joined in,' he added, with honesty that was blunt as a hammer.

For a moment my gut became clenched as if the bubblegum-sloth was doing something particularly bad again, but this was followed by a relaxing of all my tummy symptoms, leaving me at my best since waking up.

'At last,' said my mum to my dad, 'the worst of it is said.'

'I didn't love Tony Ridge,' he said, 'I destroyed him, son.' He paused. 'We called boys like Tony "moths". Moths,' he repeated, shuddering. I saw then what had happened. It was part of a long history that I'd come to understand all too well.

'Tony killed himself, didn't he?' I said.

My dad drew a big breath to calm his nerves. 'The 1950s were even harder than today,' he resumed, and then he was talking to me urgently.

Pouring his heart out, in fact.

'Say you had a friend and you got a sense of his beauty – a finely turned mouth or cute little ears like Tony's. Well, Marcus, you smashed those feelings. Almost every boy,' he insisted, while stabbing his right first finger into his left hand, 'almost every boy self-monitored every minute of every day. We called them moths,' he concluded. Shame had made his face and neck go bright red. My present, I knew, had crashed head-on with his past and I sensed that it was wisest for me to stay quiet until he was ready to offer more.

When he spoke next it was to my mum again. 'No more excuses for me, Ailsa. I was a cruel little bastard, and it's best accepted.' That, too, was blunt but at least the build-up to where we were now made sense to me. The Tony Ridge affair had been eating at my dad for over twenty years and I realised that it was why – without being cruel, like Craig's dad – he'd often blanked my queerness, hoping I would have an easier, normal life.

Suddenly I needed to be sick and my mum held the cardboard dish, which caught the pinky-green slime that came out of me. Maybe then I went a little mad. If so, it helped a lot.

On resting my spine against the pillows again, the seal I'd seen with Hugo stared out at me from where my dad's eyes now showed their full blueness. It was the purest moment of my life so far. 'Mum? Dad? I will never, ever do this again,' I promised.

It was what they'd needed to hear. That my suicide attempt was a one-off and I would not throw away my future, like Tony Ridge and Hugo.

Before I knew it my dad had half lifted me out of the bed and was giving me such a strong hug that my mum chided him. There was no anger in her voice. It seemed that on marking the end of the bubblegum-sloth's stay in my gut, the bile I'd vomited had purged something for us all. This was the moment when I began to be unafraid of my future as a gay man. And even to welcome it.

Nonetheless, the thought of going back to school was scary, but after confirming that I'd been accepted for the London sewing-machine apprenticeship, my parents announced that in the meantime I would help out at the council kennels where my mum's best friend was the vet. That was great. I loved dogs almost as much as I loved Craig, and it seemed that everything about my life was falling into place.

But I couldn't just forget Hugo, and when I became quiet again my dad wanted to know what was on my mind.

'Hugo knew,' I told them. 'When he spoke to me, he knew he was going to kill himself. The death of Robespierre and the police broke him. It wasn't suicide', I insisted, 'it was manslaughter.'

My dad kept his eyes down and I knew he was thinking about Tony Ridge.

This moment was not terrible for me. I was the lucky one with everything to look forward to. No queer-hater, past or present, could wreck that. I had survived. My mum had survived. My dad had survived. I was proud to be me. Proud to be gay.

# 55

Yet again my second sight had gone haywire. It seemed that instead of being stuck within the swirls of Jack's Elvis portrait I was now a part of its nightmare-composition. Just the sort of thing that happens when a sickly rescue dog pushes too hard. Still, my discoveries had been dramatic enough to test even a healthy rescue dog and the questions they'd raised were big.

If only Raymond had shown his feelings for Oliver by saving his life. If only Marcus's dad, Leon, had not sneered at young Tony Ridge for falling in love with him. If only Hugo hadn't killed himself, leaving Craig even more confused about being queer . . .

If only. If only. If only . . .

Rescue dogs know that the lives of humans are littered with choices that are as regrettable as their effects are long-lasting. All we can do is try to help. But ultimately the choice between survival and self-destruction is down to each individual. Realising this at least enabled me to escape Jack's painting, and I saw that when Pauline had quipped 'like father like son' to my first human, she was being ironic. Challenging him to prove the old saying wrong. That no human being was condemned to a disastrous life

Or, to put it another way, that bad bone knowledge could be defied.

After all, Marcus Wright had survived the worst that Fate could throw his way and I wanted the kid to see that, in light of this tale, his own queerness did not mean a sad little life ahead. Nonetheless, it seemed for me, Brucie-Dog, that Fate couldn't be changed with the ease Pauline had implied.

I'd escaped the painting but my weak health had landed me in another cold, black place where I expected to die. Until something remarkable happened. The seal that had come to watch Hugo and Marcus weeks before took me by the scruff of my neck and, as we rose to where sunlight was high above, he changed into Robespierre: Hugo's rescue dog.

I knew what this was about. The unused power of a rescue dog that has died early may be passed on to a younger rescue dog in need of help with its mission. Though he was well beyond his middle years when he was killed, Robespierre had still got time ahead of him, and it was this unspent energy that enabled me to return to where Marcus had called to see the kid at the workshop on his shiny yellow Raleigh Chopper.

Her Hoityness did not waste time ordering me to stop my dreaming, and get on with things.

'Before Marcus leaves!' she growled, with a wolfishness that made me shudder. Mainly because I knew she was right.

It was amazing that, after his recent go at self-offing, Marcus had come to see the kid, and to make progress with my mission I needed to explore what was occurring between the two young humans. Exactly as Her Hoityness was demanding of me and that, in contrast to my earlier self doubt, I fully believed I could achieve.

Recharged by the gift from Robespierre, I was now a wiser rescue dog who knew more than ever what he was about. I hoped Her Hoityness could see that. It had become my aim to please her as if she was my real mum, whose litter was thrown into the river from which my first human saved me.

'Get on with it!' she barked, as I shook myself from end to end.

# 56

The kid was standing on the point where the workshop met the lane. 'I wanted to say sorry,' he told Marcus, who was still astride the Raleigh Chopper. 'Really, really sorry,' he added, while my tail wagged. I hoped he might step forward into the open. Marcus waited. I waited, but on moving backwards to Big Eddie's hazy red Mustang, he once again showed a lot of whiteness.

That really set off my itching, and I saw Marcus put his left foot to the low crossbar and slip a finger into his plimsoll, where he, too, needed to scratch. Such was the effect of Craig on us both.

'Sorry for what?' he queried, setting his foot back to the ground and locking the rear brake of the Chopper. 'For laughing when I was beaten by Mr Heston?' he suggested, with an ease that, because I knew his words were hurting the kid, put the worst fire ever in my long-suffering belly.

By now he'd slid right back on the long thin saddle and was repeating his trick of levering the front of the Raleigh Chopper into the air, compelling Craig to drop his gaurd and stride forward, into the sunny lane.

'Yes, Marcus!' he blurted. 'For all that happened at school, I'm truly sorry.'

Pressing his spine against the bike's tall backrest, Marcus then widened his splayed feet and took the front wheel even further up. 'So,' he mused, 'that's it, then? You're sorry and everything's forgotten? Simple, really, isn't it, Brucie?' he added, looking down to where I'd set my bum beside him.

For some moments the kid used the side of his brogue to scuff at the long black tyre mark Marcus had laid down on his arrival. 'Do ya really reckon?' he asked, lifting his head. Marcus was watching him closely. 'I mean, that everything's so simple?' he went on, with a sadness that sent chills to the heat I was feeling.

Lowering the front wheel back to the concrete, Marcus shrugged and smiled with warmth that showed, despite the bubblegum attack and the humiliation of the school showers, his love for Craig was intact. My tail wagged and they laughed as it swept the concrete behind me.

'Listen,' Marcus said, flashing a look at the kid with eyes that were bluer and brighter than ever, 'none of it was your fault. So do us both a big favour and just forget it.'

That was well meant but, because of my powerful nose, I knew he understood that Craig would always be troubled by what had happened. His hands were the number one giveaway: I'd smelt the tightening of his hold on the Raleigh's spiked handlebar grips: the plastic had been softened by the sun.

At the same time his right foot had returned to the pedals, making me get up and stand four-square between him and the kid, who now bit his thin bottom lip.

Giving them both my biggest blue moons, I wished with all my heart that, in true rescue-dog style, Marcus could see the mass of white that signalled the likelihood of Craig also trying to off himself.

Buoyed up by the belief that the link between them was real, I saw that instead of cycling away on his own, Marcus would slide forward on the saddle and enable the kid to hold onto him from behind, making them into one and my mission a runaway success, which would have pleased Her Hoityness. It was ironic that something even more fanciful brought me to my senses.

A red ladybird landed on the polished yellow paint of the Raleigh Chopper and I realised that, after exploring Marcus's tale, it was vital for me to discover in detail why the kid was the one who'd no longer wanted them to share their lives. Arms across shoulders. Hearts beating together. Two young humans bonded by love. Aware of the drain I was about to place on the energy gifted to me by Robespierre, I Brucie-Dog drew on my second sight to become the cold, wet kid.

# 57

Cold and wet, because an old wooden roof was letting rain into the workshop where I was helping my dad fix the rear suspension of a tatty Vauxhall Victor. Again and again he cursed while hammering the head of a bolt that would not go back into place. As if the car itself was wilfully driving him into one of the rages that had lately got more frequent and ever scarier.

The more he attacked the bolt and swore, the more my gut felt as if it was being twisted, sending stinging bile into my throat. This was partly because I'd become trapped in a vicious circle. Once, I'd thrown up in the workshop, making my dad shout at me for being a cissy who was too soft to help with his cars. That was a shock, and ever since I'd worried about it happening again, which had made my insides feel knottier. Plus this was a day when I had good reason to be extra wary of what the word 'cissy' implied.

In my dreams the night before I'd been swimming in a warm sea with Marcus and Trevor from school and none of us was bothered about being queer. That was beautiful. Yet on waking up to sticky sheets I was so ashamed I'd thought about drinking the oven-cleaning fluid my mum kept under the kitchen sink.

Instead I'd asked God for help.

Please, God, make me normal. Please, God, make me dream of girls, not boys, I'd prayed, even though I believed that God allowed so much hatred of homos because he too would have preferred us dead. Nonetheless I'd repeated the prayer many times in the hope that he would see my determination and – just maybe – this had paid off.

I'd survived one of the worst nights of my life so far and, no matter what happened when Dad stopped his mad hammering – there had to be a reason why the bolt wouldn't fit – I would try to make him see that I was still his loyal deputy in the workshop. There was one clear reason why I owed him this.

Being queer was a sin, and because Dad had realised this about me he'd become a more serious drunkard than before. I was the guilty one in the family. Not him. Make me normal, I'd implored God, believing that if he did so Dad would stop boozing and be kind to my mum.

My queerness was driving him frantic. Or mad. Or both.

Hammering, hammering and hammering within the sodden workshop where, despite the thickness of my brogues, my feet were so cold that they might have been turning to ice. Finally he set the hammer aside, took his big shaggy head from within the Vauxhall's wheel arch, and fixed his marble-hard blue eyes on me. 'Well, Craig?' He held up the bolt for me to see that it was too large for the hole he'd spent ages trying to make it fit into. 'Well?' he repeated.

'But, Dad,' I protested, embarrassed that I was going beetroot, 'I gave you the right bolt. You must've dropped it and picked the wrong one up from under the car.' It was lucky for me I stopped short of adding that he'd done this because he was hung-over from the day before and half-cut from his lunchtime visit to the Gay Hussar. Pickled in booze, as my mum would have said.

The nearby hammer was picked up and thrown down with such force that a spark flew from the concrete I was standing on. 'Worthless damn cissy-boy!' he roared, yellowed teeth showing through his fag-stained grey beard and moustache.

'Socket wrench,' he ordered, clicking his fingers. Oddly, while I could now meet his eye, he couldn't meet mine. Years would pass before I understood that he was ashamed of bullying me. Years would pass before I saw that self-disgust ate at him like cancer.

The click of the wrench as he tightened the correct bolt was reassuring and, in an almost content way, I thought about 'accidentally' riding my bike off the cliff near the lighthouse at the far end of the beach. That way nobody would think I'd killed myself and Mum's oven-cleaning fluid wouldn't be wasted. The last thing I might have expected was for my big brother Jack to intrude on these thoughts.

## 58

Dad was on his knee refitting the Vauxhall's rear wheel when Jack came to the door where the workshop met the backyard at number twenty.

'Hey, Craig, me and Vanessa want a word,' he called, in a firm but friendly manner. For a moment I was worried in case Dad blew up but ever since Jack had stopped him hurting Mum in our garden, things between them had been different. Dad, I suspected, was even sort of grateful to my big brother for bringing him to heel, leaving Mum safer than she'd been for years.

'You know, son,' he remarked to Jack, who had put only his head inside the workshop, 'this place isn't toxic.'

That made my brother smile. 'It's okay, thanks, Dad,' he answered. 'I've only come outside for our Craigie.'

'We have to talk now,' he insisted, eyeballing me while Dad got up to watch us.

Under different circumstances the hard glint in Jack's eye might have set off an alarm in my head. But the cold in my feet was spreading upwards and, in my first ever rejection of Dad's company, I wanted to be in the house with my brother and sister. The call was Dad's to make and, determined to get his way, Jack entered the workshop and locked eyes with him in the gloom.

'Don't mind us talking with Craig, d'ya, Dad?' he asked, as the worry fizzing in my belly caused me to burp so loudly that they laughed.

'Go on, son.' Dad pushed me forward with a hand to my back, kindly but also like I was a gift for the older twins to do with as they would.

'Thanks, Dad!' cried Jack, and fled up the rainy yard, where Mum's potted ferns were getting their best drink in weeks.

'I'm coming, Jack! I'm coming!' I called, setting my head against the downpour to follow him, leaving Dad where the crappy old Vauxhall was ready to be lowered back onto all four wheels, restoring balance at least to one element of his life.

'Hurry up, Craig!' shouted my brother, as I reached the glass door to the kitchen off-shoot, where my meeting with him and Vanessa was to take place.

'Get inside, dolt-heads!' ordered our sister, whose over-the-top try at light-heartedness confirmed to me that they wanted to discuss something big.

# 59

Jack was wetter than me, and while he dried his hair on one of Mum's tea-towels, Vanessa set three breakfast chairs in a semi-circle before the gas fire, which was warming the kitchen. Pretty soon she was seated to my left and my brother to my right. I wanted to ask what they were about but held back because I had enough already to reckon with.

Jack had found my eyes with his in the 1930s mirror that hung at a tilt midway up the chimney breast. It felt like we were seeing ourselves on film, and Vanessa's hair, styled into blue and yellow spikes, added a theatrical touch. The mood, though, was serious.

After clearing his throat, my brother began, 'Look here, our Craig,' but was stopped by Vanessa's laughter at how up-his-bum he sounded. Annoyed, he bit his lower lip and looked at baldy old Picasso, in his domed cage on top of the fridge. The parrot's head was cocked our way.

'Oh, just get on with it, Jack!' snapped Vanessa.

That did the trick. Looking into the mirror again, her

twin was blunt as a brick. 'Half the town heard the old man having a go at you, our Craig,' he announced. 'A right tongue-lashing about being a cissy,' he added, making me squirm on my seat as if I'd got worms.

Sliding my gaze sideways at Vanessa I found that her right eyebrow was up like a question mark, reminding me that, not too long before, she'd taken me aside and said I should stop pretending the attacks from Dad in the workshop didn't matter.

'You two are ganging up!' I protested, going bright red. 'Me and Dad have just been playing-on like always.'

After scrubbing his right hand through his hair Jack shook his head and nodded at Vanessa for her to have a go. Good cop, bad cop sort of thing, but a bit mixed up.

'We know what Dad is doing is getting worse,' she was glaring into the mirror, 'so don't bloody well try and make fools of us, Craig.'

Jack's face shot towards the chimney breast and stopped when his eyes were glued to mine via the mirror. 'Agreed, our Vanessa,' he said. 'What occurs in Dad's bloody den matters a lot!'

She'd gone the same bright red as me, and when Jack's brow crinkled I knew he was scared of becoming a bully like Dad.

Maybe Picasso sensed we were all getting out of our depth. 'Matters a lot!' he squawked, and fixed on us the beadiest eye he could make. 'Matters a lot!'

I saw Vanessa's gaze soften and Jack scratch the back of his neck in a gesture that implied he wanted things to proceed with kindness rather than conflict.

'Please, Craig,' he began again, 'we're only trying to help.'

This time my heart was touched and Picasso appeared to understand our shared mood even better than he had before. 'Only trying to help!' he mimicked, making me, my brother and our sister shriek with the laughter that opened my eyes to what they had known all along. I needed to tell the story of me and Dad. Keeping it to myself had been damaging me for ages.

'When you're ready,' advised Vanessa, whose right eyebrow was up.

Clearing my throat, I got ready for the tale of Dad, cars and me. The world where I'd often been while the others were with Mum. And how over the past year it'd all gone sour.

# 60

Every Thursday evening from when I was a nipper Dad took me to the car auctions where, because he always swigged from a half-bottle of Bell's whisky, he was known as Mr Bell's, and where on account of my excitement at finding Cataloy filler on tarted-up cars I became his deputy, the Cataloy Kid. It was the kind of name that makes you feel brilliant when blokes in the motor trade say it and you're only ten – though it started when I was eight and the auctioneer, who fancied himself as a showman, closed the bidding on a dark blue Rover V8. It was identical to the prime minister's car, which I'd seen on the news outside 10 Downing Street.

'Lot number two-two-two, a performance motor-car with leather and wood, condition, it's true, all very good. Sold to Mr Bell's and the one and only Cataloy Kid!'

The fall of the hammer was accompanied by a round of laughter that made me proud to be Dad's deputy, especially when he ruffled my hair and saluted the auctioneer, who was so fast and clear with his phrasing that he'd long since earned a special name of his own: Dr Mouth.

'Thank you, kind sir,' called Dad, across the brightly lit bay that the cars were driven to for the minute or two of their sale. 'A winning performance as usual from Mouth.' He bowed his head at the surrounding bidders, some of whom roared with a different laughter – it bordered on revenge against the auctioneer, whom Dad had undermined by removing the 'Dr' from his nickname.

The bony-featured auctioneer always wore a black suit and silver-framed glasses that half hid his eyes. He was not only a showman, he was the high priest of the sale, a spruce, arrogant man who sat at a red Formica rostrum, which shone like newly let blood. An elevated post from where he held sway over the casually dressed bidders, most of whom were awed by him. Unlike Dad, who stood straight and steady as he stared across the roof of the blue Rover V8, his grey beard making him look how I imagined God to be. That was how much I'd always loved him, my car-fixing hero of a dad, who, until things began to change, had made me feel so safe that, no matter how far I strayed from his side, I felt his love.

But I couldn't help it: I was older now and felt embarrassed that other bidders at the Rover V8 sale had seen a half-cut geezer whose fingers and whiskery lips were stained by fags. A near-tramp who, despite having seven hundred quid to pay for the Rover, was wearing an overcoat with all the buttons missing so it hung over his pot-belly like half-drawn curtains. What came next was inevitable.

Dr Mouth wasn't going to be shown up by a scruff with a drink problem. From this moment on he was Dr Death to me. He could have let poor Dad have his moment of triumph without coming back at him. I will hate him to my dying day.

'Take it away,' he ordered the man who'd driven the Rover into the selling bay. Sensing his anger I tried to catch his eyes but was prevented by the gleam on his glasses. On the times that I'd been able to see beyond this, shivers went down my spine. His were cruel eyes, which made me think he hated most people. In years to come I would see him in the same light as our games master, Mr Heston. A number-one bully.

'Sold to Mr Bell's,' he repeated, and added, 'Let us pray that he finds some coat buttons in the glove box!'

After that, I was consumed by dread that all the blokes – many of whom wore donkey jackets with fat black buttons – were jeering at Dad, like he was now the joke. Except that back then he was still sharp enough to wangle his way out of most situations. 'Well, Dr Mouth,' he called, 'should I do so, sir, I'll take them to the button auction and make some of my money back.' Not a great joke but delivered like a hit for six. I was so wound up that I nearly wet my pants.

The auctioneer didn't look at Dad as he remarked, 'Whatever you say, Bell's,' and signalled for the next car from the line. He'd let Dad have a victory of sorts after all, but I'd felt in my bones how dangerous it was. The first time I'd been worried for Dad at the auctions, where he was known to be magic with cars. If he hadn't drunk too much Bell's whisky.

# 61

Five minutes of my story-telling had sped by. 'All this time and I knew nothing about Mr Bell's and the Cataloy Kid!' exclaimed Jack, who excitedly looked from me to Vanessa in the mirror. Amused, she knew I was proud to have impressed my big brother with talk of an auctioneering high priest and a Rover V8 identical to the prime minister's. It was impossible for her not to show off a little.

'Oh, but I knew,' she said – we occasionally had private chats about happier times with Dad. 'Our Craigie's told me loads,' she added.

It was then that Jack announced he was coming to the next car auction. The idea gave me the horrors. It would have been like me going to the City Art Gallery with him and Mum. Each of us kids had a number-one passion that the others did not share. Cars for me, art for him, fashion for Vanessa and sport for my twin sister, Rachael. When I scowled Jack knew what it meant.

'Okay, okay, I won't bloody be there,' he grumbled. 'But come on,' he was getting excited again, 'you can tell us more, Craigie. Can't he?' he asked Vanessa, who was smiling at the pair of us.

'Don't ask me, ask him,' she teased. She knew I was even prouder that Jack wanted more of my tale. Still, I tried to play it cool. Having the upper hand over my big brother was a novelty I didn't intend to waste.

'Give me a minute,' I said, pretending I needed to think about the next bit, which – like a reservoir held by a cardboard dam – was ready to burst free. 'I don't know. You two,' remarked Vanessa. 'Priceless as yin and yang.'

I wondered who the heck they were but didn't ask in case I lost Jack's new regard for me. Our Picasso was now having a lot of fun with himself against his plastic water butt. It was something we brothers had been laughing about for years, though this time Jack seized on it as an excuse to get me going again.

'Never mind horny bloody Picasso!' he ordered, making my green eyes return to the identical gaze of him and Vanessa in the mirror. 'Tell me more about the car auctions. And,' he added, reaching to nip my ear – the sort of tweak we gave each other when we weren't up for a proper fun-fight – 'don't forget we need to know what's gone wrong with you and Dad in the workshop.'

Unable to disguise my delight that Vanessa as well as Jack really did want to hear more, I was soon talking even more enthusiastically than before.

# 62

The last time it was great was when Dad stole a 1969 Mark II Cortina 1600E from Dr Death for three hundred and fifty quid. We knew the car already. It'd been bought new by Trevor Carlton's dad and was one reason why I became Trevor's friend. By the time it was two years old the E model was a legend.

They were the poor man's Rolls-Royce. Comfy seats. Wooden dashboard and door cappings, highly polished with a gorgeous grain to the timber. Plus dead stylish wheels, called Ro-Styles, and a leather-rimmed steering wheel. Fantastic cars that sent the blood whacking through your veins. Or, leastways, they did mine.

Plus the bonus with this one was its colour, a rare pale metallic pink called Light Orchid. A shade that suits the neat lines of the Mark II like it's almost invisible. Not fancy, just exquisite. Totally beautiful.

The first day I saw it, it was outside the small seafront hotel Trevor's parents owned, gleaming in the sun with the silver blue sea behind. One of the best things I'd ever seen. A vision. A sculpture. A work of art. In fact, I even took Dad along and we went in a dark blue '63

Morris Oxford with rotten sills and the back exhaust missing. Great fun. Sounded like the Russians had arrived. Then Dad said the car I'd taken him to see showed that, even though I was only thirteen, I had 'discernment'. Afterwards I looked it up in the dictionary and became so happy that the Light Orchid 1600E was even more special to me.

I doubted Trevor's dad would have understood this. He was fat and usually wore a white shirt, which stayed open where his belly button was. Trevor called him 'The Gorilla' because he was so hairy. I bet he didn't say it to his face. It was claimed that if anybody upset Mr Carlton in the hotel bar, he punched them. Even Dad said he wasn't a man to cross swords with, and because of the way he sometimes looked at me when I was near his car, he scared me.

But what I really disliked was that he didn't value the 1600E, which was always mucky, inside and out, especially in winter with the road salt, which made the back wheel arches and front wings go rusty. It's amazing how quickly that happens. Makes you want to cry. Made me want to cry. Sometimes I used to write messages in the dirt on its bonnet when I was doing my paper round: Save me! You're letting me rust to death.

It was little wonder that Mr Carlton seemed to dislike me more as time passed, and I stopped going by the hotel, which at least meant that I was no longer upset by witnessing the smart 1600E's slide into an eyesore.

Then, one day, it turned up at the auction, which didn't surprise me because I'd heard from Trevor that they'd bought a horrible new Daytona Yellow Mark III Cortina, which showed how much 'discernment' Mr Carlton had. Dad laughed at that, but told me not to get above myself. I suppose it's just as well he was more or less sober at the sale. At first he pretended not to be interested in the 1600E but I knew better. His nose for a bargain was still working well.

Obviously it'd come via the trade, which was how it worked. The posh dealers did the new stuff, sent the trade-ins to the auctions, and the next lot tidied them up and sold them on. Just like Dad had done since the 1950s.

He had no grand illusions about this work. Said it was a case of little fish eating off the backs of whales. That was the trade and I knew my chance to save the 1600E had come on a plate. When you looked close, the arches and wings weren't that rusty after all. Plus it had only thirty thousand on the clock. Hardly run in. But terrible to look at because the paint had become a dull salmon colour that was rough to touch where the flecks that created the metallic finish were corroded. That made it look dead in the bidding bay, directly in front of us, where even the strong overhead lighting couldn't make it shine.

'Bid for it,' I urged Dad.

'It's a heap,' he replied, amused by my eagerness.

What happened next probably surprised him. I actually got tears in my eyes, which some of the trade blokes saw. That was because I knew, given the chance, I could restore the shine, which Dad thought was impossible to recreate without a respray. 'Buy it, Dad,' I pleaded. Still he resisted but I knew I was right. He might not have been able to save the paintwork, but I could.

In the end he decided that if we bought it and lost money I had to give him my paper-round cash until it was made up. That didn't bother me. I knew we could make the 1600E beautiful without the respray Dad was predicting. And even he was surprised when Dr Death knocked it down at less than the four fifty it was worth. It put him in such a good mood that he decided it was my project to bring back the gleam.

If you'd asked me then, I would have said that the sun was going to shine out of Dad's bum forever. He wasn't just my hero. He was my super-hero.

# 63

Rain was still hitting the glass back door of number twenty, and a part of me wanted to tell Jack and Vanessa that, with the 1600E's paintwork to fix on, I'd felt less like topping myself for being a queer. I relished the task Dad had set me. It was going to straighten me out and get the likes of Trevor Carlton off my back. Or so I prayed, desperate to be normal. It was Jack, however, who unwittingly stopped me spilling the beans.

'What happened next, our Craig?' he asked, breaking into my thoughts.

For a moment I was thrown and gawped at him as if I'd lost my mind.

'I mean with getting the car to shine again!' he cried into the mirror, where Vanessa, too, seemed nonplussed by the big pause in my story.

'Vim and Brasso!' I retorted, relieved to be back on track.

'Vim and Brasso?' they cried, while each of our reflected brows went high as it could, bringing added drama to my tale of the potentially stunning Cortina 1600E. Which, for a little while, was my life-saver.

# 64

I got Mum's Vim from the bathroom and mixed it with a splash of water. Just enough to make an abrasive paste for taking the corrosion off the aluminium in the metallic paint. Stage two was to do every bit of the car again, but with shampoo in the paste, making it creamier, softer. That put the shine back on the aluminium where I'd polished away the corrosion. Then I did a panel at a time with Brasso, which removed the scratches the Vim had left in the pink. By now the surface was becoming smooth as well as shiny, with the true colour showing so well that I could hardly sleep for excitement. I was rescuing something beautiful.

After that I washed the car with scalding hot water and loads of Fairy Liquid. Big white bubbles on the gleaming paintwork that I'd brought back to life, with the rust on the arches and wings hardly showing where the brown staining was polished away. Just to protect the mirror surface I'd brought back, I waxed the 1600E three times, making the finish so extra-shiny that it was better than any respray would have been.

Next up I did the Ro-Style wheels with aluminium paint and cleaned the tyre walls with brake fluid. I made the glass and chrome sparkle, and buffed the interior, which – exactly as I'd always known it would – came up perfectly. The poor man's Rolls-Royce reborn! Luckily enough, it even smelt clean, because – if Trevor was to be believed – his dad hadn't smoked since he'd had a heart attack before he'd bought the car.

So there you go. I'd saved the 1600E I'd worried about for years. My best car moment ever. A brilliant feeling. Poor old Dad stood back, looked at it gleaming in the sun, and couldn't believe his eyes. Plus the money side of things was amazing. With Dr Death's commission plus Mum's cleaning stuff, the tally was still only four hundred quid!

'Magic!' I cried into the mirror, with pride at impressing our Jack even more than before. 'Magic!' I repeated, to the amusement of our Vanessa, though within a second of me saying this, my big brother brought us all down to earth with a crash.

'And just what did Daddio say about what you'd done?' he asked, his face scarily hard.

My heart went leaden and I looked to where the gas fire was making steam rise from my brogues, realising that, whether I wanted it or not, I was being made to see the truth about Dad more clearly than ever before.

# 65

He began calling me Retard when I was eight, but because he'd made it seem funny I wasn't upset. Then, as I got older, he'd changed to Cissy, which was what he'd accused Marcus of being. In time I saw what this was about.

Dad despised the queerness he'd spotted long before Marcus or I knew it was there, putting a cloud over our friendship and wounding Marcus. On becoming a teenager he avoided Dad's workshop, calling for me at the front of number twenty.

Often I ignored his visits because I didn't want people to think we were two full-on queers in the making. Dad said little and, to my relief, nobody seemed interested that we weren't close any more. Each of my three siblings had had best friends who'd all gone their own way too.

Secretly I missed Marcus with all my heart, and in a dream I kept having, a man in his mid-twenties urged me to embrace the love we still felt for each other. This stranger was called Oliver, and deep in my past – before I was born – I was connected to him.

Dad also figured in the dream and was obsessed with Oliver, who, like him, was a young sailor on the warship where the dream took place. As if all of this wasn't crazy enough, my queer-hating games master Mr Heston was there, too, and led a form of hide and seek in which Oliver would evade the others to advise that I should be with Marcus for the rest of my life.

Those fleeting moments were beautiful, but on finding us together in a steel-walled nook, with a single light-bulb inside a caged glass cover, Dad and Mr Heston would rant about the vileness of queers and threaten to have us thrown overboard. We wouldn't have lasted long in the cold.

Then the ship would get torpedoed and while they laughed at Oliver for being a worthless queer, a current would take him into a patch where oil was burning on the surface. That was enough torture for me. Yet on the final night I had the dream things were even uglier.

In place of being an onlooker to Oliver's death I became him in the 1940s. For a moment it seemed that Dad would save me from being burned alive, but instead of putting out the flames that were all around me, the yellow foam he sprayed from a red hose made them worse. The meaning became seared onto my heart: queers were always better off dead.

On noting my pallor in the morning Dad suggested that, rather than being in the workshop with him, I should get fresh air on the beach, where I spent ages skimming stones and weighing the pros and cons of live or die.

The last skim made ten bounces. Nine and I wouldn't have lived beyond that day, though in the weeks to come it felt that one person had died. I missed Oliver from my dreams. He gave me hope.

A squawk from Picasso brought me back to where the older twins were still watching me in the mirror and something in their shared gaze made me join up more dots about Dad.

Because of what he'd always felt about me – right back to when I was the Retard and even earlier – my urge to please him with the Light Orchid Cortina 1600E had been fated to make things worse between us.

Raising his right eyebrow, like Vanessa had earlier, Jack was ready to push things forward again. I couldn't argue with that. We'd come a long way but my tale was far from told. I was determined to keep a brave face.

## 66

'**C**'mon, our Craig,' he pressed, with a glance at his twin. 'Exactly how did things pan out?'

He sounded so adult that I feared he was going to undermine what I'd done with the car. 'It's one of Dad's best deals ever,' I replied. 'In fact, the best!' They broke into a shared smile, which reminded me that, so far, they admired what I'd done with the 1600E.

'So, tell us more about this great deal!' my brother urged, daring me to break a rule of Dad's that I must never share info about his business with anyone.

'Go on!' added Vanessa, promising they wouldn't tell Mum, who, because of how much Dad spent on booze, was always short of housekeeping money. 'I mean, without you, our Craig,' she continued, 'he wouldn't have bought the thing in the first place. Would he?'

There was no arguing with that.

'Nine hundred and eighty-five quid, he got,' I enthused, adding that the total cost to Dad was only four hundred and five pounds, including Mum's cleaning materials, and a last minute top-up with petrol.

'Nine hundred and eighty-five quid?' Jack was clearly astonished.

'Nine hundred and eighty-five quid?' echoed Vanessa, who I knew had been expecting me to say that the sale was for five hundred and fifty or so.

'Five hundred and eighty quid profit!' I boasted, while they gawped in silence and Picasso flapped his threadbare wings as if applauding.

'Five hundred and eighty quid!' he mimicked, bringing on the shared laughter that opened the way for Jack to catch me out with a sudden return to what they'd wanted to explore in the first place.

'But things have still been getting worse between our Craig and Dad,' he declared to Vanessa, who'd followed his lead in stopping her own laughter. 'Haven't they, Craigie?' he added, as their joint gaze again settled on me in the mirror.

'Listen,' he continued, giving me his hardest look so far, 'you don't have to be Dad's frigging workshop slave.'

'Exactly,' agreed his twin, who further stressed that they merely sought to discover my feelings on everything.

Little did she know how scary that was.

Mostly I feared that in disclosing too much I would let them see that the worsening of Dad's drink problem was all down to my queerness. Rather than risk them sensing my guilt, I lowered my eyes to the seahorse-patterned lino that Dad had laid ten years before. To begin with it was very bright and had inspired him to lead us all on a crazy seahorse dance, which had marked our move into number twenty. That was a happy event but the story behind it included violence against Mum and a spell in the psychiatric hospital for him, none of which I wanted to think about. Plus it saddened me that the once vivid yellow seahorses were now pale as ghosts.

'We're waiting,' remarked Jack, as a shiver went down my spine.

'Please, Craigie,' added Vanessa, as I looked up to find they were staring at me, with kindness, via the mirror.

I knew now that, though still terrified of confirming my queerness, I had to share the next bit of my story with them. It poured out of me.

'Dad started drinking more than usual and at the same time he kept looking at me as if there was something angry he couldn't say. I was puzzled. I thought he'd been well chuffed with what I'd done to the 1600E, making him a mini-fortune. Instead he was like a rumbling volcano, without the blow-up happening. I hardly dared speak for fear of saying the wrong thing. If you'd fired bullets at his eyes they would have bounced off. That's how it became for ninety per cent of the time. Much, much, worse than usual, I've got to say.

## 67

'Then at the car auctions, where the blokes had already been laughing at how drunk he was, a Corsair 2000E came through. Like a bigger version of the Cortina 1600E but not as good, especially when they've got more rot than the wreck of the *Titanic*. Which was exactly what any boozed-up maniac on a galloping horse could see was the problem with that piece of junk. Plus it'd had a colour change from light blue to glossy black, its original vinyl roof covered in overspray.

'But Dad – pissed out of his nut for days – wanted to make a point and it didn't take me long to realise what it was about, either. If a cissy-boy like me could do the 1600E, he could do the 2000E. "Another five hundred and sixty quid mark-up!" he reckoned, but really savage. Like he hated me for what I'd done and was now turning on me at the auctions.

'Then he was bidding as if his flipping life depended on it, with Dr Death, in his dark suit and silver glasses that disguised his eyes, going like the clappers, and some of the blokes tossing bids in just to see how far Dad would go.

'It was mad! The bidding went like a fire with petrol thrown on. Soon Dad was up to five hundred! Five hundred quid for a car worth three hundred, absolute tops!

'And then some of the blokes were jeering harder and Dad attempted to outsmart them by playing the clown. Except that, looking at him, he'd become exactly that. A big, scruffy, smelly clown. Laughed at. Mocked. And with all the 1600E money about to wasted on the 2000E that wasn't even firing on all cylinders.

'I hated that car. Hated Dr Death for driving Dad on. Hated the blokes for kicking him when he was down and almost hated Dad for being so crazy when we had the cash to buy better cars. Because that's how it builds. A few strong deals that lead to more deals, luck and savvy mixed up.

'But Dad was on the flipping moon or somewhere reason didn't exist. "Five hundred and eighty!" bid one man, just to make him go even further. "Seven hundred!" cried Dad, quick as lightning, causing most of those around us to roar so hard, I felt sick and scared.

'To be fair, though, some blokes didn't only stay quiet, they turned their backs. But the rest were lapping it up, and after years of being respected at the auctions, Dad looked done for. Horrible. Horrible. Horrible.

'As for Dr Death, he kept his stupid little silver hammer poised and looked from Dad to the cruel bastard who'd bid against him hardest.

"'Any further bids?" he asked, in his wicked, clear, voice.

"'Any further bids?" he said again, playing it like an ordinary sale, when really he'd got Dad snared, a crazed old thing who wouldn't give up, even though he was incapable of winning.

"'Any further bids?" Dr Death repeated twice more, still looking at the other bidder, who was tempted but wary in case Dad came to his senses and made him into the mug who'd bought an overpriced crap car.

'By now the air felt like concrete and, for a moment, I imagined every person in the bidding hall getting crushed. Also I wondered if what I'd done with the Light Orchid 1600E had been my way of bringing Dad to this destruction. At least things moved on fast.

'Dr Death was doing his selling once, selling twice thing when Dad went and upped his own bid to eight bloody hundred! At first I thought he'd got it wrong, but then saw that he was now fighting for his life.

'Eye to eye with Dr Death across the roof of the car, he'd got some kind of savvy back and it took me a moment to get how it was working. Probably nobody had ever done it before. Typical of Dad, never to be taken for granted –

"Eight ten … Eight twenty … Eight thirty … Eight forty …" Up and up he drove the price, getting many of the others to turn against Dr Death, who for once was flustered – the high priest of the sale brought low. Where, if you ask me, he deserved to be. Like a worm. But worms do good, and he was cruel and flinty and, because of what he did to Dad, worse than something you wipe off your shoe. It was then that I made my biggest mistake ever.

"Nine ten … Nine twenty … Nine thirty …" Dad was into his stride and slaughtering Dr Death, but I wanted the ground to open up and swallow me. Except that the opposite happened and, after weeks of fielding Dad's anger, it was me who now blew like a volcano. Shouting to all sundry that he didn't mean it, and was sorry for the trouble he'd caused.

'Words that spewed out because I was scared Dad had now flipped his lid forever, even if he was getting back at Dr Death, who seized my apology with one word – accepted – and brought his little hammer down with a whack that meant the shitty car was ours for nearly a grand! Destroying my success with the 1600E and taking Dad down with it. Even the frigging rats that lurked in the corners of the bidding hall must've felt something wrong had occurred.

'The whole place was ice-quiet, with all eyes on me where I'd humiliated Dad by apologising for him when I was only the Cataloy Kid, and he'd been doing cars since long before I was born.

'But the eyes I was most frightened of were his, Dad's. Cold, hard eyes that really despised me.

"'1967 Corsair 2000E," sang Dr Death. "A quality motor-car sold for nine hundred and sixty pounds only!"

'Some of the dealers laughed, rubbing salt into Dad's wounds, my wounds, and any other wounds in the hall. Perhaps even the rats were feeling sore.

'Take it away,' added Dr Death, with a nod at one of the auction flunkeys.

'It was then that the car itself seemed to pass verdict on what had happened, as on being driven up a ramp it backfired and made everybody jump. A bit like a small bomb going off.

'More laughter followed, though not from Dad, who still faced me like I was something that needed to be wiped off his shoe. There was no doubting he had something bad to say.'

# 68

I, Brucie-Dog, was used to itching on the outside and could more or less tolerate even the worst of it. This time I also itched on the inside, where it felt as if, by biting me, millions of tiny creatures were driving on my whirling thoughts about Marcus and Craig.

In particular I was shaken that the Watcher from Raymond's war years appeared to be the same queer-hating man as Mr Heston. By beating Marcus for his queerness he had caused the attempted self-offing, which in turn had left the kid even more unwilling to accept Marcus's love. 'What goes around comes around,' had been another of Pauline's ironic sayings.

Equally I was struck by how Oliver – who'd been left to die by Raymond when they were young service men – had returned via the family's bone knowledge and Craig's nightly dreams. A kindly time traveller there to help the kid with the fearsome place his young life had become. It was all too much to take in one go.

'Help me!' I prayed to Her Hoityness, as my eyes opened onto a blackness that was so much heavier than before that I felt crushed.

'Help me!' I repeated, sure that after the kid's energetic telling of his life with Raymond and the bad night at the car auction, I would die a worn-out rescue dog that had not been up to the mission he was supposed to fulfil. Maybe Her Hoityness heard me. Or perhaps there was more of Robespierre's energy left than I'd thought.

Either way, the darkness lifted and, in the moments before I adjusted to the light, which now came all round me, I thought I'd returned to the well-lit car auction, where Raymond was about to say his worst to the kid. I was wrong.

My second sight had closed for now, placing me back with Craig and Marcus in the sunny lane outside the workshop, within which Big Eddie's red Ford Mustang shimmered as before beneath the clear plastic top. At least I soon learnt why I'd become so much weaker, so fast.

'Yep!' called Marcus to the kid, as the heat of the day sent new shivers through me. 'He's too hot again. Far, far too hot,' he added, stroking one of the bigger patches of fur I'd got left. My stringy tail wagged, and for some moments I believed he and Craig had overcome their problems. That would have been a miracle. But at least they were now talking with me, Brucie-Dog, as their focus.

# 69

'I know all that,' responded the kid, who, instead of using the hubcap I'd last drunk from, was returning from filling the clear dish I'd previously dubbed my 'fish bowl'. 'But he's seeing the vet tomorrow. So if there's anything causing it, apart from the sun, it'll be getting sorted along with his mange. Won't it, Brucie-Wucie-Lucie?' he teased, peering at me through the rounded glass, causing his face to look so funny that my eyes bulged against their sore lids.

'See how he's staring back at you through the water?' asked Marcus, making my tail do more wags on the warm concrete I was lying on. 'That's because he loves you already,' he continued, with an affectionate look that made the kid blush as he set the bowl down between my outstretched front paws.

'Drink, Brucie, drink,' he encouraged, keeping his eyes low to avoid Marcus's gaze.

Soon, though, I became aware that each of them now had a hand resting on my back and I begged Her Hoityness to make their fingers entwine. Perhaps this time she was asleep.

My aches, pains and non-stop itching got worse as Craig rose from his haunches and stepped backwards until he stood still as a statue beside the Mustang's rear wheel. Deeper within the workshop than before.

'So,' said Marcus, also rising, 'still afraid of me, then, Craig? Still terrified I'm going to queer you?'

A note in his voice worried me: perhaps the gap between them could never be closed after all.

For a few moments the kid looked at me again and, on seeing my ears go up, returned his gaze to where Marcus was now retaking his place on the yellow Raleigh Chopper. 'Says who that I'm terrified of you, Marcus?' he sneered, while much whiteness showed: his eyes were like cracked dinner plates, which I half expected to fall out in pieces. Leaving him blind. Luckily, my second sight picked this moment to get going again. Rather than being returned to the car auction, though, I found myself back in the kitchen at number twenty where Jack and Vanessa awaited the rest of Craig's tale about him and Raymond on the ill-fated auction night. I, Brucie-Dog, was the unhappy kid again. We were exactly as we'd left off before my need for a life-saving drink had got the better of me.

## 70

Rain was still hitting the glass back door but a break in the sky had cast a shaft of silver, which the mirror above the fireplace reflected onto me, Vanessa and Jack. This might have been pleasant but instead it highlighted the gloom that my tale of the car auction had brought on. The air in the kitchen was thick.

'Poor Dad,' sighed Vanessa, on meeting our brother's reflected gaze.

'Poor Dad,' mimicked Picasso, spreading his tattered wings.

Jack, however, was angry. 'Never mind Dad,' he snapped at us both. 'What did the old bastard say to you, our Craig?' he demanded, as my belly started a new bout of bad fizzing.

'C'mon,' he added, his eyes now so glassy that I regretted more than ever letting my runaway tongue take me close to confirming my filthy queer nature.

'C'mon! C'mon!' he barked, uncaring that, at moments like this, he became what Dad excelled at being: a bully.

By now Vanessa was arching an eyebrow at him in

the mirror but he was in no mood to back-pedal. 'We've come this far, our Vee!' he protested. 'We're not stopping now! What did Dad actually say to you?' he demanded, as her eyes became as severe as his were. Bad cop, bad cop.

'I don't know,' I lied, hoping to make them back off by sounding upset, yet alarmed by the high pitch that terror of them outing me had given my voice.

'Then try to remember,' Jack urged, through gritted teeth. 'Try,' he repeated, unaware that in place of his and Vanessa's reflected gaze I now saw Dad's hate-filled glare after my apology to Dr Death over his bidding for the black Corsair 2000E. Eyes that had bored into me on and off ever since the minute when all the blokes from the trade – plus Dr Death and his flunkeys – had heard what he'd said in a voice that was neither loud nor quiet. Words that had been thought about and shaped in his mind, and came with all the purpose of a man digging a grave. As if, after the humiliation I'd brought to him, he was now out to bury me alive. Not that I could blame him, with what I knew about myself.

There was only one grown-up who'd told me it was okay to be gay and he was from my dreams. Oliver. Otherwise it seemed that most people truly hated homos and Dad was about to lay this fact on the line. Just to be really clear. In case I half believed that my queer nature was somehow privately acceptable to him.

## 71

'**Y**ou little shit,' he'd begun, making me feel exactly that, even though I hoped he didn't mean what he was now doing to me, the one and only Cataloy Kid, who for years had helped with his cars, when otherwise he would have been alone in the workshop.

'But, Dad -' I started before the extreme blue of his eyes stopped me and he went on with the words which even a nuclear bomb couldn't have matched for power. Words I'd feared with every bit of myself. Words that finally put my filth out there for others to see and smell. The stink of queerness. The reek of me. The vile little homo. A 'pâté'-prodder in the making.

All said with dozens of ears listening at the car auction.

'You worthless little shit. Do you think I don't know what you are? Limp-wristed little queer,' he'd concluded, while I wished I was dead. The loneliest and scariest moment of my life so far.

'Cataloy, go home,' advised one of the blokes, as Dad lurched through the silent crowd to pay for the ugly black Corsair 2000E. His death-car, as I came to think of it when, a few weeks later, he threw himself from Churchill's promontory.

It was an eight-mile walk home in the dark. For much of it the east-coast mainline was close by, and twice a London-bound train passed at great speed. But because I knew that when one twin dies the remaining twin suffers, I did not take my life. I loved Rachael and, though she couldn't know it, our bond was the thing that saved me. Just.

Still, a blowtorch flared in my gut and I knew I was being destroyed anyway. It was Vanessa who, on becoming the good cop again, spared me the misery of having to reveal too much to the older pair after all.

## 72

'I know!' she exclaimed, as her brow shot upwards again. 'Dad said in front of all those men at the auction that you were the Retard, didn't he?' She nodded to signal that she'd thrown a lifeline my way. Seizing this, I surprised myself by wrong-footing her.

'No, Vanessa.' I copied her trick of lifting one eyebrow. 'Dad did not say that.'

'Then what did he say?' snapped Jack, whose gaze flitted to where his twin wore the wounded look of one poked in the eye for trying to help me.

'He said,' I replied, with sternness to match my brother's, 'that I was a cissy-boy. So you were nearly right,' I reassured Vanessa, with a smile that made Jack wince and scrub his hair with both hands. Sort of raking things through before he got going again.

'The cissy-boy?' he mused as if trying the words for impact, when in fact he was aware Dad had often used them to imply I was a worm whose life ahead would be sad and small. 'Who needs to hear that crap in public?' he continued, with a grin, which reminded me that he was more often kind than hard.

'Especially coming from their old man,' he concluded, with a deeper look at Vanessa, which underlined that, no matter what Dad had actually said at the car auction, they knew the viciousness of his intent.

'Exactly!' agreed our sister, who'd got over her hurt feelings so fast that in gratitude I sought to lift the mood between us all.

'That's me!' I cried, unconcerned that, while determined to overcome my queerness, I could be camper than any Saturday-night showman. 'The cissy-boy!' I added.

Jack grabbed my wrist and held up my right hand to the mirror. 'With a mechanic's oily fingers!' he pointed out to Vanessa, who smiled in a way that told us she loved us.

My reflection reddened when I remembered how close I'd come to admitting my suicidal thoughts, which in our house were treacherous. Five years before, Dad had slit his wrists in the bath and Mum had loudly told the ambulance crew that it was 'the coward's way out'.

Later – when the older twins were thirteen and us younger pair were twelve – she'd apologised for letting us overhear it, and explained that, while she was furious with Dad, her biggest fear was always that one day he would succeed in killing himself. That made things easier for me to understand. But the idea of suicide as cowardly had lingered with me and Jack in particular, and we'd often used it to tease each other.

'Go kill yourself, tufty-headed coward!' That sort of thing.

Lately, though, my big brother had ended this behaviour, and because I'd learnt that tricky things had a tendency to combine, I'd been extra grateful for our new silence on the subject of suicide. After all, the very last thing I wanted was to be remembered as a 'limp-wristed little queer' who, typical of his type, had taken 'the coward's way out'.

Yet still the option of ending it all went round in my head, and I now feared that Jack and Vanessa had called me inside from the workshop precisely because they knew this. Most scarily, it also seemed that Jack was about to tackle it head-on.

Frowning, he sighed. 'I know what this Dad crap is really all about,' he announced. 'And it's nothing to do with being a retard, a cissy or anything else,' he stressed, as I braced myself for what was to come.

'Then for goodness' sake,' responded Vanessa, 'put poor Craig out of his misery and tell us what you do think!'

This time nobody laughed when Picasso mimicked her and I nodded for Jack to get on with it. Nothing could have been as bad as what was in my head anyway.

# 73

He was adamant that I should stop helping Dad. That was a shock. Even in the weeks since Dad had outed me as a limp-wristed little queer the workshop had still been the most important thing in the world to me. Dad was scary. Dad trampled all over me. But without him and his cars, my situation became even worse, making attack my best line of defence.

'What if you had to stop your stupid bloody painting?' I barked at my brother. 'What if you had to stop your wonky dressmaking?' I asked my sister. 'And what if our Rachael had to give up her effing sports?' I added, while Vanessa's brow darkened with the fury I often saw on the face of her twin.

'Oh, what utter rubbish, our Craig!' she spat, sounding just like Mum when she was annoyed. 'Nobody's saying you have to give up cars. Are they?' she snapped at Jack, who, in defiance of the tears that were now in his eyes, pointed out that he wouldn't have proposed coming to the car auctions if their aim was to stop me loving pink Cortinas.

That was funny, and because I'd been reminded of how easily he, too, could be hurt, a cold squiggle went down my spine. 'I'm sorry,' I told him, adding that his paintings were great and Vanessa's dressmaking not wonky at all. Her good mood had recovered fast.

'Wonkiness, dear brothers,' she cried, as her eyes flashed with delight, 'is precisely what I aim for!' That made me and Jack laugh and – excited by what was going on – Picasso squawked several times and set his beady eye as near to the bars of his cage as he could, watching us watching ourselves in the tilted mirror on the chimney breast.

'I swear that bloody parrot reads minds,' said Vanessa, shifting her gaze from Jack's reflection to mine. What worried her most, she said, was how, in recent weeks, Dad's bullying of me had got worse. 'Ever since Jack brought an end to Dad's violence against Mum,' she added.

I was amazed that, until then, I hadn't made a link between my big brother stopping Dad thumping Mum and Dad's harsher treatment of me. They waited, Picasso waited, and because I felt as if I was stepping onto land infested with mines, I became warier than ever.

I knew for sure that Dad loathed my queerness, yet an added reason for his attacks on me had been thrown into the mix and I needed to be certain of what the older pair were telling me.

'So,' I began, looking from Vanessa to Jack and back to her again, 'where he used to clatter Mum, he now clatters me harder than ever?'

'Exactly,' confirmed Jack.

The unkind thought that it took a bully to understand one came to me, and when Vanessa frowned I was convinced she'd read my mind, though thankfully Jack kept things going fast.

'It's simple, our Craig,' he began.

'Dad,' continued his twin, in the way that they often finished each other's sentences, 'has swapped his punchbag for a whipping boy.'

I realised from their shared expression that this was something they'd wanted to say all along. I also saw that, despite its truth, there was a context to everything, which I couldn't bring myself to share with them.

It, too, was simple.

I believed with all my heart that Dad's thirst for booze had increased after I'd become a teenager and he knew for sure I was a homo, which made me at least half responsible for his attacks on Mum when he was drunk. Or so it seemed.

The flame in my gut was bad as I faced them but I continued with care; I didn't want to cause a blow-up between us. 'Okay,' I promised. 'I'll think about spending less time in the workshop.'

Besides, I had a plan involving Dad and his cars that was less scary than taking my life.

# 74

While my brother and sisters had often discussed which colleges they were aiming for, I felt I'd already served my time in the workshop with Dad, the proof of which was the cash I kept hidden in the old brown wardrobe that always spooked me when I woke at night.

Three hundred and eleven quid I'd earned by fixing the bodywork on cars in the streets around ours. Enough to buy two tatty Ford Escorts and turn sufficient profit to repeat the same thing until I was a trader in my own right and could make Dad my partner-cum-sales-manager. A job I prayed he would accept in return for me proving to him that I would never become a full-on queer. Then he would get his self-respect back and would be called by his proper name, not Old Boozy, the staggering drunk. I still hated the men at the car auctions for that.

Mum would be impressed by his recovery too. Hadn't she always said that the man she'd loved was still somewhere inside him? And didn't I want them to love each other again, if only to stop Dad being so angry?

All of which – along with a pledge not to kill myself – I inwardly swore to God I would make happen by the time I was seventeen and had more money stashed in the wardrobe. Plus a driving licence to make things viable. Two and half years hence, with no stooping to queerness along the way and an even bigger dream to sustain me. With Dad managing sales, I would become a classic-car restorer, doing work that I loved, rather than routine welding repairs.

By now my big brother had set his chunky eyebrows on high and was smiling at me in the same bemused way as Vanessa. 'Sometimes, our Craig,' he admitted, 'you're a complete mystery to us.'

I answered with the truth: 'I bloody well hope so, Jack.' That made them laugh.

'A complete mystery,' mimicked Picasso, as I opened the glass door that led to where the sun made Mum's rained-on ferns glisten, as if their leaves were made of onyx. 'I'm coming!' I called to Dad, who stuck his shaggy head out of the black, grey and pink workshop door and grinned with a friendliness that made my chest go warm. Because, of course, I loved him with all my heart.

All I had to do for everything to work out was to stick to my plan. That much I was now certain of, thanks to the older twins. They'd wilfully forced me to think harder about the way ahead.

Unwittingly they'd also opened the way for me to become more private. My feelings were exposed by their questioning, and after Dad died I was determined not to let them pry again. Partly this was because I had a new secret. After the funeral my throat had closed tight in my sleep and I'd clutched the bedding in terror until my airways opened again. This occurred each night for a week and I could tell no one about it. I was convinced God was punishing me for Dad's suicide and also warning me against being a full-on queer. I heard the message and the scary attacks stopped – for the time being.

## 75

The cooling effect of the water that Craig and Marcus had given me, Brucie-Dog, had worn off fast and the fumes caused by the softening of the workshop's plastic top in the sun made my snout feel as if it was again being scoured within by wire wool. Even worse than this, my jaw was hurting where I'd made yet another collapse to the ground.

'Tell me he's not having a heart attack!' cried the kid, whose furry caterpillars were pulled tight over his scared eyes as he crouched opposite where Big Eddie was now supporting my underside with both hands. That was a reality check. I'd allowed myself to hope that Robespierre's gift would endure until I was fit and well but – confirming my earlier fears – its power had been sapped by my second sight. Hugo's beloved rescue dog must have been older than I'd thought when he was killed.

Big Eddie – who'd come outside with a sandwich for Craig from Viv – was upbeat, though. 'No, laddie, ya new dog isn't having a ruddy heart attack.'

He chuckled while shaking me like a toy being

tried for rattles after it'd been dropped.

Still, my thoughts were clear and I realised that, prior to this latest crash, I'd had another bout of extra-big shivers, brought on by my realisation that the kid's plan to fix Raymond's life meant he'd consciously decided there was no place for Marcus in his future. That was quite a change.

Until the car-auction night he'd never been in control of things. But after the public humiliation that had been heaped on him – the one and only Cataloy Kid – he'd attempted to take charge, which had made him his own worst enemy: rejecting Marcus's love in order to help Raymond, who'd done him so much harm that his own life was in ever greater danger, especially later when his throat went into spasm and he couldn't breathe properly.

'Are you sure Brucie's okay, Big E?' he pressed, while Big Eddie removed his hands to see if I could take my own weight.

'He'll be fine,' chipped in Marcus, who, after refilling my fish bowl at the workshop sink, now placed it on the line where the rear of number twenty met the lane. Much redness showed around him and Craig and, patting my head, Big Eddie repeated his earlier prediction that I would be a great dog. That worked wonders for my ego.

Suddenly much happier, I aimed for a yap that came

out as a squeak, and when they laughed I thought of Her Hoityness and how annoyed she would have been with them. Yet, after all that I'd witnessed so far, I was satisfied that I could make any sound at all.

Oliver was left to die in the sea that was on fire because the Watcher had made young Raymond fear he was a homo. Incredibly this man was also Mr Heston, who'd driven Marcus to take his mum's sleeping pills. Plus there was the shooting of Robespierre, the self-offing of Hugo Moncrieff, and all that I'd discovered about the distant suicide of poor Tony Ridge.

Thirty years of human life peppered with the pain, madness and self-offing of boys and men who were made to despise their own natural queerness. Or who simply feared they might be queer. Horror story after horror story after horror story.

'Better off out of it,' the kid's school caretaker had decided about Hugo, who, the newspapers reported, was found hanging in the loft by his mum.

'Limp-wristed little queer!' said Raymond, to the terrified kid, in front of the crowd at the car auction.

'Slap it in his blond-pufter hair!' Trevor Carlton had ordered, and Craig had attacked Marcus with the bubblegum.

My mission ahead was huge. Not only had the kid been born with the worst possible bone knowledge, he lived in a world where the queer-hating bone knowledge of others conspired to ruin the lives of youngsters far and wide. A double-bind, which soon made me fear that Ginger would have done far better to pick a strong-minded pedigree, like Her Hoityness. It was Craig who snapped me out of this mood. The day was at its hottest so far but he still blamed himself for my latest collapse.

## 76

'Have I been neglecting poor Brucie-Dog?' he asked Big Eddie, with so much self-doubt that, after imagining Her Hoityness going wolfish, I shook myself from end to end and lapped the water that I knew would make me feel better. It was not the only thing I concentrated on. Out the corner of my eye I saw Marcus again take his seat on the yellow Raleigh Chopper, which had been on its stand in the open. On and off the bike, like his life depended on it.

'Noooo, Craig lad,' replied Big Eddie, as he took ten backward paces out of the boiling workshop and down the lane. 'Ya not neglecting our Brucie-Bruce at all,' he added, glancing at me.

That was kind and, in a flash, I saw how he'd stepped in after Raymond's death, turning the workshop from a damp pit into a bright place where Craig could restore the snazzy red Ford Mustang. That helped the kid deal with the confusion that must have come from loving such a difficult parent as his dad had been.

Shaking the full length of my sore body again, I

made myself stay in the present.

Marcus took his right foot off the Chopper's pedal and returned it again, a move he repeated several times before reminding the kid that he'd earlier said he was soon going away to London. That was another shock for me. My second sight had kept me too involved to hear it first time round. Now I understood why he'd come visiting on his stylish bicycle. A last chance to heal their rift before everything changed forever.

'To London, Craig. To London,' he repeated, while the pale blue bits of his eyes flashed in the sun, testing my painful peepers to their limit. 'To live,' he emphasised, staring even harder at the kid, whose wounded response was to crouch low again and draw my head against his chest, his left hand caressing my throat, his right fingers tickling between my ears.

'Why?' he asked, releasing me and standing to face Marcus, who shrugged and became so sad that my tail curled right under and touched my belly as it'd rarely done before. At least I saw why it was happening.

It was a long time since Marcus and Craig had strolled on the beach, each with an arm hugging the other, and for all that I hated my thoughts, I knew that the kid no longer deserved this love. Not even Her Hoityness would have found that easy to deal with. Craig was my charge. I was his rescue dog.

I itched and itched and, on getting a whiff of just how

acidic the kid's tummy now was, I knew he was suffering.

'Tell me why you're going to London!' he shrieked, with a stamp of his foot that reminded me of Trevor Carlton when he, too, was out of his depth.

Marcus was unfazed. 'To do a special apprenticeship,' he replied, as his blond eyebrows shot upwards. 'I mean me, Craig. I'm going to London,' he continued, while, sadly, the mix of black and white that came around the kid confirmed he was at his loneliest so far. Still, the next bit was a big surprise.

After jabbing the Raleigh Chopper's easy-rider handlebars, as if to test the front tyre for hardness, Marcus eyeballed Craig and spoke in a matter-of-fact way. 'I heard about you knocking Trevor into next year,' he remarked, leaving my ears hurting even more than the last time they'd gone right up.

Several long-seeming seconds passed while they held each other's gaze, at the close of which I was saddened by the failure of my second sight to open on what had occurred between Craig and Trevor after Marcus's attempted self-offing.

Help came from Big Eddie, who was surrounded by a redness that, in being even stronger than Marcus's, made my second sight kick in after all. Whatever had been missing from my discoveries so far, I was about to learn what it was. My mission was progressing and, as I prayed to Her Hoityness for strength, the worst of the discomfort went from inside my nostrils. That was a relief. Humans will never know how important rescue-dog snouts are. Without them we're useless. For the third time that day I became the kid.

# 77

Our school dated from the 1950s and had four inner walls with big windows that opened onto a grassed quadrangle, which was used for Speech Day. Stepping onto this lawn, from the paving that bordered the twelve classrooms plus the gym and the beak's study, was otherwise forbidden.

Mr Blewitt, the caretaker, was behind this law. To most of my schoolmates he was a mysterious man, yet because my parents were older than theirs, I saw that he had the war turning non-stop in his brain. Disturbed ex-servicemen in their mid-fifties were everywhere you looked in those days. If you were tuned in.

Tellingly, Mr Blewitt was known to avoid Mr Heston, who had been at sea with my dad against the Germans in the forties. That was quite a twist of Fate and I dared not mention it at home, where it would have caused big trouble. Even before his boozing got worse in his final year, my dad could scare me to death with his temper.

Mr Blewitt, on the other hand, was a self-controlled man and it was said that if the lines where he mowed the grass were not straight, he was unable to sleep. Staff, pupils and parents alike were alert to his strict keep-off-the-grass rule. But on the morning when Marcus's dad came for Mr Heston he was on a mission that meant our caretaker's need for order counted for nothing.

From the moment I saw him enter the quadrangle via the twin glass doors beside the beak's study, I knew he would stride over the lawn to the opposing entrance of the gym. The gasps that came from several of my form-mates were followed by a remark from Trevor Carlton, which nailed what the rest of us were thinking: 'There goes one pissed-off geezer.'

By then Mr Wright had already cleared Mr Blewitt's carpet-smooth quadrangle and reached the gym. Mr Heston was within. My heart thudded. It was the first time in my life I'd seen somebody stand up publicly for a queer. Scared of letting fly a comment that would have suggested I, too, was 'one of those', I bit my lower lip, the timing of which could not have been better.

At the exact-same moment that I felt the pain Mr Wright came face to face with Mr Heston as he stepped out of the gym's blue-painted double doors.

By now twelve seas of faces were pressed to the surrounding classroom windows, including those of the teachers who, just moments before, had been ticking the morning registers. There was certainly much to look at.

Not only was Marcus's dad still young and strong he had the advantage of surprise and stabbed his finger against Mr Heston's pigeon chest. What was then said could not be heard but it didn't take much to see that Mr Heston was being threatened for what he'd done to Marcus. By now even the beak and Mr Blewitt had strayed onto the lawn but did not intervene in the confrontation. Probably they felt Mr Heston was getting his comeuppance at last.

Windows everywhere were opened, making the second part of Mr Wright's attack available for all to hear. Blunt is too subtle a word for what he said.

Mr Heston was a bullying thug. Mr Heston was a war-obsessed maniac. Mr Heston was not fit to teach. Mr Heston was a fool, with an ugly view on life that damaged young minds. Mr Heston - Mr Wright accused most furiously of all - was an out-and-out homophobe, who'd caused Marcus's suicide attempt.

At which point my belly flipped and I didn't dare look aside at Trevor, who, I suspected, was as haunted as I was by what we'd done to Marcus even before Mr Heston had been sucked in. That made us at least as guilty as our games master, who was now getting all the blame for Marcus nearly dying.

Luckily for me, the class was too interested in what was occurring outside the gym to notice that my face and neck were burning. After all, it looked as if things were set to become even more dramatic.

His attack soon over and done with, Marcus's dad backed off as beefy old Mr Heston drew himself to his full height of over six feet, at least a couple of inches taller than Marcus's dad. For the second time it was Trevor who spoke the thought we all shared.

'Here it comes. Mr H is gonna slaughter him!'

It wasn't only his tone that revealed he was now gleeful. On stressing 'slaughter' he'd tugged within his pants with the openness that even I'd often laughed at. This time, though, he was seemingly on auto-pilot, and it wasn't lost on me that if he, too, was queer, he would have been Marmite long before that day.

My thoughts returned to Mr Wright and Mr Heston, who, instead of hitting out with his fist, now sagged before Marcus's dad as if his middle was made of suet. It was a moment, I realised later, that all who'd seen it would remember for as long as they lived. If my class was anything to go by, not one person spoke and it was like the statue of a tyrant had been torn down.

We were shocked, and Susan Terry, who'd cut the bubblegum out of Marcus's hair, gave me such a sad little smile that I wished I could simply walk out of school, find Marcus and tell him I loved him. That would have been an act of madness because people would have attacked us from all sides. It might even have driven him into taking a successful shot at killing himself, making me into the one most guilty of his death.

Still, the path I needed to stay on to avoid this was at least familiar.

No matter how lonely my life became I had to keep up my fight against becoming the sort of full-on queer who was sneered about in newspapers, on the radio, on telly, in films and, most of all, in schools. Proof everywhere that such lives were repulsive to normal men and women. Apart, it seemed, from Marcus's parents.

By now his dad had left the quadrangle, where Mr Blewitt stood near the sad figure that Mr Heston had become. For a moment I believed he was going to offer help but instead he shook his head and followed the exit Mr Wright had taken. That left the beak, who was clearly unsure whether to attend Mr Heston or return to his study. In the event he chose the latter and teachers could be seen telling their pupils to come away from the windows. The event was over. Almost.

After turning his back on those of us who continued to gawp at him, Mr Heston entered the gym as tummy acid reached my throat. It was happening more often in those days and I feared my body was telling me something connected to my feelings for Marcus. Exploring this had been too scary for me, and after I'd buried my upset at his suicide attempt, I'd done my best to believe that he'd been a weakling all along. The runt of the litter. Except that, unlike me, he was an only child.

Our register was completed and each pupil had to find their way to the class where they were meant to be. In my case, though, the air darkened and it seemed that the flat top of the school was being hit by rain.

But it wasn't a downfall from the heavens. It was a cascade from the chromed shower head where Marcus had been on the day when his body had made him into an object of scorn and violence. I'd been wrong about the limited amount of energy gifted to me from Robespierre. My second sight was going harder than ever and, much to my surprise, I, Brucie Dog, was now becoming the watcher of Mr Heston. After discarding his red track suit he was crying as he sat naked beneath the cold-running shower. I was saddened by his vulnerability. This was not easy for me.

It had been confusing enough to feel pity for Raymond, who'd been violent towards Ginger and destructive against the kid. My second sight, however, was not about to let me off without revealing how Mr Heston had become the Watcher he was when young. I was in for a trial to test my rescue-dog compassion to its limit.

# 78

It started beautifully. My itching was gone, my eyes felt good, and as I saw a man of about twenty kiss another young man, the air around them went red and warm, proving that this was how life for natural-born queers was meant be. Freedom to love without judgement from others, just as I wanted for Craig and Marcus, who, I knew in my doggie-bones, could have decades of shared love ahead. If only the kid might find the courage to be who he really was.

Then everything went black as tar again, and I found myself in a small windowless cell, which had two steel-framed chairs, a bare Formica table and dark green brick walls that glared where an overhead bulb was reflected as it shone within a wire cage. That made my eyes sting. Yet on spotting the first of the young men I'd just watched kissing so happily, I didn't care about my own discomfort.

In place of the redness that had made me optimistic he was surrounded by even more whiteness than the kid had shown when I'd first encountered him. The meaning was obvious.

Something terrible had occurred since the kiss and, as if hiding from the world in shame, he was squatting on the rough concrete floor, his curved back touching the wall opposite a grey metal door.

'Help me,' he prayed, while I realised that here was Mr Heston before hate had corrupted him into a blackmailer of his own sort. The door went and a burly police sergeant entered and spoke without delay.

'Get up, George,' he ordered. 'Get up and sit,' he added, aiming his right hand at where I noticed the chairs and table were bolted in situ.

Terrified, young 'George', as I now knew Mr Heston to be, rose from his haunches and was halfway to the nearest seat when his face was punched so hard that he reeled aside, hit his head against the wall and slid downwards to where he lay sobbing, like a child.

This did not mean that the sergeant was about to show mercy and his booted foot came to rest on George's exposed left cheek, crushing the other side of his face to the hard surface below. 'Listen carefully, sonny,' he began. 'The only reason you're out of here without charge is because it's your first time and we're taking the view that your friend, the one you were caught with,' he added more pressure with his boot, 'has taken certain liberties with you. That's right for the official record, isn't it, George?' he asked. 'The filthy pervert dragged you into the cesspit where these people – these damn queers – enact their disgusting practices on each other.'

By now my red-raw skin was burning and desperate for the boot to be taken off George's face. I wanted him to blame the other young man.

Incredibly he held back, and for some moments I hoped that the sergeant would admire his courage and allow him to get up without more torture.

Instead he gave several jabs with his foot and I saw blood where the rough finish of the floor had cut into skin. No young man could have withstood such treatment for long. No rescue dog could have tolerated it. It had to end. At any cost.

'Yes,' George finally said, to my relief.

'Yes what?' asked the sergeant, keeping up the pressure.

'Yes, yes,' responded George, in a rush, 'it was him who said we should do it. But me, Sergeant,' he added, as the boot was withdrawn and he met the hard eyes staring down at him, 'I never wanted to do it. It's disgusting,' he concluded, as a big shiver went through his body, telling me that the joy he'd previously taken in being true to himself was now destroyed forever. It had made him into a typical queer-hater, just like the sergeant. I wished with all my heart Her Hoityness was there to turn wolfish with him.

But that was pointless dreaming. What was done was

done, and thirty years later I, Brucie-Dog, was only there to learn what I needed to know. Things sped on and I was whisked away from the cell to another part of the station.

A corridor built of the same dark green bricks led to a store where a fleet of black pushbikes had their front wheels slotted on high within a metal rack. Not far away a young copper, who was preparing for his beat, was putting on the clips that would keep his uniform trousers clear of the pedals.

'Another one back on the straight and narrow, Sarge?' he asked cheerfully, as George was led towards what I guessed was the back exit of the station.

'You just mind your own business,' retorted the sergeant, with equal good humour, as he undid the first of six bolts that were keeping a pair of wide metal doors shut tight. 'Might as well take your bike out this way,' he added, getting rid of his junior colleague before offering George some advice.

'Listen, son,' he said, 'find some skirt and do the normal thing. And as for these blasted queers,' he added, 'they're like rats and you'll find them everywhere.'

For a moment George appeared to be nonplussed and I saw that he already knew a lot about where queers might be encountered. Perhaps the sergeant realised this too. Before continuing he tugged at a sprout of hair that grew from his right nostril. Getting himself back on track, perhaps.

'Now listen,' he resumed, touching George's frayed shirt collar, 'a chap like you always needs extra money. Correct?' he asked.

A glint that was suggestive of the Watcher came to George's blue eyes, and I shuddered from end to end. The sergeant was on to something tantalising, and after the punishment he'd just taken, corruptible young George Heston was interested in wringing something out of the trap in which he was caught. A bottom-of-the-heap young queer living at a time when police officers were free to make the lives of queers into hell. 'I can't say I'm exactly swimming in cash,' he warily admitted.

That made the sergeant laugh hard and declare that cash was the thing, all right. Moving closer he smiled at George. 'These vile beasts, son, who prey on decent young chaps such as you, they'll pay whatever it takes to keep the law off their backs. Hard cash.' He rubbed his first finger and thumb together.

By now he looked and sounded like an uncle who was offering the best life-advice in the world. Even I, Brucie-Dog, was touched by his tone, which reminded me of my first human, whose cruelty often worked best when glossed with kindness.

'All it takes is for you to watch carefully and move in

at the right moment,' the sergeant explained, as he guided George off the premises.

'Look at it this way,' he continued, as he held the closing edge of each metal door as if they were curtains and a show was ending, 'you'll be helping the law to keep our rodent-queers under control.' He laughed his loudest so far and was lost from sight behind the fortress-like exit. One by one he slid home the six bolts, keeping the police station safe and leaving the young man, who was now primed to become the Watcher, alone in the lane. There, he became lost in thought and blackness streaked the air around him.

It was impossible for me to hate him. It was impossible for me to love him. I needed to escape the barbed tangle that was his life. Even Her Hoityness could not have sorted that out. Hell was an understatement. It was no wonder that he would become the Watcher.

# 79

I knew right away that the middle-aged woman standing near Mr Heston was his wife. He was sitting beneath the chromed shower head, and the water had been turned off. 'You can't stay here all morning, George,' she said, offering him the red track suit and large white underpants she was holding.

Slowly Mr Heston accepted these and she stepped back to give him room to get dressed. As he did so she spoke with authority.

Mr Gold the headmaster had been clear. For three months Mr Heston would receive sick pay and then his pension would come early, meaning he would never have to teach again. That sounded like good news to me, but Mr Heston became almost lost within the whiteness that I was tired of seeing that day. Unable to see this shroud as a rescue dog could, Mrs Heston was tuned into what it might have meant.

'Planning the coward's way out, George?' she asked, with brittle fear that I understood was for both of them.

Mr Heston had been tying the lace of his right sports shoe and looked up. Anger now entered her blue-green eyes. That made me like her. She had strength.

The lace was pulled tight and they were soon standing face to face. 'Listen to me, George,' she urged, putting her hand flat to the right side of his chest. 'You know that the boy who took the tablets is going to be okay. You can't be held wholly responsible for it all.'

I realised that she must have been feeling the rhythm of his heart, and when he laughed, it sounded like glass being ground in his throat. Her hand twitched as if she had taken an electric shock, such as I'd done so many times when just a pup.

'You ought to leave me, Dorothea,' he insisted, removing her palm from his chest and hooking behind his ears the wet strands of hair that hung at the sides of his otherwise bald head.

'You do know the truth of what I am,' he told her.

She shot back that that sort of thing no longer mattered to her. 'Didn't we all have to do our best after the war, catching what we could when everything had been thrown into the air, and was falling back all around us?'

Mr Heston weighed her words as if wanting to agree but was cynical.

Seeing this, she took some car keys from the jacket of her light blue trouser suit. 'It's too late for either us to jump ship,' she snapped. 'We're too old, you and I,' she added, flicking a strand of hair he'd missed into place over his right ear.

A long silence followed until he raised her right hand, took the car keys from her fingers and set her palm back to the beat of his heart. That was the weirdest moment. I was still there but my second sight was jammed and I doubt even Her Hoityness could have got it working again. I knew what this meant. Mr and Mrs Heston were stuck and nothing could change for them. Still, I didn't want Mr Heston to off himself. I'd seen enough of that. It was an answer to things but not a good one. Or so it seemed to me – and them.

Instead of leaving via the main entrance of the gym they headed for the twin doors that spilled onto the playing field and the start of what I wanted to be thirty years of retirement for them. Because, despite Mr Heston's time as the Watcher and what he'd done to Marcus in particular, I saw that my role as a rescue dog would not be strengthened by wishing ill-fortune on him. He knew he was a disaster and that was enough.

After all, Mr Heston was also a victim of the hate that was everywhere for queers, especially when he was young. I sensed that Dorothea understood this and couldn't stop myself loving her for it.

That might have been that. I was exhausted again. But one thing in particular had to be tied up and it was big. The fight between Craig and Trevor, which Marcus had spoken of at the kid's workshop. There was no escaping it: I had to see how the nastiness between them had finished.

# 80

The young teacher who was the new games master stood on the spot where Mr Heston had waited for Marcus as he came out of the showers having been turned on by Trevor Carlton. Several of the boys in this man's care were still towelling themselves and others were already dressed, including Craig, who could not stop looking to where Trevor had his eye fixed on a tall boy that I smelt he wanted as his latest victim. Their young teacher, though, was on the ball.

'Get dressed, Carlton,' he instructed, flicking a look of reassurance at the worried-seeming kid. 'You too, please, Woodman,' he told the tall boy, confident that he was in full control of the class. Still, things were set to get rocky.

Woodman was putting on his underpants when Trevor pointed at his skinny bum and cried for all to hear, 'Hey, Woodworm! Ya'll not get a bum-chum with an arse like that! Will ya?' he added.

Woodman sagged as if hit in the gut and Craig went cherry-red from the neck up. Two hits with one stone.

That was tough to see and I wondered why the young teacher was not reacting. But then I saw that a boy who had given the thumbs-up when Marcus was turned on and had tried to stop things going bad was stepping up to eyeball Trevor, who quickly shrivelled and looked scared.

'Carlton,' the thumbs-up boy said, right into his face, 'if you do any more of this shit to anybody, ever, I'm gonna break your arm.'

Everybody else in the group was quiet and watched. The boy prodded Trevor's chest so hard that he staggered backwards and looked even smaller. A prime queer-hater stopped in his tracks. Apparently.

It was the end of the day and Woodman was first out of the changing room, then Craig, then Trevor, who'd barely bothered getting dried. I knew why. Any rescue dog would have sensed the same thing. Humiliated by the thumbs-up boy, he was out to get the kid, and for the last time that day, I, Brucie-Dog, became Craig, taking a different route home from usual to avoid Trevor, who, after what had happened in the changing rooms, had given me looks to kill.

# 81

I went down an alley that opened onto a bombsite, which was bordered on three sides by the back gardens of houses built about five years before. Sometimes this was used as a spill-over car park for a nearby sports club, but on that occasion it was empty and I thought I'd successfully avoided Trevor. I was wrong.

I was about halfway over when he strode from behind a large shrub that was on a rough strip to the side without houses and socked my left cheek, hard. That was a big shock and my face felt worse than when, a year before, I'd cracked my cheekbone after crashing my racing bike into a wall.

'Hurts, does it, Craig?' he asked, prodding my chest as the thumbs-up boy had done to him.

'Get lost, Trevor!' I spat, using my right hand to feel where I hoped my cheekbone was not broken again.

'Missing your boyfriend, who's not coming back to school, are you?' he sneered, blocking my path and pushing me backwards as I attempted to leave.

'I mean poor little nancy-boy-Marcus,' he continued,

while I felt sick at heart that queers like me could be shoved around by anyone who took a fancy to doing so.

'Ha!' cried Trevor, on seeing the tears I could not prevent. 'He does! He does! He misses his queer other half!' he jeered, while I swallowed the puke that had come to my throat.

Even then I kept trying to get away but all of a sudden his bright red face was so close to mine that our noses briefly touched.

'You fucking puff!' he screamed, while a string of spit came off his bottom lip. I glimpsed his right fist again coming my way. My brother Jack would have applauded what happened next. My time to fight back had come. Just like him standing up to Dad in our garden.

Lifting my left arm to block him I punched Trevor's face so hard that, for all he was bigger than me, he went down like a dropped brick. That was fantastic and, driven by fury, I knelt on his chest and slammed a second blow into his right eye.

'Enough, Craig!' he cried, as tears poured down the sides of his face. 'Enough!' he repeated, writhing beneath my weight.

By now a bruise that thrilled me had come to the side of his nose and I raised my arm in readiness to thump his other eye. 'He nearly died, you bastard!' I yelled, while he sobbed hard. Somewhere deep within me, I realised that he, too, cared about Marcus.

But I'd never been angry like that before.

'Not so much fun destroying people now, is it?' I spat, gripping his frail-seeming throat in my left hand. Instead of his terrified face, though, I was now looking into the eyes of Oliver, the kindly queer in my dreams after Dad's suicide. This was not the only odd thing to occur.

My fist had stopped mid-air, and while I felt as if I were pressing my knuckles against a power greater than me, I recalled my parents once saying I should be kind to Trevor. His worn-out old mum had left his thuggish dad to bring him up alone. Tingles went down my spine, and as Trevor's face came back into focus, his blue eyes were so big and desperate that I felt sad for him. There was no doubting that he saw this and, on controlling his crying, he asked me to let him get up. Please.

'You've made your point, mate,' he added, as I took my knee from his chest.

Within ten seconds he'd run clear of the bombsite. When I thought about Oliver's role in ending the fight I wondered if I'd at last gone mad. If so it didn't bother me. I'd been stopped when I was doing a bad thing and, for some reason I couldn't pin down, I sensed this was connected to Dad.

Instead of going straight home I went to the seafront

and sat on the wide wooden bench where he'd jumped over the railing. I asked the stone face of Sir Winston Churchill why he'd allowed it to happen on his watch.

Laughing at myself for talking to a statue, I watched several gulls that whirled and squawked as if they knew something difficult lurked below the mirror-like surface of the sea. The words that came out of me were as unplanned as my counter-attack on Trevor had been. They were from my heart.

'I'm not limp-wristed,' I told Dad. 'And I'm never gonna be pushed about again.'

Then I sobbed hard. Just like Trevor had done. Because my dad was dead and my long-term plan to make him into my partner was sunk. An hour passed before I got cold and rose to go home. Dad was gone and nothing could bring him back. But at least I could honour him by never becoming actively queer.

That night I slept well and had no fear of my throat closing, which reassured me that, if I was vigilant against queerness, I was safe from suffocation.

# 82

It was the same as before. My second sight had taken me deep into the kid's story but in reality no more than a minute had passed. This time it was harder to adjust and the redness of Big Eddie's car dazzled me. That was a warning. Robespierre's gift was at last used up and my life was back in the balance.

But at least I knew that in overpowering Trevor and accepting the death of his dad, Raymond, Craig had found strengths within himself that he had been unaware of. For some moments my tail wagged, but as my vision cleared I saw that any hope of bringing him and Marcus together remained slim.

The kid had clearly shrugged off his fight with Trevor and, to shorten the talk with Marcus, had sunk deep into the workshop again. He was so pale that I almost growled. Big Eddie, too, was wolfish in his own way.

Annoyed at Craig's surly behaviour, he shook his head so hard that his crash–helmet hair came apart like rats' tails. 'Congratulate ya friend on his 'prenticeship, won't ya, Craig laddie?' he boomed, glancing to where Marcus was still sitting on the Raleigh Chopper in the lane.

The kid did not react and, avoiding the searching look Marcus now gave him, he became surrounded by the thickest white possible without death occurring. I realised that, because he knew Marcus was leaving the area where they had been boys joined at the hip, he was at an even bigger risk of offing himself.

That made things much scarier for me and, despite the heat, I shivered hard. The tang from the kid's acid-attacked gut was only just bearable and further confirmed to me that life itself was destroying him.

He loved Marcus but could not accept it. He needed Marcus but could not concede it. He was lonely but tried not to show it. All of which I knew young Marcus understood. He must also have realised that Craig was going to fight his queerness even at the cost of his life, leaving me in a quandary.

Nothing could be done to save the situation and, because he deserved to be happy, I wanted Marcus to follow the advice of his parents and leave the kid to his fate. Maybe he sensed this message coming off me.

After lifting his left leg from where it had been bracing the Raleigh Chopper on the lane, he back-kicked the bike's stand into its off position and rode several circles in the sun, his silver-blue eyes searching for Craig less and less until he stood on the pedals for the uphill slog back the way he'd come. 'Ta-ra, Craig! Ta-ra, Mr Heartbreak Hotel! Ta-ra, Brucie-Wucie-Lucie-Darling!'

he called, over his shoulder, as he rode off.

I went to the kid, who looked even paler than he had a minute before. As if a rock had been smashed into his brain. Or his heart. Or both. Despite my earlier cockiness about Her Hoityness, begging was not beneath me and I needed her more than ever.

'Help me,' I prayed, certain that, without her help, I was about to die and Craig soon after. A disastrous pairing by poor old Ginger, whose intentions for us had been driven by love.

'Brucie's really ill!' Craig shrieked, as the redness of the Ford Mustang thickened and I became fixated on the broken-egg shape of Big Eddie's right pupil, the old wound that spoke of his recovery from a difficult start. His memories and interior voice abruptly became mine. Another powerful move by my second sight, which scared me: perhaps before I could return to being me, I'd have the heart attack that had Big Eddie's number written on it. In case that sounds dramatic, it was generally accepted that, if he wanted to make old bones, Big Eddie needed to lose four stones of fat.

But the fear was gone as quickly as it came and my focus was where I wanted it to be.

Because that was what I'd promised Craig's father Raymond shortly before his death. That I – Big Eddie Clarkson – would always look out for his younger son, Craig lad.

# 83

I met Vivienne when we were teenagers and now
her ill-health frightened me: I wouldn't have traded
an extra moment with her for all the gold in the
world. Her love had made me believe in myself as a
man. So, when Raymond from across the lane asked
me if I thought love between men was wrong, my reply
came readily. Love was all that mattered to any of us.

Since I knew he was asking about the nature of
young Craig, I added that all four of his children were
loving youngsters, who would surely bring happiness
to themselves and others.

I spoke sense, he decided, making me ashamed of
my behaviour an hour before when, from the backyard of my hotel, I'd heard him bawling at Craig.
Hard, hard words. My blood had boiled until I'd
wanted to shake him and ask what on God's earth he
was doing, hammering a youngster who worshipped
him. And who – above all – needed his approval. His
love.

I'd waited in the rain, all the while spying from a
knot-hole in the back gate, determined, against my

wife's wishes, to tackle Raymond when the laddie was out of the way. As it happened, that came about when his brother Jack called for him to go inside.

Raymond had been working on an old brown Vauxhall. Given the combination of my height and the fact that he was squatting in readiness to lower its side jack, I towered over him. I promised that if I ever heard him bullying Craig again I'd punch his lights out. I was braced for anger but received a weary nod of understanding that suggested he was relieved somebody was at last putting the brakes on his fury with his son.

'Help me finish this damn thing, Eddie mate,' he said, which in fact was unnecessary as all he had left to do was to get the car off its jack. No reference was made to my having called him a gutless coward who, if not punching his wife, was hurting his children. Just an hour of quiet companionability during which we wiped the car down and made it look less of an eyesore.

Soon after that the sun came out and did away with the rain, which had turned his garage into a sodden Hell that would have tested Mother Teresa. By then Craig had come outside and made friends with his dad, and I'd reported on my meeting with Raymond to Viv, who'd told me to go back outside and be with him. She was like that. Kind to a fault.

Craig had gone off somewhere and Raymond was

alone. 'Walk with me,' he suggested, and set off towards the sea, which had turned from a dark grey to a shiny blue that underlined one thing. No matter how violent he was with his fists or his tongue, I couldn't judge this troubled man. His aloneness with his pain was profound and, if anything, I wanted to protect him against doing further harm to himself and others.

'Sure I'll walk with you, Raymond,' I said, as curious as I was moved that he appeared to have faith in me.

# 84

I see three on the promontory that day. First, the round-bellied figure of Sir Winston, his back ramrod straight as he looks across the sea from where he stands high on his stone plinth, his white marble body sparkling in the sun. Then there's me sitting on the seaward bench below the statue, my carefully done hair destroyed by the rain.

And finally there's a heavily bearded man, lost in thought as he rests his left hand on the railing while staring out to sea, his right fingers holding a cigarette and his oily red jumper made comical by the bits of white shirt that stick out of its holey elbows. His feet are protected by black wellingtons, cut down to ankle-height. Almost, in truth, a tramp.

'You'll have to let me know where you got the boots, Raymond,' I said, to break the tricky silence that'd also marked our walk down the lane from the garage. 'Could do with some of those,' I added. 'No offence intended.'

He flicked his cigarette aside, turned to me and asked if I could imagine the ocean on fire. As he did so, his blue eyes became brighter and I sensed what had wounded him so deeply. It was the tale of many men who were his age, the war and its long-term effects on them.

'No,' I replied, I could not imagine the sea on fire. My gaze was held fast as he drew his hand up the whiskery side of his face and through his wild grey hair. His head tilted back so I saw yellowed teeth as he appeared to offer a silent prayer to Sir Winston.

'Ah!' he said, lowering his eyes back to me. 'It's only those who were there that have the damnable imagining of it, the sea on fire. Only us who were there.'

His aloneness made me slide my hands beneath my thighs on the bench, as if this simple action would prevent me talking when it was clear no words could be right – at least, not unless I'd been there when the ocean was ablaze, and was part of an exclusive group with a right to discuss it.

With an appreciative nod, he turned back to the horizon and lit another cigarette. The smoke that was soon swirling around his shaggy outline reached my nostrils and stirred a need in me to speak of a horror that I most certainly did comprehend: Vivienne's lung cancer and the loss I would soon be facing. But, just as strongly as I understood that Raymond was not yet done with his confessional, I felt it would be wrong for me to compete with him in the pain stakes. I also kept to myself the memory of a young father who was killed at Dunkirk when I – his only child – was still in short pants, and the story of my mother, who, on her death when I was in my mid-thirties, was convinced that the attending male nurse was the love of her life back from where he'd been fighting in France.

Such was the war and how it affected us all, I thought, as I sat on the bench beneath Sir Winston, whose gravelly drawl made me smile as I recalled a young laddie pressing his ear to his mother's parlour door to catch a speech about fighting on the beaches. I was puzzled that we were to resist the Germans in our breeches.

# 85

I looked to Raymond's right and watched a few gulls swooping and soaring, their freedom to be nothing but themselves as readily expressed by their ear-splitting squawks as it was by the flashes of their diamond white undersides when they rose on high.

'Noisy damn beasts,' said Raymond, who was watching me. 'In fact,' he continued, as he raised the bushy eyebrows he'd passed on to his children, 'they're despised by many as vermin.'

'Ah,' I said. "Despised" is a strong word.'

'I suppose it is,' he agreed, his eyes sliding to where he now crushed his cigarette end beneath his boot.

Then his head snapped up and, on meeting my gaze, he asked if I truly believed that love between men was acceptable. By now this had become a theme and I didn't need to be a genius to sense that it was connected to his war experiences.

But it was my concern for young Craig that made me straighten my back and hold my head high – as if that could defend the lad against his father's behaviour. Words were not necessary. My silence was my reply.

Raymond's lips widened and the yellowish skin around his eyes crinkled. I feared an explosion, but it was the start of a grin, the only occasion when I saw him beam with fatherly pride.

'Eddie, my friend,' he said, 'you're a man of great distinction.'

I laughed at being teased by a neighbour who wore rags and cut-down wellingtons, but I was glad about the point we'd got to. 'Whatever you say, Raymond lad,' I responded, trying to sound casual, when in reality our words had been as loaded as the silence that again hung between us. A silence I was careful not to break as I fixed my eyes on the distant meeting of the darker blue sea with the paler blue sky, a line so neat it might have been painted by God's hand.

'I want you to do something for me,' he said, his voice cracking as the gulls flew away with their claws swept back.

'I'm listening,' I said, softening my voice as best I could while gripping a slat of the bench beneath my thighs with both hands. As if otherwise I might have tumbled into the blue expanse that was before us. 'I need you always to look out for my second son,' he said.

His request made me think two things. First, that he was a brave man who, to protect his wife and children from his own chaos, was preparing to leave them; and second, that being invited to care for young

Craig was the best thing that'd happened to me, apart from marrying Vivienne.

Ever since he'd first caught my attention by using Vim, Brasso and a ton of elbow grease to put the shine back on a dulled pink Ford Cortina, I'd been as smitten by the lad's passion for cars as I was concerned by Raymond's attitude towards him. That was why I'd quietly added a couple of hundred quid to an old mate's offer for what he called the pink projectile: it was worth every penny when Craig's pride at making such a strong sale had him walking ten feet tall – and I escaped the ear-bashing I would otherwise have copped for being a spendthrift.

To be fair to my wife, she, too, was so taken by the liveliness of the family across the lane that hardly a day passed without a report on which one she'd seen doing what. Her deepest laughs mostly came after she'd settled by the kitchen door to the yard, the cigarette smoke that was so much a part of all I cherished about her chuffing from her nose and mouth.

'Well, Eddie, Rachael was at the bus station with a trampolining trophy as big as a bucket!'

'Well, Edwin' – I must have been in her bad books – 'young Jack's in the paper for winning a painting competition!'

Such was the nature of her constant reporting. Such, in fact, was our mutual infatuation with all the family from across the lane.

# 86

Apoliceman who was known, apparently, as Bill the Copper brought the news that, after getting drunk at the Gay Hussar, Raymond was seen by a motorist – who at first thought he was a streaker – to remove his clothes, salute Sir Winston and go over the sea rail.

Knocked sideways by this turn of events – it happened only hours after our talk – I can't claim I was surprised. I'd already reached the conclusion that here was a man who'd struggled in a particularly cruel sea for a long time.

And while my heart and Vivienne's went out to all his young 'uns I have to say it was the older lad, Jack, who made the greatest impression when he called for the vicar to delay the sending off of his father, his face set with love as he stepped up to kiss the coffin lid, say, 'Goodbye, Dad,' and press the away button himself.

Then he returned to his twin sister, Vanessa, whose grief – in Vivienne's surprisingly blunt words – made her look as if a fist had been punched into the middle of her brain. Not that Rachael, Craig or even Jack appeared to be much better, but where the younger pair had withdrawn into themselves, their older brother was already looking out for at least one of them.

'Hey, Big Man,' he said, his eyes locking with mine as I came out of the crematorium, 'I reckon our kid would love to fix up that rusty old American car of yours.' Maybe he thought this was something I needed to get done and, if so, he was right.

'Happen he would, Jack lad,' I agreed, with less trouble in my heart than before. 'Happen he would,' I repeated, with a wink of thanks, leaving the sharp young fellow to shake the hand of the next mourner.

# 87

After our wedding in 1955 we went to America. I was a welder in the Texas oil business and Vivienne was a high-school secretary. With a bit of juggling on my part, we always had the summer to explore the States. For two years we drove around in a clapped-out pre-war Chevy, then bought a blue and yellow Ford Edsel, an immense car of the late fifties that, because of its upright radiator grille, was known as the Ford Ethel.

After ten years we had enough cash to come home and buy a B-and-B. Our acceptance of childlessness made our marriage even stronger than it already was. I was happy, Vivienne was happy, and as proof of our buccaneering years, we were still the fairly young couple who flashed around town in a red Ford Mustang. A car that real-life speed fanatic Steve McQueen had made iconic in *Bullit*, the film we'd been to see the night my fingertips turned to iron as they happened on a lump in the lower curve of Vivienne's right breast. Its removal came as swiftly as her consultant's follow-up promise that they'd 'got it all'.

That same year, 1969, Elvis Presley, whose 1950s rock-and-roll had meant nothing to me, staged his mighty comeback as a singer of ballads about love. His voice smoothed away my fear of losing the person I loved so much that thoughts of life without her brought on an unbearable darkness. It was somewhere I absolutely could not be.

One year later we underwent the whole trial again when part of her lower bowel was removed: bad luck but not secondaries, explained another consultant, who added that maybe it was time for Vivienne to stop smoking, a warning she laughed off with a quip that he obviously thought she smoked through her bum.

Elvis had a new loneliness in his voice as he sang of a love that was always on his mind, and somehow it felt right for us to sell the B-and-B and open our own Heartbreak Hotel. The only thing that spoilt the image we worked so hard to create was the rust that several British winters had given our Ford Mustang. Neither of us could bear to part with it, and it still looked a million dollars, parked on the forecourt beneath our neon Elvis in one of his glittering jumpsuits.

We were fine again. We were great again. Until the day not so long ago when Vivienne had a coughing fit. Afterwards the tea-towel I'd given her as a makeshift hanky was bright red with blood. Warnings didn't come much bigger than that.

# 88

I had everything planned with jackpot certainty before we were out of the crematorium grounds. First, young Craig and I were going to rip the sodden roof off the garage and replace it with something that would keep the rain out but let the light flood in. Then we'd clean away the oil that, under Raymond's control, had been compressed into a thick carpet that made your feet stick to the ground.

Plus we'd do the tatty old brick walls in white, completing the transformation of a depressing cave into a cheery place where I'd teach the young 'un how to gas weld. It was a skill I'd been so proud of when I was young that many Texan pipelines had my flowing signature welded on to them.

'If he can cut out the rot and weld in new steel, he'll be a proper car restorer,' I said, with such enthusiasm that Vivienne urged me to be quiet in case I seemed disrespectful to Raymond's memory. I'd forgotten Craig's father as soon as I'd locked onto the idea that, with the lad doing the repairs, the condition of our Ford Mustang would not be terminal, proving that a bad diagnosis could always be beaten.

A renewal of hope that had me seeing a future in which Vivienne, the laddie and I would be together in our iconic car, now cured of its rot. My vision, if you like, that everything would be okay after all. What more could I have wanted from life? Everything was still to play for.

## 89

On my arrival at number twenty from the kennels I, Brucie-Dog, had been struck by the huge blueness of the sea. After the many capers on which my second sight had just led me, I was now surrounded by an identical blueness that soothed my skin. The reason was clear. Everything I'd learnt that day was coming together and made sense to me. Even the craziest bits.

For example, I was no longer surprised that I'd earlier become a part of Jack's portrait of Elvis, which I now saw was the key to so much of what was going on in the kid's life. Jack was bold-hearted and, with the instinct of a true artist, had felt the pain that, one way or another, connects all humans. Sadly he'd painted only Elvis's despair and missed the comfort that millions took from his soulful voice. I knew why this was so and, in relation to Craig, it was ironic.

Unlike his immature younger brother, Jack was yet to fall in love but when he did so I had no doubt that the side of him with the potential for bullying would go. In showing green as his primary shade he'd proved to me that he also had the bully-free strength I'd found in Craig and his two sisters.

What else do human beings need to rise above old hurts but a combination of self-discipline and creativity allied to love? Big Eddie had done it. Oliver would have done it. Even Mr Heston, who'd been the Watcher, had accepted his wife's effort to help him. Hope: with the right things in place, I believed in salvation for all humans. I also knew that Her Hoityness might go wolfish with me for being glib. Probably she would have been right to do so.

My second sight had shown me the cruellest of human antics during war, and the worst and best of human behaviour when private hurts were struggled with. Two big forces that the kid had been scissored by non-stop since birth, and against which even the love of his family and the restoration of Big Eddie's car were unlikely to be enough to save him. Leaving me, Brucie the rescue dog, chosen by Ginger to help him make it in a queer-hating world where self-offing by young men was an everyday fact that few people cared about.

The suicide boys: better of out of it, as the school caretaker had said within earshot of young Marcus. Plus I had more pressing reasons to be extra scared for Craig.

Marcus had finally pedalled out of his life on the shiny yellow Raleigh Chopper, and Oliver no longer visited his dreams, placing him even more at the mercy of his bad bone knowledge and all that Raymond and school had done to him. I wanted to be stronger than ever. I needed to be stronger than ever. I was a rescue dog whose purpose was as clear as could be.

But the blueness that had been so soothing grew hotter and, with Robespierre's gift completely used up, I feared that this time I really was about to die. A rescue dog that had learnt everything and done nothing. In sum, a failure that the other mutts at the kennels had been right to yap at for being useless.

Perhaps my thinking box had been fried by rabies, and everything that had occurred since Ginger had first called me an artful bugger was a dream. What happened next proved that, in part, this conclusion was plausible.

## 90

I was being boiled alive and, from high above, I heard Ginger's explanation to the four twins. 'The emergency vet warned that his fever will become truly dreadful. We might lose him at any minute,' she'd cautioned. That really got my shivers going and, to resist them, I curled into a tight ball, the last-resort position of all rescue dogs, everywhere.

My shivers lessened but if my first human had turned up with his special electric cable I would have welcomed a final round of punishment as an escape from the place where I was now trapped.

Something equally odd happened.

I, Brucie-Dog, became the hub of a carousel that had dozens of fast-moving seahorses, which on closer look I realised were also the sailors lost when Raymond's ship was sunk. They were soon joined by the German survivors he was ordered to machine-gun while they bobbed in the sea. By now anything was credible to me, including seahorses that were men and men who were seahorses. They were not smooth in their swimming.

Having died as young men decades before, they thrashed as if their new lives depended on them going ever quicker. Clenching my sore eyes I wanted them to be gone but two in particular had a power I could not resist. I had to face them.

The first was the bearded captain who had picked up Oliver, the Watcher and Raymond from the sea before his ship, too, was torpedoed. 'I was just an ordinary family man,' he exclaimed, and zoomed back into the swirl of seahorses-cum-men. I wanted to reply that he was still a queer-hater but the second sailor was too quick for me to get a word in. It did not surprise me that this was Oliver.

'You can still save him, Brucie-Dog!' he cried. 'You can still save your kid if you've a real mind to!'

That was like being picked up by my scruff and shaken hard.

Next to Marcus, Oliver understood Craig better than anybody, yet as part of the kid's bone knowledge he was central to the events that had borne on everything since the 1940s. Though he'd meant well, his words frightened me. I was only a rescue dog, not a challenger of Fate.

Oliver must have been reading my mind. 'You can do it, Brucie!' he insisted. 'You must do it!'

The carousel went, leaving me in the same very blue place, which was now heavy as well as hot. Ideal for suffocation of a sick, exhausted dog.

'Please, let me die now,' I begged of Her Hoityness, who I hoped would understand that, in accepting failure, I was at least setting the family free to pick a rescue dog worthy of devotion. One that might save Craig after all.

In choosing me over the healthier mutts, Ginger had opted for the runt of the litter. The reply to my pleading came not from Her Hoityness and I welcomed the healthy scent of young Rachael. 'Don't you bloody dare die on us, Brucie,' she hissed right into my ear. 'If you do my stupid twin will become the biggest drama-queen on earth.'

I know that my tail wagged because it hurt at the root.

'Fight for us, Brucie,' she added. 'Fight for our Craig,' she insisted.

I sensed Raymond lurking and that in his silence I was accused of treachery against the family. Doing as Oliver and Rachael had asked felt impossible and I expected to die at any moment. What actually came about was as strange as my carousel of seahorses-cum-men had been.

# 91

A shiny patch formed on the darkness I was looking into. At first I thought it was an opening through which I had to pass. I was wrong. It was a big version of Picasso's beady eye, and though I wanted to break its hold, I could not. The baldy old parrot was once again entrancing me.

Then I saw movement and Her Hoityness emerged from within the eye and padded to where I was now resting on a sandy area of seabed. As she did so a silver light came from the body of her lifeless white pup, held between her fangs. Only then did I grasp that, throughout our shared time at the kennels, she was grieving and had self-offed by becoming wolfish with Psycho Vet.

I watched as she released the little body to where a current took it into the dark. Then she lay at my side and lifted a leg to permit access to her milk. 'Drink,' she instructed, as I understood that this was her special gift to me. 'Drink,' she repeated, as I also saw that, despite being a pedigree, she too had been a rescue dog whose life was cut short, just like Robespierre's.

'Drink!' she growled, with anger I could not ignore, meaning that through her gift I would be there for Ginger, Jack, Vanessa, Rachael and especially Craig: the young human who needed me to save his life.

The warm milk was sweet and the more I drank the better I felt. I wasn't the runt any more. I was Brucie the Rescue Dog, and after all I'd learnt that day, I knew I could meet the demands of my mission. I loved my new family so much that nothing would ever again make me doubt my role as the kid's rescue dog. Our life together was about to begin. Ginger had made a good choice with me. Pauline had been right all along. Fate could be challenged. Even as a very old rescue dog I remain sure of that.

The kid. My kid. I, Brucie-Dog, was going to save him.

# PART TWO

# WINSTON LOSES HIS HEAD

# 1

I t was the summer of 1982. Big Eddie and Ginger had been married for five years and were touring the South of France, leaving me, Brucie–Dog, and Picasso the parrot as Craig's only companions at number twenty, which had once buzzed with life.

It was a long time since Jack, Vanessa and Rachael had left home for the universities that paved the way for their adult lives, but the kid was like a hamster on a wheel, constantly welding up cars that had failed the MOT because of rust. This was a compliment to him: Raymond's former contacts in the motor trade trusted Craig and supplied work without knowing that his old dream of being a classic-car restorer had soured. Even the outlook from the wide door of the workshop had lost its sparkle, with few touches to lift the drab view.

Big Eddie had sold the Heartbreak Hotel to a developer, who had replaced it with flats so dull that he'd regretted his decision not to employ a care-taker-manager. Still, not everything about the kid's world had changed beyond recognition, and one of the best bits was still letting much-needed light into his life. When Raymond had died, Big Eddie had fitted a clear plastic roof to the workshop, and after ten years it was unclouded, just as I'd found it when Ginger urged me to be with Craig on day one of my rescue. This was when he already had a fair sum saved from fixing cars, two years before passing his driving test in late 1974, since when I'd accompanied him on the hundreds of car journeys that had helped keep his life in balance.

Twenty-four-year-old Craig was bored with his work but his self-image remained car-based, and in the eyes of others this defined who he was.

His car was a powerful red Capri 3000E, suggesting that, far from being a queer, he was a manly sort. I couldn't blame him for almost believing this self-deception. For a long time it had made his life bearable.

Yet, as all rescue dogs know, it's a rare human who can deny his true self without paying a big price. Everything was about to change but, shamefully, I Brucie Dog didn't see it coming.

# 2

Most rescue dogs cannot get enough of riding in cars, and I'd come to associate sitting up front in the Capri with being close to the kid's heart. I knew every inch of the surrounding roads and took comfort from all that was familiar, especially the nearby seafront strip, Sir Winston's promontory, and the huge spread of the sea.

It seemed that, short of a tidal wave, nothing would surprise me about my life with Craig. For a plain mutt this might have been a good thing, but as a rescue dog I was soon to find that my many years of cosiness had misled me. The truth behind this was harsh and, from her equally long period of silence, I saw later that Her Hoityness was angry with me for letting the question of the kid's queerness slide. I was failing in my mission, and by mid-1982, there was little time left for me to wake up and help him accept the love that would have enriched his life. Satisfied with my routine, I saw nothing wrong with being lazy and it was small wonder that the coming changes for me and Craig started with a bang. We both deserved a good shaking-up.

The kid had taken me with him in the growling red Capri to the breaker's yard where he'd settled the account for parts bought over the past three months. This was a regular trip and, because of the sun's strength, the sea was at its bluest, affecting me hard. I was an old dog with cloudy eyes. Bright colours plus heat always made me drowsy, especially when I was on a car ride. Still, I should at least have tried to be alert.

Craig hadn't been at his sharpest for a day or two and maybe his driving was sloppy. A slumbering rescue dog still knows what's going on around him but it had been easier for me not to sniff out trouble. Humans are up and down with their moods and the kid was typical. Did it matter that he was a bit out of sorts?

It was after he'd changed down for the left turn onto Sea View Road that a large Alsatian, which appeared to be Her Hoityness, bounded off the steps from the beach. They were connected to the promontory where the life-sized marble statue of Sir Winston Churchill faced the sea, before the bench where Raymond had offed himself a decade before. Sometimes Sir Winston was grey but on this occasion he sparkled as if he was plugged into a power station and, to my surprise, I felt a twin surge of energy zip to my nose and tail. Never had my mood changed so fast.

The Alsatian – which was actually a young he – had

cleared the wide pavement and was padding at an angle towards the front of the Capri. Everything became fast and slow at the same time. As Craig grabbed my scruff to stop me hitting the windscreen, he stamped on the brakes. A thump from behind made me howl, as if my time with the living was up.

'What the heck?' the kid cried, flicking a look at the rear-view mirror. 'What the heck?' he repeated, releasing me.

By now the Capri was stopped with its nearside wheels high on the granite kerb, slightly beyond Sea View Road. Setting his fingers on the door handle in readiness to get out of the heavily slanted car, Craig turned his top half to face me and I saw that his spinach-green eyes were wide with concern. 'You okay, Brucie?' he asked, stroking my head with his free hand. 'You okay?' he repeated, in a tone that showed he knew I understood every word. This and his touch were re-assuring and I licked his big straight nose. The next bit was odd and made me worried.

Craig was laughing at my antics but I knew that something important, which I couldn't put my paw on, was missing from our connection.

'Ya big daft mutt!' he exclaimed, in relief that I was unharmed. 'Howling like a bliddy wolf,' he teased, stroking me for a little longer. Before he left the car he wound down the driver's window an extra bit, so I could breathe but not get out.

I watched his every move closely: a random-seeming event had occurred and partly because of the riddle as to what was absent between us, I needed to study what was going on. My ears were on high alert too.

3

You might think a car crash was the most alarming thing I experienced on that hot day in August 1982. That would be to overlook an event from the early hours of the morning when I woke up suddenly: my throat was tight as a vice, making my lungs burn. I threw myself face down to the floor and clenched the carpet so hard that afterwards my fingernails were painful. The more I tried to breathe, the worse my insides felt and the wilder the storm in my head became.

For the minute that this lasted a high-pitched whistle escaped me, somehow mocking the situation. When my throat unlocked I could breathe and think again with ease.

Ten years had passed since Dad's suicide, when my airways had closed several times while I slept. Nobody had known about this. It was the secret of a boy who believed he'd caused his dad's death by being queer and that his breathing problems were a warning from God. My thinking was simple. Dad's life had been sacrificed because of me and if

I ever turned actively gay my throat would stay tight until I was dead. This was a tough deal to take but I saw that God was no harsher towards queers than most people were. We were despised at worst, tolerated at best, and one of my hardest moments came when Dad called me a limp-wristed little queer before loads of blokes at a car auction. After that, nothing was right between us, but we'd been heading the wrong way for a long time.

Dad was a back-lane car dealer and I'd been his sidekick in the workshop at the rear of our house since I was small. For much of the time we were happy. He loved me and I loved him. But because he'd always spouted on about homos and sneered at me for growing into what he called a cissy, things got dark between us and I was clearly to blame: the queer-boy whose nature had driven his father to drink and suicide. Or so I felt.

In the moments after the seafront car crash I knew something else. This time it was accurate. I'd been so off the ball while I was driving that when a big Alsatian strayed onto the road I didn't react soon enough, causing a shunt from behind when at last I stamped on the brakes. At least my excuse for this lapse was true. Some hours before, when my throat seized up, it seemed that my survival was again under threat. It put me on red alert against a long-running suicide-theme in my life.

Ironically Dad had set an example when he went over the sea rail. Then Hugo Moncrieff had hanged himself and poor old Marcus had taken his mum's pills after he was mocked in the showers, leaving me more scared than ever that I might be a homo. This was not drama-queen stuff.

Teenagers such as Hugo, Marcus and I weren't only queer. We were the suicide boys, and my seemingly out-of-the-blue car crash had brought me back to this point with a bang, which included the other driver's injuries, even if they were down to more than my bad driving. I saw that the windscreen of his big gold Ford Zodiac was blood-spattered above the steering wheel, proving he was not wearing a seatbelt when the collision occurred. I sprinted to kill the ignition before a fire started.

Nothing could have prepared me for what came next. It was my worst nightmare come true and the best thing ever.

# 4

The door of the Zodiac dropped to the road when I pulled it open. The front end had caved in more than I'd thought and the driver was lying on the flattened seat, facing me with grey-blue eyes. My heart warmed. It was as if liquid gold pumped where my blood should have been.

'Are you okay?' I heard myself ask, as he gave a smile that made him seem familiar to me. He was cheeky with words too.

'Good as I'll ever be after nutting a windscreen at thirty miles an hour,' he replied. This time I found his voice beautiful. Later I would discover that, despite his discomfort, my transparency tickled him.

Even the damaged gold car was on my side in whatever was starting up between me and its owner. Somehow he'd wiped out my defences so I had to disguise my emotions as best I could. This was not easily done but, satisfied that with its power turned off the car was less likely to burn, I met his gaze again. This was a mistake. He was so handsome and vulnerable and my sense of knowing him grew stronger.

The blood that had thickened on his moustache and beard was a barrier to recognition and I made the only comment one bloke could offer another who was in a dodgy way.

'You'll be okay, mate,' I said.

'Sure I will,' he replied, teasing.

A shiver went down my spine.

'Sure I will,' he repeated, wriggling into a less uncomfortable position. Weirdly I felt as if he was reassuring me that I would be fine and I felt the heat of a familiar rash on the left side of my neck. Usually this on-off blotch was strawberry-coloured but it could be purple, and I knew that because the stakes between me and the driver were high, this was one of those rare times. Things were beautiful but nightmarish, and I dreaded that in my excitement I might tell him he was handsome and that I wanted to take his pain for him. Worse, I wanted to kiss him and promise that if the Zodiac caught fire I would stay at his side.

Luckily at that moment a taxi driver who had radioed for help said: 'Ambulance is on its way. Few minutes at the most, I reckon.'

By now several more people were near to us. In the past I would have shied away from all close contact with another young man, but this time I stayed put. The thing between us didn't only come from my side and what I did next surprised us both.

# 5

**W**ithout thinking about it I set one hand to his denim-clad knee and cupped his head with the other, bracing him against further harm. Sirens were sounding from the south end of the prom. Maybe I should have taken them as a warning. They were louder and more urgent-seeming by the second.

'Thank you,' the Zodiac driver said. Soon his pale blue eyes were closed and I was scared he might die in my hands.

'Mind ya don't hurt the lad!' barked a man from behind, shattering what had felt like a private space between me and the driver.

No sooner did I release him than his eyes opened and my insides flipped so hard that I had to catch my breath. 'Do I know you, mate?' I blurted. The rash on my neck was becoming hotter.

The man who'd barked at me to be careful now instructed me to move aside. That was rough. I was there to help but at least one person saw me as a threat to the driver. Maybe he was right and I was in shock after my car had been rear-ended by the Zodiac. What I did next supports this view and I must have sounded odd to all onlookers.

'Can you tell me please? Do I know this driver? I mean, are we connected in some way?' I asked.

The angry man scowled as if I might infect him with the plague, and years of defending myself against homo-haters enabled me to understand why. I was an obvious queer sticking my nose where it had no right to be. His wife, though, was fair.

'You've had a little bump is all, darling,' she advised, as I looked to where her husband was now crouched beside the woozy driver, who lifted my mood by looking past him with a smile just for me.

'I know him. I'm sure I know him,' I told the woman, who shrugged, but not unkindly.

An ambulance was now coming to a halt on the red tarmac strip behind the Zodiac. The woman advised that I should take some deep breaths and leave the crew to do their best for the driver, who was again writhing on the seat. This was sounder advice than she knew. For half a second my throat had gone tight and I'd feared a closure that might have seen me carted off to hospital as the second casualty of the crash. Relieved that that wouldn't happen, I was struck by the contrast between the wrecked Zodiac and my Capri, which appeared to have only a broken exhaust tail.

Weighing this up, I put the survival of my car down to the tow bar I'd fitted for when I was taking my oxy-acetylene bottles to be refilled. It made the back of the Capri stronger than a tank – most cars hitting it would have come off badly.

Then the woman made a suggestion that gave me good reason to step away from her husband. 'Perhaps you might double-check your lovely dog's unharmed,' she said, pointing to where our Brucie was watching everything through the rear windscreen of my car. That was welcome and I avoided looking back to where the stretcher was being prepared for the Zodiac driver. My jealousy of the ambulance crew made me ashamed, but for the first time in my adult life I knew that I was not the outsider. Brucie might have smelt the thrill that gave me. His nose twitched, his eyes were bluer than usual and, after clambering into the front seat of the Capri, he gave me his paw. Sometimes it seemed he understood life better than I did.

The bearded driver who'd seized my heart was taken off in the ambulance. All I could do now was wait and see how things panned out between us. There was no doubt in my mind that he was part of what lay ahead. My life had changed but exactly how I didn't yet know.

# 6

I, Brucie–Dog, had been giving the kid my biggest blue moons but it was impossible for him to know why I was so switched on by what I'd seen at the seafront. The spook of his grey-bearded dad had been lurking beside the wrecked Zodiac and, without Raymond knowing it, I realised what was missing from my life with Craig.

Redness flared around the kid when the spook was close. It was many months since I'd last associated any colours with him at all. That was shocking: as a young dog my reading of colour was so powerful it could exhaust me. Yet recently I'd allowed it to go. Burning with shame, I soon saw another bad thing. My sense of smell was turned off, reducing me to even less than the lazy creature I knew I'd become. Sad as this was for the kid, it could have been fatal for me.

A rescue dog that loses his sense of smell is in the same place as humans who no longer cry when they're peeling onions. The close-down of life is under way. It was no wonder that, in my case, Raymond was back. After all, for older rescue dogs, such as I, everything is linked, making any neglect of care dangerous.

Craig had reached a make-or-break point in his life and there was a lot I needed to be reminded about.

The kennel lad who had led Her Hoityness to her final meeting with Psycho Vet was none other than Marcus Wright, whom, until Raymond's queer-hating had worsened in his last months, the kid had loved more or less openly. On the day of my rescue from the kennels Marcus had attempted to repair his relationship with Craig, who, because of his dislike of queers, which was passed on in his bone knowledge, and Raymond's influence, despised himself too much to accept this last-minute chance of shared happiness. Standing high on the pedals of his gleaming yellow Raleigh Chopper bicycle, Marcus had pedalled away from the workshop, soon to quit the area for a specialist apprenticeship with a sewing-machine manufacturer, three hundred miles away. Stories of broken love did not come sadder than the tale of these two young humans, and now even my own body was reminding me of the worst of it. That's how it is for rescue dogs. Our health mirrors the state of those we love and even at my laziest I'd always been tuned in to the kid.

It was a long time since I'd had mange but I itched as if the disease was back to punish me. If so it was deserved and I half expected my fur to drop out in clumps. Under my care Craig had fought his true nature so strongly that he'd even managed to drive Marcus almost out of his conscious memory. No human being can do such a thing and thrive and no rescue dog can be satisfied if his mission has withered.

Now gold as well as red exploded around the kid and those onlookers beside the mangled Ford Zodiac. That was scary and exhilarating. It was a long time since I'd been so alive and the salty sea breeze coming through the part-open window of the Capri caught my nostrils. I, Brucie–Dog, was reborn eager to support Craig, who settled on the driver's seat, ready to drive us off the high granite kerb.

It was only eighteen minutes since the crash but, after years of stillness, we were set to go forward together.

# 7

He took the next turn off the seafront and headed for number twenty via the high street, a short ride during which the spook appeared on the back seat and set his startling blue gaze on me. 'Now then, Bruce!' he barked, as the black interior was lit by silver flashes that again made me wary of my weak bowel. 'Our Vanessa loves her young man! Our Rachael loves her young man! And our Jack,' he concluded, 'adores his Lisa-Jane!' That was quite an outpouring, and because he'd always scared me a little, I had trouble resisting the shakes, which I knew Craig would put down to the crash. And I didn't need to be a pedigree, like Her Hoityness, to see what Raymond was getting at with the love that had enriched the lives of Rachael, Vanessa and Jack. It was simple. He regretted his role in bringing about the solitude that had been the kid's lot since he was a teenager.

The shine that had brightened his grey hair and beard dulled and, as if to mock his despair at what he'd done to Craig, one of the Capri's twin exhausts fell and dragged on the road.

'Shit,' muttered the kid, who glanced in the mirror for cars behind.

'Shit,' he repeated, on double-declutching to the five miles an hour that stopped the mid-section of the pipe departing its hanger.

'Not far now, Brucie-Lucie,' he commented, as the scratch of steel on tarmac made me whimper in protest at the pain within my head. That's how it is with all older dogs. Noises skewer into us and we suffer for it.

The spook was smiling at Craig's handling of the wounded car and I couldn't stop my tail wagging. My mixed feelings about Raymond were hard to balance and I knew that this was a two-way situation. He'd doubted me from day one, but I was the only rescue dog the kid had, obliging the spook to be grateful to me.

Very soon his gaze came my way again. There was no unkindness beneath what came next. Just a clear wish for the kid to find the happiness I also wanted for him. 'I hope you're up to what my boy needs,' he remarked, as my tail stilled.

'He, too, must have love,' he insisted. Craig was showing lavish streaks of black and gold, proof that he was at the edge of the happiness we both wanted for him.

# 8

I'd never seen the kid so restless but the Zodiac driver's name wouldn't be known until the police visited number twenty, leaving long hours that Craig tried to fill with tasks such as weeding Ginger's small front garden – she'd packed it with irises of every shade so it was admired by anyone who passed the house. I wasn't up to its mix of colours and scents. My eyes smarted, my snout hurt, and although the kid was normally a keen gardener, he was only half interested that day in weeding. Clumsy with it too.

When he trod on a thick root that showed above the soil he cursed and came over to me. I'd parked my rump on the short concrete path that led from the rusty metal gate to Ginger's liquorice allsort front door. 'Strange times, eh, Brucie?' he mused, tickling the spot between my ear flaps. 'All this flipping heat,' he continued, as I saw my quizzical face reflected in his eyes.

'Ya big old champ,' he remarked, with love. I felt extra-glad to be his rescue dog, though before I could shoot my tongue at him he stood up, cupped his hand to his brow and faced the sun, which, since the car crash, had moved from the rear of number twenty to the front.

'Know what?' he asked, without looking down at me. 'I woulda preferred full-on fire to this torture.'

I understood what he meant: things had got over-heated in more ways than one but there was nothing he could do about it. The reek of his stomach acid became so strong that it even overwhelmed the effect of the irises on my snout.

I had to be less uncomfortable. I got up and padded beyond the wide-open liquorice allsort into the cool heart of the house where, through the glass door of the kitchen extension, I saw Picasso dozing in apparent unconcern about Craig. On any other day the ancient parrot's beady eye might have made me wolfish, yet when I needed his help with the kid he was sleeping on the job.

That didn't mean I was working alone. I had an old ally to call upon. 'Please,' I prayed to Her Hoityness, 'make the police come soon with the driver's name. Please,' I repeated.

I worried that, because I couldn't see whiteness around the kid, my powers might fail again, leaving him stuck with new dangers. It was disloyal of me not to see that, despite his obsession with the handsome driver of the gold Zodiac, he was still looking out for me, his treasured rescue dog.

# 9

For twenty years the lino in the kitchen had had yellow seahorses on a blue background but Big Eddie had replaced it with hard green tiles that were scratchy beneath my claws. Sometimes I left the room because of that, but after being outside in the heat I wanted to lap my water bowl dry.

The kid saw that I needed to cool down. 'Drink it all up, Brucie-Wucie-Lucie darling,' he encouraged, showing a touch of red, which reassured me that my powers were fully back.

By now Picasso had been awake for several minutes and was gazing at us from where his domed cage sat atop one of the new benches that were also among Big Eddie's home improvements at number twenty. 'Drink it all up, Brucie-Wucie-Lucie darling,' he mimicked.

I couldn't hide from the kid or the know-it-all parrot that I was exhausted, so after my drink I padded to the sofa cushion Ginger had given me to keep my old bones comfortable. I raked its cloth surface with my paw to make it mine and flopped into the tightly curled shape of all ageing rescue dogs that seek restorative sleep. My hope for a good rest was limited.

In wake of the crash, the return of the spook, Craig's aimlessness, Picasso's odd behaviour and the question of the Zodiac driver's name, I might have had my wildest dreams in years. Oddly that was not the case. And I knew I'd need every bit of my strength for what was coming down the line. I slept better than any sheep dog but was unable to keep one eye open . . . even though Craig needed me to be at my most watchful.

Still, many dogs kick the air or even move around while they're asleep and at some point I padded upstairs to be near him, the smell of soap causing the sneeze that woke me up. Hours had passed since the crash and I was lying on my side in a pool of light that spilled from the bathroom. The kid had left the door open. Very soon I sneezed again.

A splash came from the tub as he sat up to look my way, which under normal circumstances would have been fine. Now, though, his hair was flat and his eyes disturbingly wide, marring the off-beat good looks he shared with his older brother Jack. This wasn't important. Truly serious stuff was occurring.

Despite the red and gold he'd shown earlier, the air around him was so thin it made everything transparent, as if we were inside a world of ice, the meaning of which was scarily clear to me. The crash had pushed

Craig beyond his daily point of being and he was closer than ever to offing himself. Quick as a whippet I was four-square and doing blue moons.

'You'll never guess who the other bloke is, Brucie!' he declared, as his furry caterpillars went so high that they might have left his brow. 'Back after all these bloody years,' he continued, and his infatuation with the Zodiac driver clouded his face. It was as if he'd sipped a cocktail and found it bitter. It irritated me that my tail wagged hard: the kid was more conflicted than ever. On returning his gaze to the tap-end of the tub he slid back below its rolled rim, frustratingly out of sight. My heart thumped and I hoped that the Zodiac driver was Marcus Wright, back to fix things with Craig before my life reached its end.

This was a fairytale: the young man from the crash had dark hair where Marcus was fair, and if it was Marcus, Craig would have known. Full stop.

Ten years had passed but I'd never doubted that if the kid found the guts to rise above his bad feelings about being a natural-born queer, he and Marcus would be happy for the rest of their lives. Facts, however, were facts. The chances of Craig leaving the closet felt about as likely as Picasso fleeing the cage that had been his since Ginger's parents had given him to her as a fledg-ling on her fifteenth birthday.

For half a century steel bars had shaped the parrot's

life and without them he would have crashed and broken his neck. Exactly as I feared might now happen to the kid, whose defences had been wiped out at a stroke. Still, I saw that on balance his life had taken a turn for the better. He was young enough to risk leaving his old ways and I was pained that he held onto the name of the Zodiac driver as if it sealed his fate as the lonely old queer-hater I was meant to stop him becoming.

Willing my second sight to open I aimed to witness the kid's encounter with the police, who had visited number twenty while I'd slept. Instead the light from the bathroom became a ball of silver ringed by black and I soon saw why this was. My mind-of-its-own second sight had things it wanted me to learn: I'd been drawn into an outsized version of Picasso's all-seeing eye. It erupted into sunshine, wiping out ten years of my life. My aches and pains were gone. I was young again and up for anything.

# 10

The concrete of the lane was warm beneath my paws as I sped beside the fourteen-year-old kid, whose hands embraced Marcus's slim waist while he steered the Raleigh Chopper towards the seafront. Their hair flew back, their faces were red and they laughed as one, proving that if Craig could find the will to drop his war against queerness, they would share a happy future. That would have been perfect.

'Faster! Faster!' cried the kid, as they cleared the red-topped seafront road, where I saw the spook clapping them on so hard that I felt his need for the kid to heal from the queer-hating that had damaged his life so far.

For once Raymond was joyous and I was pleased for him.

'Yes! Yes! Faster! Faster!' he roared, stepping backwards and onto Churchill's promontory, where he clasped his hands as if in prayer to the statue as it twinkled in the sun. That made sense.

I knew the spook loved the kid and understood that, until Craig became happy with Marcus, he couldn't rest in the peace that Ginger, the four twins and even Picasso had wanted for him. Plus Marcus and Craig were at a handicap too. Only a minority of humans see spooks and they were blind to Raymond's joy. This might have made me sad but something key to my life as a rescue dog occurred instead. At last I saw what made us so important and I felt stronger for knowing it.

Even the most alert people are largely removed from the pre-birth events that influence their lives and the kid was a prime example of this. To say that for much of the time he lived within a fog of half-understanding is fair. There was so much he couldn't know that was obvious to me, especially where Raymond, Oliver and their old war experiences were concerned.

It wasn't only that the spook was invisible to Craig: he couldn't possibly see that the fair-haired young man who'd first come to his dreams after his dad died was born with him as part of his bone knowledge. Or that Raymond had betrayed Oliver during the war, where queer love was feared by men on each side, especially those who hid their needs, like the Watcher.

Still, the ride of the two boys on the Raleigh Chopper was speeding up, and as we left the spook behind us with Sir Winston, I drew power from his high spirits, making me quicker than a greyhound. Otherwise I might have dropped dead before my renewed mission to save Craig had really got going. Everything was beautiful and my tail wagged so hard it was a miracle it didn't break.

'It's me 'n' you, Craig!' hollered Marcus, as the far end of the promenade came to a rocky point. Beyond, on St Christine's Island, the white lighthouse, which could be seen from the bottom of Sea View Road, also twinkled in the sun.

'We're in luck!' he added, as they became surrounded by the deepest redness I'd known any humans to show. 'Causeway's clear!' he continued, splashing the Raleigh Chopper through the shallows left by the tide. 'To the lighthouse!' he shouted, while my heart pounded as if it might burst.

'To the lighthouse!' repeated the kid, whose joy at hugging Marcus from behind as he pedalled the Raleigh Chopper misled me into believing that my mission was unnecessary. Rescue dogs must be clear-sighted or our lives are pointless. Marcus and Craig had almost reached the thick base of the lighthouse when there was a bang and a flash, as if the sun was exploding all around us.

I was back to being me, Brucie the old collie cross, whose purpose was to save twenty-four-year-old Craig before my days ended. To my shame Her Hoityness was snarling for me to get on with things. It didn't matter that years had passed since I'd last seen her alive. She would be with me until my mission was done and without her I'd be lost. She was my conscience.

Her anger stung, and what I couldn't know was that while I'd been dreaming, the post-car-crash situation for Craig was becoming critical. I would soon discover why this was so, and it was much scarier than Her Hoityness had ever been. That was for sure.

# 11

The crash between the gold Zodiac and the red Capri was tough for an old dog to take and I'd gone back to sleep on the carpet where the light of the bathroom spilled from its open door. On a normal day that would have been fine, but for the second time I was unable to keep an eye open. Luckily Craig's thrashing soon woke me. I stood on my back legs, front paws against the edge of the tub, and saw why Her Hoityness had been fierce with me.

The kid's thick black hair was floating like strands of seaweed around his lobster-red face below the surface. Even as I took in this image his flailing arms slowed and I realised that, because his throat was closed, he was incapable of saving himself. Nothing could have been starker: if he didn't suffocate he would open his mouth with a gasp and fill his lungs.

'Sit up! Sit up! Sit up!' I barked, as my snout dipped to where the acid-reek of extreme danger scorched my airways.

'Sit up! Sit up! Sit up!' I repeated, then took a decision that would otherwise have been unthinkable. I would lock my teeth around his right arm and try to pull him above the water. But the kid was solid with muscle and my back legs were already so tired that my paws slid where bathwater had splashed the lino. The more I tried to reach him the more I fell and banged my chin on the tub. I was old. I was pathetic, and I never should have slept with both eyes closed. It was me who deserved to die, not him.

Collie crosses are known for their sense of duty but I'd been more like a poodle. As if to punish me for this, his arm got wedged between his ribs and the tub, ruining my last hope of getting a bite on him. The situation was desperate. I barked, slipped and fell many times but knew my efforts were pointless.

After all our years together he wouldn't have the chance to be happy with Marcus after all. 'Look out for my younger boy,' Ginger had said, following my rescue from Psycho Vet. It was pitiable. I'd failed them both, and as the life left Craig's body, there was no chance of things changing. Or so it seemed.

## 12

The spook came from nowhere, lifted me high and dropped me onto the kid, who sat up and coughed so hard that I was thrown against the taps, causing a wave that went up the tiled walls.

'Jesus Christ!' he cried, as I scrabbled over the rim to where I slid this way and that, eventually finding my balance near the tub. It was hard to believe what was happening but the welts where my claws had snagged his skin proved that all this was real. Things kept changing fast too.

The spook was gone and for a moment I became sad that Craig would never know who'd really saved his life. Perhaps this was just as well. He'd also suffered a big shock and I didn't want him to fear that madness had him in its grip. Those rare humans who saw spooks were often given drugs, locked up and even zapped with electricity.

'Jesus Christ!' the kid repeated, as I shook away the wetness that had made my fur claggier than mud. 'Brucie-Wucie-Lucie-Darling!' he cried. 'You bloody great mutt!' he added, as I gave my biggest blue moons and sniffed the air, confirming there was no longer an acid-smell of danger. Even more happily I spotted small yellow spikes in the greens of his eyes and my tail wagged hard, pushing him at last to say the Zodiac driver's name. 'Would ya believe,' he remarked, scrubbing the top of my head, 'that Trevor bloody Carlton is back.'

For several seconds I didn't know what to think or how to react but my body took care of that for me. It always had and sometimes I'd even wondered if I was in control of my own life, let alone influencing the kid's days for the better.

My tail suddenly hurt, as if it was knotted, and at last I saw the link between the thick-bearded young man in the gold Zodiac and the queer-hating teenager of a decade before. I wanted to bark but held back. As I parked my rump on the landing, I saw that the crash wasn't just about a gold car hitting a red one. The kid's past and present had collided, and with all that I'd discovered through my second sight, I understood his long struggle against being a natural-born queer even better than the spook did. Especially in the period after Raymond's self-offing, when Craig's throat had closed for the first time and young Trevor had done so much harm to him and Marcus. It was an effort to bring my attention back to the moment. The past was an unruly place where any rescue dog might perish, especially an older mutt.

The kid had dropped his towel and was using it to mop the lino. I expected a dense show of white, which would make me essential. That was exciting. Rescue dogs are not humble. We enjoy our glory . . . but I was soon reminded of how misleading that can be.

Craig showed the crimson that was all around the Raleigh Chopper when Marcus had pedalled them to the lighthouse. Something most odd was happening and I knew that, so far, things could have been far worse for him and me.

At least I hadn't been seen off by the crash or its after-shocks and would still be around to watch my kid beat the queer-hating odds that had been stacked against him from day one. Depending on how things went for us both, of course.

My tail lost its knot but my second sight kept up the pressure. I was old yet my mission was incomplete. That needed to be put right. The return of Trevor Carlton – who had largely caused Marcus's suicide bid – had to be put in context.

# 13

Not all of my work was for the motor trade. Those who lived in the area knew that I was good at what I did and often came to me direct at number twenty. Sometimes they were ex-schoolmates who expected I'd knock off a few quid for old times' sake. That was ironic. Most of them had been scared of me because I was queer and, now that we were older, were unlikely to suggest going for a pint.

One of these customers was Howler. In the days after Marcus's release from hospital he'd stopped Trevor queer-bashing a boy called Woody so I'd replaced the sills of his orange Avenger GT for the cost of parts only, a freebie I enjoyed doing. He had an open face, a copper tinge to his brown hair, and hazel eyes, which intrigued me. Beyond this I avoided contemplating his good looks and neat build. Later, when I'd wised up, I could nail him in four words: happy, daring, attractive and likeable. But that's me getting ahead of myself. Howler was just Howler, an old pal to whom a favour was owed.

The Avenger needed to be in good shape because he

was moving to the South of France, where he and his girlfriend were to manage a sporty campsite for keep-fit fanatics. That seemed a good plan and, with the repairs to his car done, I'd expected him to drive off, putting me out of his mind. It was what I was used to, staying put while others moved on.

Years had passed since I'd learnt from Dad and school that I must never be a hands-on homo, and if being in love meant coming out of the closet, there was no alternative way ahead for me. I had to be alone and it was Howler who put this old belief to the test.

Instead of firing up the engine for his departure he wound down the driver's window and cocked his head. I knelt in the lane in front of the flats where the Heartbreak Hotel had been. We were eye to eye and when he didn't speak straight away I did my big sister Vanessa's trick of raising one eyebrow above its neighbour. In my case this was the left but for her it was the right. If Howler wondered why I gave him that quizzical look he was right to do so. It worried me that he was after a freebie paint-job for the Avenger, whose new sills I'd done my best to colour-match. I was wrong, and it didn't take him long to blindside me with something else entirely.

'She was married when we met,' he announced, referring to his girlfriend, who I knew was called Zoe because she was the older sister of Susan Terry, who had helped Marcus after Trevor had made me put bubblegum in his hair. Which I felt to have been just before he'd called to the workshop to show me the Avenger's rusty sills.

I often awoke to the reek of the lurid pink bubblegum because of my lingering guilt over what I'd done to Marcus, especially when I'd joined in with the chant of 'Punish the queer' in our school changing rooms.

Howler was not about to rake over this history. 'Never been bitten by crazy love, have ya, Craig?' he probed, causing my second eyebrow to shoot upwards, as if a tiny bomb had gone off beneath it. 'Never, never, never,' he added, looking down the lane at the sea and laughing to himself, but without the spite of Trevor or others who, over the years, had asked why I didn't have a girlfriend. 'Oh, I'm not saying it's always a good thing, crazy love,' he shifted his gaze to where the wide-open workshop hadn't changed since Big Eddie's revamp after Dad's time, 'but it sure as heck moves life on from one place to another.' A shudder went down my spine. We'd known each other a long time, and for some reason it bothered him that I was a loner stuck in a back-lane garage.

He knew I was closeted and was willing me to trust him, but I was tongue-tied. After slapping the steering wheel, he faced me with a beautiful smile. That was a relief. The last thing I wanted before he and Zoe left for France was for us to be out of tune with each other. He had his future, I had mine – such as it was.

Still he'd provoked me, and I wanted to know what it felt like to fall in love and be free of guilt about it. Things livened up. He spilled the beans and it was great.

# 14

When I was young my teeth were bodged by a dentist called Nosgood, and on discovering that Howler had become his patient a year before, I almost asked to see inside his mouth. He was on a roll and it was clear that eight questionable fillings was the price he'd paid to stick with Nosgood's surgery.

'The gorgeous nurse,' he continued, keeping his left hand to the top of the Avenger's steering wheel, 'was Zoe and from one appointment to the next,' he confessed, 'I couldn't get her out of my mind. I thought about her every minute and felt something that, until then, I'd no idea about.' He shrugged, then looked away, over the satsuma-coloured bonnet, to the sea. 'Pure crazy love,' he concluded. I sighed and he faced me again.

'Ah, but, Craig, man,' he chuckled, 'it's brutal. Like your heart gets grabbed so hard you can't breathe properly.'

That struck a chord and I got near to revealing how, after Dad's suicide, my throat had shut in my sleep. That would have been a selfish confession. Howler's mood was too good to wreck and he soon repeated his wonderful smile, which melted my heart. 'Drenched, Craig,' he went on. 'The long and the short of it is that I was drenched by crazy love,' he concluded. I wanted to hear more, but his talking was now done and he reached for the ignition, which was on the side of the steering column.

The engine fired into life and he winked at me, just like Trevor had done at school often while tugging on his bits, which Susan Terry had once said would be worn out before he was thirty. That was Trevor's power. He was brazen by nature and had used it to embarrass others into submission – especially me, the biggest closet-case of all.

Still, Howler's message from the driver's seat of the Avenger had been mindfully given and I read it with ease. So what if I was a homo? It was time to flee the workshop and let crazy love drench me, as it had him. He grinned and a mild crunch from the Avenger's gearbox told me he'd selected first gear.

'Look after yerself, Craig,' he called, and left me where I stood with Brucie in the middle of the lane, bang on the dip that fed rainwater to the drains, which served an outfall pipe on the beach.

My focus stayed on the Avenger. Its orange bodywork glared in the sun and appeared to become a ball of moving flame. As I heard the car's twin-carbs open up on the seafront road I feared that my stand against being a full-on homo was weakening.

It was little wonder that as I slept that night my throat closed for the first time in a decade. Since when is anybody in full control of their life? Especially if they're trying to crush their need to be loved and to give love in return.

Things were all jumbled and the very next day my red Capri was rear-ended by the gold Zodiac, whose injured driver I'd had a mad need to hold in my arms. It was only after the police called at number twenty that I saw a bigger picture. The tide that, long before, had taken me, Marcus and Trevor out of our depth was turning and there was nothing I could do to stop it.

# 15

If it wasn't for our Brucie I would have drowned, and it amazed me that, despite his age, he'd scaled the bathtub. On the other hand he'd always been strong and for years I'd loved Big Eddie's joke that Brucie was my rescuer, though recently I'd grown ashamed of what some might read into this.

Why would any closet case want others to see the loneliness in which their only close companion was a dog? Still, Big Eddie was right about Brucie's role in my life and there'd been times when, without him, I would have gone the way of Hugo Moncrieff, which – sad to say – would not have been exceptional.

Queer boys all over tried to take their lives and many did not survive. Out-and-out homophobes alone couldn't be blamed. Everybody had a hand in what was happening and no one spoke out against it, leaving the situation to self-perpetuate. We were the suicide boys, the disposables, and I'd even heard kind-hearted people reiterate what our gruff school caretaker had remarked about Hugo's death: queers were better off out of their misery. I knew this was evil, yet at twenty-four, I still couldn't guarantee my own survival.

Wary of going to bed in case my throat closed, I took Brucie to the promontory and sat on Dad's suicide bench at the base of Sir Winston's statue. The night was dark and the nearest part of the black sea had a thick gleam, making me want to write on it with my finger, cartoon-style. It was typical of Brucie to be tuned into this mood and his wise old gaze stayed on me as I looked to the ships – their lights seemed to have been on the horizon since our move to the coast twenty years before.

Of course I saw this illusion for what it was: the ships had changed, proving that patterns could shift unseen until the unexpected occurred, such as Trevor Carlton crashing back into my world. I might have been a little mad after the crash. Never mind the weakening of my defences against being a full-on queer, I was tortured that while I'd survived the seafront collision unscathed Trevor had been kept in hospital with suspected neck damage. It was true that he'd been driving too close and without a seatbelt, but I'd hit the Capri's brakes without checking the rear-view mirror.

It seemed I was a near-murderer, and now I regretted that when we were teenagers and fighting I'd punched his face twice and that, without the help of Oliver from my dreams, I would have hit him again. It was fantastical and I didn't want my old fears around Dad's periods in the psychiatric hospital stirred up. I had enough to reflect on, and the fact that Trevor had started our fight, coming out of the blue to sock my cheek – which was still healing after a cycling accident – did not cross my mind. In the long term I was guiltier than him, especially in light of an old warning from my parents: his life with his father was hard, and Trevor played out his pain on others.

Whether or not Hugo and Marcus might have agreed with this did not come to mind, though in all likelihood they would have urged me to go with the flow. It was an odd thing: nobody I knew of had actually disliked Trevor who, when younger, was sometimes lovely. I recalled how he'd smiled at me when he was stuck in the buckled gold Zodiac. His vulnerability then was profound, and I was angry with myself for not recognising him when it was clear that he knew me.

It was ironic: my old attacker and the prime-bully behind Marcus's decision to take his mum's happy pills was now my potential saviour from aloneness. I ached to help him in any way I could. He would be happy. I would be happy. Our crash would be forgotten.

Everything was complicated and as plain as the nose on my face.

Brucie was still peering hard and, because the statue was uplit by purple spotlights, his intense eyes shone with whiteness and magenta, giving me an escape from my tangled thoughts. 'Brucie-Wucie-Lucie-Darling!' I cried, as his tail got going. 'Brucie-Wucie-Lucie-Darling!' I repeated, plonking a kiss between his ears and moving back a little to observe him, watching me, just as always.

All I had to do was make it through the night, then visit Trevor in hospital. The thought made me so happy that when I tilted my head back and looked up at the statue's face, I laughed in gratitude, as if Sir Winston was giving me strength. Dad had entered the sea from the exact spot where I was sitting, yet I was quite happy there. My old friend Trevor needed me and, my heart open to whatever lay ahead, I recalled the angry man at the crash scene who'd ordered me to move aside. He'd seen I was queer and didn't want me touching Trevor, who'd required comforting. Nobody like him would be around to spoil things in the morning, and I was sure that my old school friend wanted me at his bedside.

# 16

The hospital had opened the year before on former grassland close to the school that I'd attended with Marcus, Trevor, Howler, Susan Terry, Woodman and the rest. Word had it that the William Shatner lookalike who'd replaced Mr Heston as the head of sports ten years earlier was now to become the headmaster and I liked the idea.

For once my drive by the gates didn't make me mull over the past and, without glancing at the place where so much had happened to shape my life, I was eager for the start of morning visiting hours on Trevor's ward.

Howler's notion of being drenched by new feelings couldn't have been more fitting. I understood him 100 per cent.

On the short walk from where I'd left the customer's car which was with me for welding repairs, the brightness of the sun spotlighted that I was at my happiest since my early days with Marcus, before he left for London.

It had taken me a long time to accept this loss and as I neared Trevor's ward I felt the same butterflies that being with Marcus had caused. There was no doubt that their return was wonderful, but it also put me on my guard against being excited before the nurses and others. Howler would have laughed at this wariness, but my upbeat mood placed me at my most conflicted ever. Closet cases do not come out overnight. We fight to the end and often at the cost of the exact happiness that would save us from loneliness.

Still, I was convinced that Trevor and I needed to see each other and on nearing the side room where I'd been told he was under observation, I expected him to be lying flat, connected to monitors. In fact he was sitting up in bed, flirting with a young nurse who smiled and said, 'Hello, you must be his friend, Craig.'

Then she was gone and I realised that because I was gawping at him, Trevor had a watchful shine to his eye. For once in my life I didn't know what to say, but above all I was relieved that, despite the blood of the day before, his bearded face was unharmed.

He grinned and pinched his pyjama top at either side of his chest: 'It's all they had in my size,' he explained. The pale blue cloth was patterned with yellow bunnies that had dewy eyes and white tails. He shrugged: 'Actually they're jimmy-jams for girls.'

That did it for us both, and as we laughed, I sat on a salmon-coloured plastic seat beside the bed. Soon we were quiet, and because I had an urge to admit what it meant for me to be there, I locked on to a topic that I understood better than my own feelings.

'That gold Zodiac of yours?' I queried, bringing a wary glint to his face. 'Its front end didn't half fold up easily,' I added, sure there was something dodgy about the car before Trevor drove it into the Capri. Three seconds passed while he peered at me. Then he did a single clap, which made me start.

'Straight to the point, Craig mate!' he cried, with a laugh. 'Straight to the point!' he repeated, as I did my raised-eyebrow trick, wondering what he had to reveal about the pre-crash state of his car.

Touching the side of his nose, he muttered, 'Cut and shut,' and all at once the big damage to the Zodiac, compared to the light wounding of my Capri, made sense.

The coffin-shaped gold Ford was built from sections cut out of wrecks, and when put to the test it had given way. I might have been concerned that it was on the road at all but our secret of its history marked my renewed happiness. Life had been flat for too long. Trevor was home and he was a tonic.

'Penny for them,' he quipped, flashing a grin which brought shudders to my spine.

'Last time I saw you,' I replied, 'you were all mashed up. Like, really badly,' I insisted, as if deep down I feared that he'd wilfully driven into harm's way. This note of blame surprised us both and, from the widening of his eyes, it seemed that my mind was being read, just as he'd often done when we were young.

'Sorry,' I shrugged, aware from its heat that the left side of my neck would soon be purple. This was embarrassing and, to block him from reading too much into it, I admitted that the risk of the Zodiac catching fire had terrified me. Nothing was truer or more selective. I chose not to comment on the angry queer-hater who'd wanted me to quit Trevor's side, or how wounding this had been.

'You were nearly cinders,' I persisted, unable to keep the emotion that threatened to overwhelm me out of my voice.

There was a time when he would have dismissed me as a willy-woofter for this, exactly as he'd done to Hugo after he'd hanged himself. But I could almost hear Oliver and my dad ordering me to cut Trevor the slack he now needed.

Ten years had passed. Don't we owe others the right to change? And if we deny them this, what does it say about our own chances of getting things right?

Besides, I was genuinely shaken by our crash and Trevor understood this.

'But I'm not cinders,' he carefully replied. 'Am I, Craigie?' he added, with a smile in his eyes, which were even bluer than I remembered from school.

'No,' I agreed, touched that the new Trevor Carlton had trodden softly, where his younger self would have trampled all over me.

'And I'm not going to die,' he concluded, making me so grateful for his survival that if he'd wanted a million-pound loan, I would have found a way to get it.

He was beautiful. He was flawless. He was Trevor, and in the space where my loneliness had sat for years, my butterflies fluttered at their gayest.

# 17

He got me to shut the door and asked if I would do something for him, my instant hope being that he needed money after all. Years later I became ashamed of this. Buying into his life was an easy option, but Trevor was wiser than I knew.

'Get this bloody fuzz off. ' He laughed, drawing fingers through his beard. 'It itches like hell,' he complained, getting higher against the pillows. 'I mean, the nurse was going to do it,' he added, pointing to some scissors, a hand towel and shaving gear on the far side of the bed,' but it seems you've scared her off. Doesn't it, Craig?' he ended, with a wink.

My neck had been hot a minute before but now it had gone cold, and I knew I was pale. It was only eighteen hours since his beard had been matted with blood and I was scared to use the scissors and the razor. One slip-up between us had already put him in hospital.

'I might cut your throat,' I protested.

'You'll be fine.' He laughed. 'I trust you, Craig,' he insisted, as our eyes locked for what felt an age, but was five seconds at most. I trembled and he knew it.

After covering his front with the hand towel he set his chin forward, as if a point of no return had been reached – which I guess was fair. This was a special shave. Its pull on me was strong, and Trevor was determined. 'When you're ready,' he remarked, without looking at me. 'Make me beautiful,' he instructed, with a smile that was oddly innocent.

On a different day that might have been that, but because so much had occurred since the crash, I needed more pressure to begin and he stayed on my case.

'Go for it,' he urged, with a nod at the scissors I was holding. 'It's now or never,' he declared.

That was true. Trevor had returned in the nick of time to save me from becoming a bloodless sort of man, as I'd seen happen to several locals, who were dulled at thirty, wasting their lives.

Still, I held back and by default that helped us both.

Trevor gave off a sternness that drove me to accept that, if shaving him was a queer thing to do, it also proved I could smash old taboos, just as Marcus had done when he came out as gay at school. That had been the start of so much, and now I couldn't stop my mind going into overdrive.

Dad and my old sports master Mr Heston were queer-haters, whose weaknesses were exposed by time.

I wished Hugo Moncrieff had survived, as Marcus had, and proved his strength to the world. It was criminal that young men took their lives because they feared being gay.

None of this was easy, but Trevor wanted proof of the spine that was being put into my back and I couldn't be a coward any longer.

'Snip-snip away,' he quipped, flicking a glance at me.

'Snip-snip away,' he repeated, with an edge that could have chipped granite.

To my surprise, I took up the scissors and began to cut his beard. That would have been routine to the nurse but for me it was ground-breaking. My biggest worry for years was that I would find myself involved with another young man, yet now I was up close with Trevor and grooming him.

It helped that he was witty.

'Try not to cut my throat,' he pleaded.

I was elated to be his barber. It made me important to him. It made me close to him. It put me under his spell and I was happy to be there.

'Feels good,' he reassured me, when I protected his Adam's apple with my fingers and trimmed his neck hair, ready for the razor.

He smelt musty. My skin tingled, and when my eye caught his, he smiled. 'I'm glad we're friends,' he confided, with the innocence I'd already noted. He was turning me upside down and I loved it.

# 18

I shook the cuttings from the towel into the small bin, which was nearby, and splayed my right hand before my eyes. Its steadiness amazed me. Laughing hard, Trevor was boyish: 'You see, Craig? Nerves of steel!' That delighted me, and I saw, with the thickness of his beard gone, he resembled George Best, the handsome footie star.

Setting his fingertips to his face, he rubbed what remained of his beard and urged me to press on with the razor.

This time he didn't need to repeat himself and I filled a plastic kidney bowl – which the nurse had also left – with warm water at a washbasin near the door. We were making great progress.

As I moved the shaving brush towards his chin our eyes locked again, and a couple of questions popped out of me: little rebels seizing their moment to stir things up.

'Trevor mate, why are you here? Home again after all these years?' I was abrupt, but fair: he'd literally crashed back into my life and I was yet to discover why.

His eyes lowered to where the soapy brush was suspended in mid-air and we shared a sad smile. I swear that I felt him think his next words before they came. They were firm, shrewd and not unkind.

'You're saying you want me to go away?' he asked. 'When I'm only just back?' he continued, as a lump came to my throat.

I turned aside and coughed while still holding the shaving brush. That did it, as far as clearing the lump went, and I even risked some teasing of my own. 'You can sod off any time you like,' I replied, praying he saw that this was the last thing I wanted. A shared journey was under way and my sixth sense told me that our lives depended on its completion.

He placed his first finger on the upper side of my hand and applied pressure, which made me lower the brush to the kidney bowl, ready for when we started again. It hurt me that he now looked small on the bed, and several seconds passed while he gathered his thoughts.

'Why am I back after all these years?' he mused, so serious that I wished I'd shaved his whiskers off while the mood was upbeat. After all, I'd had years of unhappiness, and although our car crash had been as scary as my old throat problems, a door had been opened on a renewed friendship between us.

That was what I had Trevor to thank for, and I

couldn't return to my life as it had been before I'd braked to save the stray Alsatian. Things were critical and my gut tensed at the delay I'd caused in making Trevor clean-shaven. It worried me that something good was now being destroyed.

'Don't look like that.' He grinned. 'I'm going to answer you,' he promised, with a shrug. 'It's a bit of a tale,' he added, while I kept dead calm for fear he would see how much I wanted to fold my arms about him against all harm, forever.

# 19

Three years earlier he'd married a Polish girl called Karina, who'd come to work at his uncle's hotel in Brighton, where he'd lived since leaving the north after our fight. Things had gone wrong, and now that they were having a trial separation, he'd returned to run his dad's old seafront hotel, caretaker-managed after Mr Carlton died in 1980. This covered a lot but the main point had grabbed me.

'Trevor!' I cried, when he paused. 'You're a husband?' I pointed at his bare marriage finger. 'Like, where's the band of gold?'

My voice had gone high, then hit gravel, leaving me sore behind my tongue. That was because of my two recent throat closures. I'd done my reading and knew that each spasm strained the voice box.

Trevor smiled but mini-sharks swam in his eyes and I saw what this meant. He was troubled at heart and couldn't hide it from me, any more than I could disguise my feelings for him. Still, he put up a brave front.

'So long as we're at different ends of the country, me and Karina,' he explained, 'I'll keep the evidence out of sight from nosy-parkers. But trust me,' he held up his finger to show the mark where the ring had been, 'it exists, Craig. It exists and I'm married,' he ended, with finality, which made me feel cheap for suspecting he was up to his old tricks.

Why wouldn't Trevor be married? I was the one who'd shied away from life, and his sharpness with me for querying his tale was a reminder of where we stood. He'd taken a punt at being an adult but I was still pretty much a boy, torn between wanting things fixed for him and Karina and being his number-one friend. I must have looked perplexed and he clearly thought I needed convincing of his sincerity.

'I'm ashamed,' he confessed, taking me by surprise. 'Ashamed to find I'm a bastard like my old man,' he admitted.

That struck a chord. He couldn't get free of Mr Carlton any more than I could escape Dad, who, even when I wasn't thinking about him directly, had always lurked in my mind.

Instinct told me that Trevor hadn't previously confronted his feelings about Mr Carlton in the way he'd now shared with me. I held my tongue, waiting for more. Instead he looked downwards at where his hands were knitted on his tum and I got the impression that within my face he'd seen a reflection of himself: the flawed son of a flawed father. That skewered me. Being queer had always been my biggest terror, but a close second was my fear that I'd become like Dad, who'd broken Mum's nose with his fist.

Why wouldn't young men like us be wary? Even my big brother Jack had faced up to an angry streak that came from Dad.

'Keep a grip on your temper, Craig,' he'd advised, touching on something our Vanessa had said about Dad being the exact person who'd least wanted to be like Dad. That was sharp, but when she'd added that he was a pacifist at heart, I'd been conflicted. Looking for goodness in Dad felt like panning for gold. Shiny bits were hard to find.

Besides, Dad was long gone, and I hadn't crashed into Trevor's life. He'd crashed into mine, making me keen to explore the young men we'd become, not ancient history. Trevor's trial separation from Karina seemed to be the starting point.

'So what went wrong with married life?' I probed, taking a seat on the bed, resting my left foot on the salmon chair, yet keeping us eye to eye.

Several moments passed and I noted that his mini-sharks were gone. Lifting his right hand to his mouth, he gestured as if drinking deeply from a beer glass.

This was the best, most powerful mime I'd ever seen, and despite my wish to go forward I realised then that his suicide had been on the cards for years. A shudder went through me. Trevor jiggled his spine, remarking that booze always wrecked everything.

Nobody could tell me more than I already knew on that subject: alcohol had poisoned Dad's life and a lot of it was in his blood when he'd thrown himself into the sea. The mood I'd gone into was dark, and because I was sick of booze, weary of Dad and unwilling to discuss Mr Carlton, I began to get up, ready to use the soap and shaving brush.

Trevor stalled me. 'There's something else about my marriage,' he disclosed. 'Women, Craig,' he continued, making a sexy outline in the air with his hands. 'I just can't stop myself,' he admitted. It was impossible not to smile.

When I'd entered the room he was flirting with the nurse. That was his nature. What this meant for Karina or any other woman who loved him I couldn't say. I was a virgin and knew nothing of relationships. But I did grasp one more thing and it put the focus back on me with a bang.

It would have taken courage for any queer to admit that men were likewise irresistible. This was the double standard of the day. I wanted to be kind but it was impossible to hide my envy at Trevor's freedom. Where he would be indulged as a ladies' man, I would be reviled as a predator.

The air went heavy, and it bothered me that I could be sour about him. If anything, though, I was now an even more eager listener to his tale.

# 20

Karina had given him three months in which to join Alcoholics Anonymous or their marriage was over, but it was what he said next that shocked me.

'I was already knocking it back at school,' he confessed. 'Old Lard Arse,' he continued, meaning his dad, 'scared me so much that I needed a drink just to sleep. Every night,' he stressed, grabbing the air with his fist. His eyes were so bright that I felt the terror he was speaking about. Dad had been violent but I knew Mum was right about each swing of his fist being a nail in his own coffin. Mr Carlton was different. Something at his heart was cruel and I was sure that even Dad was disturbed by this. It came to mind that he'd been a hypocrite but that didn't make sense, and it was because of his fury at his own behaviour that I felt right in forgiving him. This was just as well. It was impossible to thrive without ditching my old pain and, though Mum had suffered most at Dad's hands, I knew she would have encouraged me to move on, as she had with Big Eddie.

It eased me to imagine Dad applauding their happiness, and as I did so another bit of understanding opened up to test me, something that, because of Dad's extreme behaviour in his last year, I'd avoided accepting.

There had been a streak of fairness in my booze-wrecked father that was wider than the Mississippi, and it was wrong to keep denying it now that I was older. I had to be fair to his memory. To make him into a monster was convenient but did nothing good for my head.

My pressing wish to see things in their roundness was part of what Trevor had brought on his return from Brighton. We were changing each other for the better, though nothing could have improved my take on Mr Carlton. He was bad and my mum saw it long before I did.

Those were the days when he'd bought a new Cortina 1600E, which was a shade of pink called Light Orchid, a fantastic car that really excited me.

For reasons I was too young to understand, I was wary of showing this enthusiasm before Mr Carlton. It was my big brother Jack who'd later explained what I'd sensed about him: he had a calm front but was a psychopath, and that was why Mrs Carlton had fled.

The intimidating atmosphere in Trevor's home made sense to me after that, though there was more to clarify when it came to the lingering influences of both our fathers. Their histories were like whirlpools within the bigger tide we were struggling against, and avoiding them was impossible.

Still, my up-and-down life with Dad in the workshop differed from Trevor's boyhood at the hotel, where Mr Carlton no doubt hated himself most of all. It wasn't that I was going soft on Dad, far from it. His loathing of queers did me great harm, but I had to admit that, while Trevor never got warmth, Dad always loved me. He was destructive yet it wasn't unusual for him to be magical, and it helped that Mum had always cared for him.

The distinction between Dad and Mr Carlton was undeniable, and in the hours since Trevor's gold Zodiac had hit my red Capri, I'd become acutely alert to the regrets that had driven Dad's suicide. He was a man who had suffered, and I had to be big enough to see it. I couldn't be a boy any longer and it was almost as if Dad's ghost was willing me to accept my queer nature and be happy with life, as I expected Marcus was: out, proud and touching the hearts of many with his laughter. I doubted I could do the same. It wasn't so much cowardice as the fear of being overwhelmed. I was born into an overhang of the Dark Ages and had fought hard to be 'normal'.

Coming out as gay was one thing but facing down

an everyday army of casual queer-haters was another, making me the potential hypocrite of the family, not Dad.

Still, coming half out of the closet would at least have brought me comfort in numbers, but that was not what I sought for my future either.

My eyes had been wide open for years and part of what I'd seen was a shadowy world of queer men, marked by the shame Dad had driven into me.

My butterflies were not at work now and a new well of loneliness opened up. I loved Dad. I hated Dad. I needed to forgive him but didn't know how to do so, any more than I could see myself thriving, like Marcus.

Trevor cut into my thoughts. I needed his help to move forward and he was on a mission to confess all about his boozing.

'Vodka when I was twelve, Craig mate!' he cried, setting my mind racing with a new insight into what had occurred when Mr Heston had belted Marcus's bum in front of us all.

Was Trevor half drunk? Had that led to Marcus being queer-bashed by our teacher? Was that why he was so brazen? The booze his scary dad had driven him to?

It was as well that our car crash had not put him on the life support that had saved Marcus after he'd taken his mum's pills. For half a minute I might have pulled out the plug, but I also understood that, whatever his wickedness towards Marcus, Trevor was out of his depth. We were frightened boys growing up in a period when to be gentle was to invite violence.

But now we were adults and there was a new cast to Trevor's face that implored me to be kind, which made me consider Oliver's role in my life. He'd stopped me hurting Trevor when I was young and I hoped he would soon visit my dreams and help me again.

I shivered. I knew that Marcus and Dad would also have also wanted me to go easy on Trevor, already a long-term boozer, hanging on by his fingertips.

'Vodka, Craig.' He grimaced. 'Nicked from the hotel bar and down the hatch like Coca-Cola.' He avoided my eye. It was easy to see why. He was scared that I thought he'd been a loser all along but that was not the case, and I wanted him to see that I didn't stand in judgement. How could I? He'd sought refuge in drink, my sanctuary was the closet, and it was a dead cert that the result of each would be self-destruction.

It was an added twist that many closet cases got through their days by becoming boozers, paying the price inflicted by bigots with their mangled lives and early deaths.

Trevor accepted all this. I saw he did and my heart ached, but I didn't take it as a bad sign. That was another thing I'd learnt from his return: pain enabled us to see our mistakes. Trevor had been screwed over and so had I, but at least we were talking and maybe this would take us somewhere better than we'd been for years.

# 21

Whatever his mistakes, he was the savviest person I'd known, making it ironic that he was now in danger. I'd seen what booze had done to Dad and the harm it caused everyone he'd loved. I might have said a lot about this but felt it was wiser to flag up Big Eddie's period of boozing.

'Thing is, Trevor mate,' I explained, 'it took a heart attack to get him on the wagon. Otherwise.' I drew a finger across my throat, 'his last round would've been with the Grim Reaper. The way it goes for most alkies,' I concluded.

Trevor winced, and I realised that although I didn't want to go on about Dad, I'd now summed them both up as being two of life's losers.

Still, it helped that Trevor had knowledge of Dad's last two years, when my schoolmates often saw him bouncing off garden walls as he came home from the Gay Hussar: a basket case, tormented by demons, which, because I could only guess at them, scared me more than if I'd known every detail of his life. It was Trevor's turn to be mindful and I was grateful for it.

'You've got your ghost, Craig, I've got mine,' he reasoned, aiming to help us both cope better with the two men who had refused to lie down and be dead.

By now he was sitting upright again and the air thickened with the subject that had underpinned everything so far. We couldn't be friends without addressing it.

Never mind Dad and Mr Carlton, much of my life had hinged around Trevor's past queer-hating behaviour and it even crossed my mind that he might need a slug of vodka to open up on this. Something hostile must have shown in my eye.

He looked at me with added interest, taking me back to the day when Howler had called him a Svengali. Even Susan Terry had laughed and said that a nail was hit on the head. I sensed she was right but checked 'Svengali' in the dictionary and, Trevor's eyes now fixed on me, I saw that, growing up with Mr Carlton, he'd become a watcher of other people.

That was how he'd survived being alone with his psycho-dad, who'd known that his ability to control lay in reading the fears of those around him. Could there have been a better starting point for an unhappy teenager out to prove his self-worth by tormenting others than queerness?

For half a minute I hated Trevor again, and there's no doubt that this also showed in my face. Bad things had happened because of him, and despite my elation at his return, they were impossible to overlook. Still, when his eyes went grey I worried that this had more to do with the car crash than our shared history.

I was much younger when a friend of Big Eddie's had fallen from a kerb. He seemed to be okay but two days later he passed out and was taken to hospital with blood clots on his brain. It was a relief that Trevor had not lost consciousness.

Drawing a sigh that dragged like a lead blanket, he raised his hand for me to wait before he spoke. My throat burned and I hoped he couldn't smell my breath, which stank whenever my insides played up.

We saw that where we must go would be dark. I wondered how he hadn't already drunk himself to death. Never was a touch of pity so firmly rejected. The smile he gave me was sly and left no doubt about something that defined me as well as him.

I, too, was a watcher, a survivor of hurt who had coped by learning to read others. The name that now hung in the air around Trevor had been seared onto my mind for a decade and we both understood why.

'That clever lad from the other school,' he said, after a short while.

'Hugo Moncrieff.'

'His death terrified me, Craig,' he admitted.

He cocked his head in sorrow, and I saw that he was

expecting me to rip into him. He wouldn't have fought back but I needed to escape the bleak moment. That didn't say anything special about me. I was simply joining dots like never before and was struck by just how unseeing I'd been as a teenager. Beneath his mockery of Hugo's suicide, Trevor had been on the verge of taking his own life, and to keep going after his willy-woofter campaign, he'd turned his queer-bashing on Marcus, causing a whirlpool that had drawn us all in.

Marcus took his mum's happy pills. Howler stopped Trevor destroying Woody. Trevor lay in wait to attack me. Oliver prevented this fight from being worse, and finally Trevor fled south - escaping Mr Carlton. But not, of course, the pain that had shaped him as a queer-basher and also brought about his craving of vodka.

There was a time when going over all of this might have floored me, but in recent months I'd thought so much about men, boys and suicide that I was matter-of-fact. Hard, even.

Trevor could have killed himself a decade before but he didn't, and I almost asked what difference it might have made. That scared me. My thoughts had swerved from his life to my own. Was there any point in a closet case being alive?

Acid flooded my throat and the sound I made when

clearing it caused Trevor to flinch, as if I'd poked his eye. That felt cruel but I was glad he didn't see me having a full-on spasm, deflecting us from what had happened to Hugo after the killing of Robespierre.

A bright young homo had died and to many it was a big joke. Of course it was. Worst of all, Hugo's parents had even seemed to apologise in the *Gazette* for the fuss he'd caused, making my mum angry with them, as I now was with Trevor.

He had made everybody laugh at Hugo's death. He had trashed Hugo's life.

'Your willy-woofter campaign,' I told him, 'was the wickedest thing I've ever seen. You mocked what happened because Hugo was gay.' I knew he could hit back with my betrayal of Marcus, making each of us as bad as the other.

Instead he said gently, 'Don't we both have big regrets? You and me, Craig.'

My anger melted, leaving me keen to keep things right between us. We'd survived the smash-up of our cars and could surely manage to talk without another collision occurring.

It was my turn to be mindful. 'I never blamed you alone, Trevor. Never.'

He responded with a nod.

'What we did at school,' I continued, 'the bubblegum, Mr Heston, the changing rooms, Marcus could've died.'

Trevor was calm but the unease that creased his face made me feel so ashamed I had to say something that, prior to his return, had always been too hard for me to accept. It was brutally simple.

'I was cruellest to Marcus,' I said, 'not you, Trevor mate.'

Things might have stopped there but Marcus's role in my life counted most and I had to be open about it.

'He loved me and I loved him,' I told Trevor. 'He wanted us to share our lives,' I added, fighting back more tummy acid. What my body had been telling me for years was clear: I needed to accept guilt for what I'd done. Marcus had loved me and I'd ruined it. My war against queerness was a venture in self-destruction that I should have quit long before. Also it was ridiculous. My brother, my sisters, my mum and Big Eddie all loved me for who I was.

Trevor's eyes had recovered their blue, but I was wary of his pity.

It seemed certain that by now Marcus would be settled with somebody else. He was the best of us all, and the biggest loser was me, not Dad.

Half a minute passed while Trevor looked to the window, which fronted the area where I'd earlier parked. As he did so a shine returned to the many windscreens, suggesting that a cloud, which had been blocking the sun, had gone.

# 22

'There is good news,' he announced, with a grin that brought a return of my butterflies. 'In five years my uncle will sign over the hotel to me. The whole lot,' he beamed, 'bricks, mortar, the business itself. That is,' he added, while I waited for the catch, 'once I've proved myself to be reliable, Craig.'

Reliable meant sober and we both knew that staying dry would be a big challenge for him. My dad had tried many times but never lasted longer than a month before he went on a bender.

I decided against asking Trevor why it might be different for him, and wished the thought hadn't entered my mind. When I was young I'd hurt Marcus badly and the last thing I wanted to do now was undermine Trevor, who needed me to believe in him.

'I know what you're thinking, Craig,' he said, eyeballing me. 'And I know it's going to be hard. But I promise I'm giving it my best shot. I've got to. I mean, what else is there?'

We were at a bitter-sweet moment: Trevor had shared his vulnerability but I'd spent too much time avoiding all closeness with others to trust myself with any sort of intimacy. It felt like something I might drop and shatter. Otherwise I was still upbeat and, from the shine of the cars outside, it seemed that the sun was even brighter than it had been when I'd left number twenty that morning.

Staying bold was important, and Trevor was waiting for me to seal our closeness with words of my own. Besides, supporting him made sense of my own life. He needed me, I needed him, and above all, I craved to leave my aloneness in the past.

'Listen, mate,' I said, 'I'm so glad you're back. Really and truly.'

He gave a sigh of relief, and I realised he'd been scared I might reject him as a friend.

'C'mon, Craig!' he cried, clicking his fingers. 'Get this fuzz off my face! Before it turns grey!'

Knitting his hands at the back of his neck, he braced his head and I soaped his whiskers in readiness for the razor, which I had no fear of handling. Despite my self-doubt his faith had eased me and it was beautiful to be close to him. Luckily, I stayed on my guard against mishaps.

While shaving close to his right ear, I found a honey-brown mole that hadn't been there when we were at school. That stilled me. Years earlier Mum had had a man in one of her art classes who'd accidentally shaved off a mole, making his neck bleed heavily.

The real problem, though, was that the site was found to be nasty, leaving me wary of the two moles that had been on my pecs from birth: one black, the other like milky tea.

'Oh, do stop fiddling with them,' Mum had said, when I got paranoid that they needed cutting out. 'Moles should always be left alone.'

He watched me shake my hand. 'Aah,' he teased, 'you've discovered my silky spot. Haven't you, Craig?' He winked.

I rinsed the razor and took a few moments to calm my nerves. There was still so much between us that I didn't understand.

'It's dodgy to muck about with moles,' I said, thinking of Mum's student, who'd died of cancer in his forties, with no health worries until he'd needed A and E to stop his shaved mole bleeding. 'They're not always what they seem.' I seized my chance to look deeper at him.

A few beats passed before he nodded, then stole back the initiative. I was puzzled to hear that he knew I'd recently seen our old classmate Howler who, three years before, had been his best man. The odd mood of the past minute now made sense. Trevor had needed to speak up, and it seemed that quicksand now sucked at my heels, tugging against our eye contact.

'You mean Howler went to Brighton to be your best

man?' I asked, regaining my balance. 'Like, you've been mates since school?' I persisted, as he wiped his bottom lip with the back of his hand.

These were not questions that required answers, and to manage my awkwardness I went to the far edge of the bed, leaving the right side of his face to complete last. His response came after I'd used the shaving brush to soften the soap, which had begun to harden on his bristles.

'You don't mind that I'm his friend, do you, Craig?' he queried, directing his eyes to the upper right corner of the room.

This was another question that did not need a reply. We both understood that I minded a lot about the bond between him and Howler, though at least he couldn't know the pettiest result of this: my sudden suspicion that when I'd fixed the sills on Howler's Avenger GT at cost only, I'd somehow been taken for a ride.

Trevor's eyes flicked back to mine and, sweat trickling from my underarms, I knew that if he smelt anything different on me, it was a return of the bitterness I'd been dodging for years.

Still, the better part of me understood that Howler hadn't ripped me off, and as Trevor held my gaze with just inches between our noses, I understood exactly what he was seeing and it wasn't flattering.

I was a fool who'd spent years in a crappy workshop

while my old friends got on with life, and blaming others for that was easier than being honest about my failings.

It was true that I'd been hammered by Dad and school but my error was to let this define me. I was cowardly, and sick of being at odds with everybody.

He broke from my eye and looked back to the corner, freeing me to  finish the removal of his whiskers, which up close had a hint of red in their black. This was something else about him that was new to me. He truly was beautiful, and being able to say this to myself made it even more important that I did a good job as his barber.

'There,' I declared, when the last bit was done. 'Smooth as a baby's bum and not a drop of blood,' I boasted.

He bounded in his bunny pyjamas to the small mirror above the basin. 'Just look at that man, Craig!' he cried. 'I get handsomer every year!'

Another question popped out of my mouth: 'Trevor, why are you still in hospital?'

He returned to the bed, sat in the lotus position and explained that, because the men in his family were prone to blood clotting, he would be kept under observation for the day. 'Old Lard Arse is pushing up daisies and my uncle takes rat poison,' he quipped, referring to the blood-thinner Big Eddie had been on since his heart attack. Typically, though, my mind made a trickier connection, overwhelming my relief that he had not been badly hurt in the crash.

On remembering our fight, I was disturbed at what the result might have been, with his dodgy blood. Fortunately I was now better at being positive and soon lifted the mood again.

'You know what?' I said, right from my heart. 'I've a lot to thank a bloke called Oliver for.'

He laughed. He was too smart to ask who Oliver was. That, too, was typical. Trevor always avoided being on the back foot and knew when to let stuff go. Plus, even I found it strange that a man from my dreams had stopped me hitting Trevor more times than I had.

'Forget the bloody past, Craig!' he said. 'I started that fight between us! And you,' he wagged a finger, 'you gave me what I deserved.'

That was a key moment. I had to reveal my feelings for him. Or what I believed I felt.

'We're brothers now, you and me. Anything you want, it's yours,' I promised, sure that after years of loneliness I was connected to his soul. Old habits died hard, though, and I was kidding nobody. I didn't need another brother, and Trevor saw this as strongly as he knew that I was obsessed with him. Still, he was unfazed and my announcement had made it easy for us to move on.

'Well, brother,' he teased, 'there is something you can do.'

'Anything,' I repeated, feeling more valued than at any time in my adult life.

'Get me some new wheels for when I'm outta this dump! Something with grunt!' he continued, making it clear that despite the destruction of his gold Zodiac he intended to remain a king of the road.

That pressed a button. It was a long time since I'd fallen in love with Mr Carlton's pink Cortina 1600E and, thanks to Trevor, my enthusiasm for cars now returned with a bang.

'Something with grunt?' I pondered, as he came out of the lotus position, braced his palms on the bed, and made a wide V of his legs.

The pause that followed was sweet but, because of my stare, Trevor was compelled to break it. 'What, Craig mate? What?' He was daring me to comment on the wetness in his eyes.

'I don't know,' I answered. 'I guess you're a survivor,' I concluded.

He held my eye a moment longer and clapped once, just like earlier. 'Something with grunt!' he repeated, with a wink .

'Something with grunt,' I agreed.

If he was still reading my mind when I left the room,

he would have known that I intended to fulfil this promise with style and crazy excess.

My ten-year-old red Capri was a top-of-the-range 1972 3000E that I'd bought a month after Viv died, on the same day as Elvis Presley in 1977. Almost right away Big Eddie was boozing, and because of the wedge this put between us, I'd sought a new project to focus on. When it was caught in a pile-up on the M1, it came to me as a salvage job whose front end was damaged. I repaired it with new body parts from Ford. Different from a cut-and-shut fix-it, my Capri had full strength and I was proud of my work.

Plus the tow bar I fitted made it a dead-cert that while Trevor's bodged Zodiac was destroyed in our crash my car had minimal damage. Otherwise, history was set to repeat itself.

On my fourteenth birthday I'd begged Dad to bid for Mr Carlton's 1600E after he'd traded it in for a new Cortina and it came up at the car auction. It wasn't old but the special metallic paint was drab and Dad bought it on condition that I polished it up.

That was thrilling and I wanted to prove myself to him by making it shine again, which I excelled at doing.

Eleven years on, my plan was to likewise shine up the 3000E for Trevor as the car he'd asked me to find anyway. It excited me that in terms of the grunt he sought, the Capri and the Zodiac had the same V6 engine, known for its power, torque and toughness.

I wanted this gift to underline how strong my care for Trevor was, and I almost couldn't believe the luck a random car crash had brought me. Everything had changed, and nothing could have made things return to how they were before Trevor came home.

# 23

It was some time since Craig had noticed my eyes were cloudy yet I remained a good-looker with all the hallmarks that make collie crosses a cut above. But I was old, and when brightness spilled into my sleep, my eyes ached hard.

I was shocked that the kid had tumbled into love with Trevor Carlton, and so was the spook.

'Be-bloody-sotted, Bruce!' he barked, as his face zoomed close to mine. 'Be-bloody-sotted, with the wrong young man!' he raged, stamping his foot, deep into a layer of whiteness that signalled danger for Craig, though I didn't have time to ponder this.

Raymond stared at where his wartime lover Oliver had come between us, making my eyes ache more. That's another price we pay for being rescue dogs. We are receptors of human pain and the spook's fear was so great that I could have been blinded. At least this risk passed quickly.

I realised that revenge was not Oliver's aim: spooks only come to put old wrongs right and the time was close for Raymond to be at rest. This was deserved. He'd looked out for Craig over many years and had done all he could for him.

'There's no reason to be scared,' Oliver reassured him. He had kept his young looks but had an air of wisdom.

'What happened to me was not your fault,' he told Raymond, echoing Marcus's old reassurance to Craig that he wasn't responsible for what had occurred between them. I had doubts about each case and my pricked ears became strained at their roots: past and present had collided again, and as Raymond sobbed, I wished for the power to make everything come right for all humans, always.

This was madness, such as rabies might cause, and a growl from Her Hoityness proved that she was still looking over me.

The whiteness left the ground and mercifully Raymond's crying stopped. Whatever his flaws when alive, I loved him for being a part of Ginger's history, especially when they were young, before the war roughed up their lives.

Oliver set his amazing silver-blue eyes upon me. 'Stick with it, Brucie-Bruce,' he instructed, making my tail wag. That had been Big Eddie's special way of saying my name, which I had not thought he could know.

'Stick with your kid,' he stressed, as the two spooks held hands and faded away, leaving me less wary about the make-or-break point to which the crash had brought Craig. Still, I could have easily curled up to rest for ever.

It's not uncommon for rescue dogs to die before our missions are done, leaving our humans half fixed, as I feared for the kid, who was tantalisingly close to accepting the happiness that was waiting for him. I had to be alert and Her Hoityness stayed on my case.

'Oh, do get on with it,' she barked.

'Now!' she snarled, making my heart race.

That felt right. Speed had marked the day, and in the half-second before I, Brucie–Dog, was the kid again, I was fired up by his renewed passion for cars.

I, Craig, was on a mission to prepare my Capri for Trevor, and to avoid the heat within the clear-roofed workshop, I parked the car in the lane. There, I found that, because the exhaust had been shoved forward by Trevor's Zodiac, the joint in the engine bay was damaged. After heating the bent bits with my oxy-torch, I refitted the system, and polished the car with the valetting machine I'd bought years earlier. All of this was done in two hours and I paid little heed to our Brucie when he yapped at where the red acetylene and black oxygen cylinders were held in a steel frame, clipped to the wall. He was an old dog, and so long as there was water in his bowl, I didn't worry about him. Time was marching on and there was much to do.

Left unprotected the Capri's red paint would have soon dulled again, and I hand-waxed each panel three times, creating a deep gleam in which my face was clear. The chrome came up perfectly, and the original steel wheels looked so good that I shook my head at the day when I'd nearly swapped them for a set of alloy rims. Very soon the glass was sparkling and the black interior looked brand new.

This was all thrilling, but what really made me disregard our Brucie's odd behaviour was anticipating the joy my work would bring to Trevor. I should have paused to consider why my dog yapped at the gas cylinders, whose rubber tubes lay in random coils on the ground.

I had an end-of-afternoon target, when Trevor would come from the hospital to find his gleaming new car outside the hotel. It seemed that nothing could go wrong.

# 24

Dad had taught me that old brake fluid was handy for making tyre walls shine and Trevor arrived at number twenty just as I was jazzing up the last of the Capri radials.

'Hello, Craig,' he said, across the car's front, giving me such a start that I knocked over the plastic bottle of the fluid. That made me curse. It was nasty stuff and I feared our Bruce might tread in it. Luckily the cloth I'd used to buff the tyres absorbed the spill with one wipe that saved me from appearing clumsy before Trevor, who, because he wore the clothes of the day before, I realised had come straight from the hospital.

Still, I'd been caught on the hoof: the Capri was prepared but there had not been time for me to sort out its documents, ready for the handover I'd planned. It was all meant to be so special.

'Trevor mate,' I responded awkwardly. 'Weren't you meant to be under observation all day?' I was gathering my wits as best I could.

He smiled, charming me. 'Nuts to observation.' He laughed as a whine started up inside the workshop, like a siren heard through cotton wool.

'I had to find you, Craig,' he said, from the far side of the Capri's bonnet, which had a power-bulge, suggesting the grunt he'd wanted that I could provide.

Less than a minute had passed but it seemed that we had been together all day, and as my butterflies returned, I felt woozy. What might have been said next didn't stand a chance of making it into words. The whine became an ear-splitting roar. This and a howl from our Brucie made my gaze spin to where a split had opened at the top of the acetylene cylinder, which shook so hard that the clip holding the metal frame broke from the wall, causing the welding kit to topple with a crash, shattering its four pressure dials.

That was it for my poor old dog. He flattened himself under the Capri and continued to howl, as if he was competing with the roar from where the damaged cylinder now projected a bright yellow flame, rocket-style. Propelled by this energy, the five-feet-long steel tube left the ground and turned in mid-air, until its fiery top was its base.

I feared my number was up but Trevor threw himself across the bonnet to bring me down and lock his body over mine. With a loud splintering of wood and plastic the cylinder launched through the workshop roof, into the sunny sky.

There was a nanosecond before we raced to the far side of the lane, and the apartments that had replaced the Heartbreak Hotel. What we saw next was incredible. Our accidental missile ended its zigzagging flight with a dive towards the promontory, where Sir Winston Churchill had stood for ten years. A loud crack was followed by cries from those who were on the promenade and several cars stopped so suddenly that their tyres squealed. 'Bloody hellfire, Craig,' whispered Trevor, putting an arm across my shoulders. 'Bloody hellfire,' he repeated, as we looked to the bottom of the lane where the statue was to our left, out of sight.

Soon, a man who lived in the end house ran into view. Even this was an event. He was big and normally moved at a snail's pace. 'Hoi! You two clowns!' he called up to us. 'Sir Winston's lost his ruddy head! You've decapitated him!'

A leaden feeling came over me. I eased free of Trevor's arm, looking beyond the Capri, into the workshop, where bits of plastic roofing and cables for the strip lights Big Eddie had fitted dangled above the lonesome oxygen cylinder where it lay on the ground. It hit me that I'd repeated the error I'd made with the welding torch on the day we'd rescued our Bruce from the kennels.

Big Eddie had prevented an explosion then and I now believed that the destruction of the workshop and the beheading of Sir Winston were caused by a queer-rooted madness that had overwhelmed me since the crash. My determination not to be a hands-on homo had always been steely but in those moments – when I took stock of the explosion – it seemed to become case-hardened: I would never, ever live in that way.

A car crash had thrown me off course for twenty-four hours. That was all. Or so I thought, as all the self-hating stuff I'd tried to cast out of my life boomeranged back. It'd been crazy to hope I could live as a happy queer.

# 25

I, Brucie–Dog, had squeezed behind the front wheel of the Capri, where the wax the kid had used to rust-proof its underside with made my black and tan coat sticky. This was a small price to pay to avoid the blast, but because a suffocating whiteness soon blanked everything, I believed I was dying of shock.

To my surprise, Raymond was within this fog and even for a spook his eyes were deeply shrunken. I thought he had gone with Oliver forever but obviously that was wrong. I was glad. No rescue dog wants to pass away alone, and I was scared.

'Well, Bruce,' he declared, 'that's it. Time's up.' He sighed, confirming that my mission to save Craig from a lonely life was over.

The spot hurt where my first human had most often put the electric cable to my spine, and I knew this was because of the spook's old regret at punishing the kid for being queer. He tried to make the best of things for me.

'You've been a fair rescue dog.' He smiled. 'Tried your

damnedest,' he concluded, as my tail wagged a little.

I expected to disappear into the white, a flop that, after years of laziness, had woken up to his mission when it was too late. But Raymond's turn to prove that he, too, was a mind-reader had come. 'We would have lost him without you, Bruce,' he said, 'if not years ago, then last night for sure.' That was true, and kind of him.

When the kid's throat had closed while he was bathing, Raymond had dropped me into the tub, bringing Craig to his senses before his lungs failed.

For the first time since I was saved from Psycho Vet, it seemed that I'd also been the spook's rescue dog. When it really counted we had worked together to save the kid, who now at least had Trevor Carlton as a friend.

And Raymond reminded me that Ginger had sought me out as a rescue dog to help all her family cope with their grief for him, not just the kid. He did not need to add more for his meaning to be clear. Every rescue dog has a day of reckoning and I knew that Her Hoityness would have expected me to review how things now stood for all of my lovable, argumentative young humans.

The spook opened a scene from earlier in the summer, before my colours went dead, and just after Jack had made the news as the latest up-and-coming artist to win the backing of two famous arty brothers, called

Sweinhart and Sweinhart. Ginger could not have been prouder, and when word came from Jack that two of their staff would visit number twenty to pick six of his early paintings, redness had showed around her for days.

Raymond's eyes were less shrunken, and my second sight chased hares at a pace that made me dizzy.

# 26

I t had rained on the morning when they came to see the paintings, which were stored in Jack's old bedroom-cum-studio, the only bit of number twenty that Big Eddie had not redecorated. But as they entered Ginger's garden the sun was out, raising steam from her many irises, whose petals shone like velvet.

'I'm Mr Kipper,' announced the first, who had the same square build as the kid, green eyes, and thick curly hair, which was red like Ginger's.

'And I'm Mr Brash,' smiled the second man, who, like the first, was in his late twenties but with black hair, chocolate eyes and tawny colouring.

It was obvious that they were together, and because their combined scent was what I'd always wanted for Marcus and Craig, I leaped up to them. They fussed me as if I were their dog.

'Hey, Brucie,' cried the kid, coming off the doorstep onto the short path. 'Let them past the gate,' he added. The Sweinhart and Sweinhart car parked at the kerb was a red and gold 1970 Rolls-Royce Silver Shadow shooting-brake. Then he spotted it. 'Wow!' he cried to

Big Eddie, who had followed him outside with Ginger. 'I mean, like, wow!'

So many colours showed around Mr Brash that my eyes seemed young again.

Still, it was Mr Kipper who had been watching Craig most closely and bits of silver zipped around him as he disclosed that the 'two Swines' were also car collectors. The year before they had commissioned a coachbuilder to convert the Silver Shadow from a saloon to 'something fit for carrying works of art around the country'.

It felt as if he and Mr Brash had known my family for a thousand years, and as more shades swirled around the Rolls-Royce, my tail wagged so hard it's a wonder it didn't break – which does happen to excited rescue dogs.

Soon the little party was gathered in the middle of the path. Big Eddie was so taken by everything that he asked why Mr Kipper and Mr Brash wore identical dark blue suits, maroon shirts and yellow ties. Craig answered before either of them could get a word in. 'Image,' he exclaimed. 'Sweinhart and Sweinhart create an impression everywhere they go.' He wasn't fazed by the two visitors, who had seen his queerness straight away, and I was proud.

It intrigued me that he'd shown no white, and maybe I could have taken this as the moment when he could have embraced his potential for becoming happy with his own nature. Sadly it would take a car crash for that to happen, and the conversation in the garden shifted to Ginger's liquorice allsort front door, the pink, black and grey of which she had refreshed for the occasion.

'They need to be careful with that,' commented Mr Kipper.

'The two Swines would have it,' agreed Mr Brash.

This was also great, and as the kid grinned at the pair, I made blue moons for Ginger, who, despite her happiness for Jack, was showing a small amount of white. Her artist-son would easily surpass the fifty years of painting that had left her big, beautiful hands all knobbly with arthritis.

Still, a yap of excitement for Jack escaped me, drawing laughter from them all, and putting a full stop to the first part of the Sweinhart and Sweinhart visit to number twenty. The serious business of choosing half a dozen paintings was the purpose of Mr Kipper and Mr Brash's drive from London, and Ginger knew from Jack that their bosses expected them to make a quick turn-around.

They spoke as if they were one.

'If we miss a masterpiece . . .' Mr Brash advised Big Eddie.

'. . . our blood will be boiled,' Mr Kipper told Ginger, who was wearing an old pea-green trouser suit that I loved to see her in.

Craig's scent was healthy, but he made an excuse to return to the workshop. That didn't surprise me. He liked Mr Kipper and Mr Brash too much to risk being relaxed for longer, and when more white showed around Ginger, I understood that she was sad for him.

Big Eddie led the guests upstairs to where Jack had spent many of his teenage hours at the easel Ginger had set up dead-centre on the bare floor. Now it held the strange painting of Elvis Presley, completed on my first ever trip to Jack's room.

Ten summers had passed but it seemed that time had stood still and, from the fleeting black that showed around Big Eddie, I realised Ginger had not disclosed that she was going to make the portrait prominent.

There were times when the skin around her eyes became wrinkled and her back seemed to shrink, making her look older than her sixty-five years. If Mr Kipper or Mr Brash had noticed this occurring since their entry into the room, they hid it well. Big Eddie was mindful too. He knew that after her latest stroke Ginger could quickly become difficult.

All human eyes were on the painting and, because the air was thick, I focused on the many smudges of old paint on the floor around the easel. They were caught by the silver light that came through the window, and as their colours grew richer I wanted to snuffle them for secrets. No one glanced down, but I knew what was going on above my head. Rescue dogs always do.

# 27

It was years since Big Eddie had styled himself on Elvis but with his silver hair, straight back and un-lined features he was impressive in his own right. And he was calm when Ginger demanded to know why he'd refused the Elvis painting as a gift from young Jack. It was an old theme. Each time Ginger raised it she had forgotten the previous occasions.

Scattered bits of white came, suggesting he was not going to protest, as he usually did, that he was losing interest in Elvis. Everybody knew that was untrue. He'd only dropped his impersonator-act after Viv died, when, for a time, he was a boozer.

'I mean why, Edwin?' Ginger pressed as Mr Kipper and Mr Brash politely studied the canvas. 'Why didn't you accept it?' This was putting it unfairly.

The memory of a rescue dog is always good: I knew that when Big Eddie was shown the portrait on his fifty-sixth birthday, Jack had not offered it as a present. He'd suggested it should be hung at the Heartbreak Hotel reception, but Big Eddie was evasive.

The air in the room thickened, and as he faced the

portrait it turned so bright that I felt something bigger than a quest for six of Jack's early paintings was going on. Ginger waited, Mr Kipper waited, and Mr Brash tested the floorboard smudges with the edge of his well-polished right shoe, bringing a soft wag to my tail.

Big Eddie cleared his throat, and I expected that what came next would be more for the Sweinhart and Sweinhart guests than for Ginger. They needed to understand the story of Jack's work and Big Eddie saw the importance of that to his success. Another thing I loved about him: he'd always backed the two sets of twins as if he was their father.

'The laddie didn't realise what his own painting was about,' he stated, with a certainty that made Mr Brash raise an eyebrow and nod to himself. 'I thought it wrong to take it,' he continued, with a shrug at Ginger, who looked back to the canvas with sadness for Jack. He had poured so much grief at Raymond's suicide into his art that he'd added a slash of crimson to its top right corner. As if the canvas would bleed forever.

'The boy was in too much pain,' Big Eddie added, while Mr Kipper took his chance to test the floor smudges with the side of his shoe. A rainbow grew in the sky beyond the window. Everything felt epic, and I yearned to be with Ginger for longer than the brief time left to me.

'My Jack,' she calmly explained, 'knew you were

grieving in advance of Vivienne dying, Edwin.' She was like that. Lost one moment and found the next.

Big Eddie took a hanky from his hip pocket and wiped his eyes. He didn't need to reply and kept his gaze fixed on the garish swirls of colour that suggested Elvis's plump belly and sickness of heart. I prayed to Her Hoityness for my legs to remain firm. Human vulnerability is exhausting.

Still, at last I understood my mixed response to Big Eddie's Elvis phase and its relevance to my life before Ginger rescued me from Psycho Vet. It had been confusing that where my first human would have offed me with his electric cable, Big Eddie had treated Craig so well that his war against being queer was less harmful than it might have been. I only had to think of Hugo Moncrieff to know that.

Yet what both Big Eddie and my first human had found in the voice of Elvis Presley was a balm to soothe their pain, proving that they had an area of common feeling. Even the kid's twin sister had once said that Elvis's voice was a cry for those who struggled. My first human died of unhappiness at forty-two, just like Elvis. Big Eddie, of course, was luckier.

'A study of grief in many ways,' murmured Mr Brash to Mr Kipper, who glanced at the floor and added, 'Precisely.'

If Big Eddie took a few moments to realise what was

occurring, Ginger saw it right away and it almost set off my seal wiggle.

Her left eyebrow rose as she watched Mr Brash and Mr Kipper kneel and touch the limpet-like smudges that spread from Big Eddie's black loafers to the easel's triangulated legs, the exact area where Jack had done his early work as a painter.

'A portrait of our young man . . .' began Mr Kipper.

'. . . as an artist at work,' concluded Mr Brash, in satisfaction.

Redness glowed around them while Big Eddie and Ginger held hands and listened to the plan that was hatched on behalf of Sweinhart and Sweinhart. The Elvis portrait, the easel, the paint-smudged floorboards, plus old tubes of oils, brushes, palette knives and more would form the centrepiece of a big Sweinhart and Sweinhart London exhibition.

'They've found their masterpiece,' Big Eddie advised Ginger, as she cried for Jack, who had made the tale of his alkie dad into art, which would now be celebrated. Success did not come bigger and I hoped that the spook was lurking to enjoy it as much as I was.

# 28

Big Eddie had served the breakfast I was watching him eat with the kid and Ginger, whose unusual watchfulness made me itchy.

Picasso felt something in the air, too, and because his beady eye was fixed on me, I had to resist yelping just to make my humans say something. This went on until Craig rose from the table for the start of his day in the workshop.

'Those smashing young chaps from yesterday,' Big Eddie began, hooking Ginger's eye from where he sat opposite her, 'they do make each other happy,' he declared, turning to the kid, who shrugged as if Mr Kipper and Mr Brash were of no interest to him.

'Yup,' continued Big Eddie, wiping bacon smears from his plate with a gobbet of bread he popped into his mouth. 'Happy is as happy does,' he concluded, point made to Craig, who looked as if he'd now been zapped with my first human's electric cable.

Picasso's eye had gone so big it might have popped from its socket, and as a purple rash came to the kid's neck, Ginger put her head down, scooping breadcrumbs from the table into her cupped hand. Yellow showed all around her. It was years since the air in the kitchen had been so dense, and after turning from the table to dump his plate in the sink, Craig slammed the back door behind him.

Probably that was the moment when my colours began to go but my number one worry was Ginger. She was supposed to avoid stress and, mercifully, Big Eddie reassured her that, despite the kid's tantrum, things were not as bad for him as they appeared. 'Don't worry, love,' he said. 'He'll be fine.'

By now he had wrapped his hands over hers on the table and I padded close, intending that my blue moons would make them smile, but Picasso had a cannier trick to pull. They're like that, parrots. Always ready to upstage a rescue dog.

'Swineheart and Swineheart,' he squawked, making them break into laughter.

'Swineheart and Swineheart,' he repeated, reminding me that I loved him as much as I did Big Eddie and Ginger, who now cast off her worry for the kid in the same way as I shook away my fears for her. There was much good stuff for me to explore and I had only to dwell on the success of the kid's twin sister, Rachael, for my tail to wag hard.

After just three years of teaching PE, she was a county-wide physical-education adviser, pushing for the inclusion of girls in sports previously open to boys only. It amused Ginger that where neither of her sons could kick a ball, her younger daughter was a ferocious centre-forward. I was proud of her and saw the importance of the love of her slightly older husband, whose business in car seatbelts spanned much of the world.

That left Vanessa and her husband Zenon, an engineer on the Isle of Man, where parts of the railway were still powered by steam, his specialist field. Even more happily for me, she had found her niche, designing, making and selling what Jack teasingly called 'hot couture' at her own boutique on the island. It was years since she had swiped one of Ginger's gold velvet curtains to make an outfit that had gone down in the family's history, and everybody was chuffed when a big name in fashion put her on a retainer that would make her well known.

Still, I knew that in going over the lives of Rachael, Vanessa and Jack I was avoiding my lack of success at nudging the kid out of the workshop. Could I be blamed that he was self-destructive? Wasn't it too much to expect me to save him anyway? Maybe that was what the spook had felt after Sir Winston had lost his head.

'No rescue dog could have done more,' he'd concluded, leaving me sad but no less determined to protect the kid.

It was not two cars that had crashed. It was two lives and I needed to be clear-sighted. My bones were old but I was up to the job.

# 29

The sun was sinking over the town, and the sea was as pink as I'd ever known it. It was beautiful, but as we sat on the bench in front of the headless statue of Sir Winston, I knew Trevor was troubled.

It was five hours since somebody had reported the explosion as a bomb, with fire engines, ambulances and police cars arriving fast. We were grilled about the acetylene cylinder, whose flight had even led the regional news. Plus a reporter had come with a photographer who, after snapping Sir Winston's marble face as he peered up from the rocks below the promontory, had cheerily suggested that the old PM would be livid about me taking him out.

Trevor and the police had laughed, but because Dad died on the spot where Sir Winston's head awaited rescue, I was glad the tide would soon cover his marble eyes. It was odd. A part of me I couldn't control felt that a real death had occurred, and maybe that was sort of true.

It was thirty hours since Trevor's car had hit mine, and my crazy need to embrace him as my brother was gone, piquing my curiosity as to why he'd discharged himself from hospital.

'C'mon, mate,' I said, keeping my eyes on the horizon, where the lights of a dozen ships twinkled. 'What's it all about? You, turning up at the workshop,' I went on, surprised by a hard note that stole into my voice.

If this was upsetting for him it didn't show and I realised that the hysteria that had often made him shriek when we were fifteen had been replaced by the control he was now exhibiting.

Pushing for a quick reply would have been pointless. He was deciding what to say. After looking to where several yellow-beaked gulls glided onto the salmon-red mirror that the sea now was, he finally opened up.

'You made an assumption this morning, Craig,' he remarked. 'A big one,' he added, as I twisted my upper half towards him, concerned that I was why he had left the hospital early.

'How so?' I asked, while he kept his eyes on the gulls, whose white feathers were somehow resistant to the reflection of the sunset on the water.

'C'mon, please, mate,' I persisted, eager for the moment to be over. 'What big assumption?'

Trevor turned and looked into me in a way that made me certain he loathed what he was seeing: a kinky homo who had got the shaving of a hospitalised friend out of proportion.

That was me. I had stalked him to his sick room and caused the explosion he had saved me from. I cringed at my plan for my red Capri 3000E. Trevor might stick a match down the fuel filler and I couldn't blame him for it.

Squawks came from the floating gulls and I looked away from his piercing stare to where they now spread their wings and rose from the sea, as if the tension from the promontory was too much to bear.

'Look at me, please, Craig,' said Trevor, levelly. 'Look at me,' he repeated, as I shifted my gaze to where the lighthouse threw one sweep after another, just as I had seen thousands of times, with nothing new to find. Streaks of black were coming into the red sky.

'Sunset's dying,' I commented, for the sake of something to say. 'Like they all do.' I was bracing myself for the attack I thought was coming.

Maybe this was how it had to be, first the crash, then the explosion, compelling us to confront past, present and future, with no time to draw a breath between events that had literally left me gasping. If Sir Winston's head was not lost under the sea fifty feet below us, I might have believed that he now cleared his throat to make me pay attention to Trevor.

A rush of hope made me face him, and as I did so a smile lit his eyes, which were now more silver than blue.

Nothing could have been lovelier. I'd got the wrong end of the stick about everything and my exciting plan for the Capri was back on the cards.

The next bit simply happened, catching me unawares, though probably Trevor had expected it from the second that I crouched at his side as he lay in the wrecked gold Zodiac. Tingles shot down my spine and I moved in to kiss his lips but the gentlest shake of his head cautioned against it.

'You're still picking me up all wrong,' he said, with affection. I marvelled that I felt no guilt about wanting to kiss a man. When he shrugged, I knew that the insane queer-hating behaviour we had been through had to stay where it belonged: in the past. Plus I was sick of thinking about me. It had got me nowhere, and Trevor was a welcome alternative to self-obsession.

I wanted to run my fingers through his thick black hair. It was so like mine, which had never been cut nicely. In his beauty I found mine. To this day I hope he got stronger by likewise glimpsing himself in me.

Everything I had been told about being queer was wrong, and I shuddered to think of Hugo Moncrieff and all the boys who had died because of what they had been told by their parents, teachers and classmates.

It was a huge blessing that Marcus had survived. I saw that when he'd called to number twenty for me on his Raleigh Chopper, he'd known his self-worth and was there to help me find mine. I'd been blind. I'd been a fool. I'd been cruel.

But at least I understood this and, oddly, the person I wanted to tell most of all was Dad. I had the most profound sense that he would have been happy for me and I wished he was there.

The sun was gone and the sea's thickening darkness was made shiny by the moon.

Whatever Trevor needed to tell me, I could have waited forever to hear. I was queer and there was nothing wrong with the life that I intended to live.

The words I heard next were marked by a note that, because it humbled Trevor, was achingly beautiful.

'You wrongly assumed that Howler was my best man,' he announced. 'And I wrongly let you believe it, Craig. Very wrongly,' he confessed, leaving no doubt that he had discharged himself from hospital to correct things between us.

A lone gull returned to float about fifty yards off, and when it squawked loudly I faced my old friend again. 'Marcus,' I said. 'Your best man was Marcus,' I concluded, unperturbed that he was looking into me just as I was doing to him.

'You spent too long in that bloody workshop, Craig.' He shrugged. 'Slowly pickling in old stuff while the rest of us moved on,' he added.

I loved Marcus, and if he was back in my life there

would be no more stomach pain, no more throat closures, no more rough sleep, no more fear of madness,
no more danger of suicide, no more risk of becoming
a boozer, no more playing the straight type, no more
battling against being who I was, no more living a lie,
no more loneliness, no more self-destruction, no more
carrying a secret hunger for Marcus, every second of
every day. No more, no more. I'd had my fill.

Still, I was practical, and as the gull took off and flew
overhead towards the town, I asked Trevor if Marcus had
a boyfriend. 'Someone who loves him properly,' I said, as
we became bathed in purple cast by the spotlights that
suddenly uplit the statue. I thought it should be turned
off until the council had refitted the head.

He smiled and slid his gaze upwards to the stump of
Sir Winston's neck. 'There you go again,' he said, 'always
expecting the worst. Never mind the one-night stands,'
he continued, bringing his eye back to mine. 'He was
with Peter for a year, a lad called Tony for longer, and he's
only recently split with Malcolm. The only other one,' he
stressed, as if accusing me of wrecking the relationship
from afar, 'who might have been with Marcus forever,
Craig. Forever,' he repeated.

Still, I was worried: 'We both know he'll want a relationship with somebody more like himself. Somebody
well practised,' I argued, with a deep wish to be wrong.

'Bollocks!' exclaimed Trevor, with a toothy laugh.

'Peter, Tony, Malcolm,' he added, reaching along the bench to tap-tap my shoulder, 'each was handsome in a big-nosed way, each was dark-haired with green eyes, and all three were oddballs. Remind you of anyone, Craig?' he teased, looking hard at my face, which was seemingly a dead-ringer for those of Marcus's exes.

My heart thumped and as the silver, purple, white and black of the evening went fuzzy, I braced myself against sliding onto the granite paving that was laid when the statue was put up in 1972. It was the sea breeze that stopped me passing out, and I hardly dared trust what Trevor was revealing. The tips of his fingers stayed on my shoulder, sending tingles through me.

'You're the only one for him, Craig,' he emphasised. 'Always the only one,' he added, with wistfulness that made me look beyond my own life at a much bigger picture.

It wasn't only queer boys who were harmed by a world that expected young men to be tough. Maleness itself was kicked about, like a football, and it was unsurprising that Trevor was already a boozer, risking his marriage to Karina, who I was certain would be his saviour. He didn't need to ask why I had become serious, and we knew that if I succeeded with Marcus his own chances would be boosted, so entwined were our lives.

'Who would've thought where that bubblegum malarkey would take us all?' I quipped to keep us upbeat, though when he frowned it seemed this had backfired. But too much good stuff was going on for him to be glum.

'For you, Craigie,' he announced, taking a piece of folded paper from the breast pocket of his denim jacket, which was stained with blood from when he had crashed the Zodiac.

He didn't need to say that this was Marcus's address, which I assumed was in London. I was wrong. It was no wonder that he'd frowned at my quip about where he, Marcus and I had got to with our lives. Things were not what I expected.

## 30

**M**arcus had followed up on his City and Guilds with a degree in education and was now back to teach Design and Technology at our school, where Mr Heston had queer-bashed him. Wow. Trevor had an air of triumph, and as we watched the moon go from silver to corn yellow, I fancied it was hanging over the sea by a single steel thread.

That was typical. My mind had a way of doing things that I rarely understood but which kept me sane. And I was still bang in the moment with Trevor, who soon underlined what was most important about all that he had told me.

'Marcus is back.' He smiled. 'For you, Craig,' he stressed.

By now he was standing between the bench where I was still sitting and the pale blue safety rail that Dad had gone over. It seemed that all our bits of conflict were done with. Still, a rebellious thought popped out of me. 'Then why hasn't he come to see me?' I demanded.

Trevor looked to the ground, then faced me again.

'Didn't he try that last time? Isn't it your turn to do some running?' he asked, as his face tightened.

That hit home. Marcus had never given up on me and I needed to prove that I was ready to return his love and loyalty. It was Trevor's long stare that made me become truthful with myself.

'I'm frightened I won't meet his expectations. That I'll be a disappointment,' I explained, feeling myself go small all over.

'You think you're the one taking a risk?' Trevor asked, putting his left hand out and gripping the top bar of the sea rail, which was round and rusty on its underside. 'What about Marcus?'

Placing his right hand on the back of my head, he brought his face down and gave me a deep kiss that made being alive a thing of wonder. I had never felt anything like it, and when I opened my eyes he was striding off towards the small hotel where he was bullied as a youth and might thrive as a man.

'Are you going to be okay?' I called.

He turned to give me his best-ever football-star grin. 'Me, Craig?' he replied, parodying his old cockiness. 'I'm gonna make my marriage work.'

The next bit had to be said. 'Our crash? The cars?' I called, cupping my eyes against the big promenade lamp that was making him into a dark outline. 'It was planned? Right?'

Trevor burst out laughing. 'You think I'd deliberately head-butt a windscreen at thirty miles an hour?' he teased.

'But you were coming to see me,' I insisted.

'With Marcus's address!' he cried. 'You weren't supposed to hit the bloody brakes!'

That was funny but I could not resist sparring some more.

'You do know that insurance companies always hold the driver behind responsible,' I said, making him dismiss the point with a wave of his hand. That was fair enough. We had much more important stuff to think about.

'You make it work with Marcus,' he insisted. 'I'll make it work with Karina. We owe that to them and us,' he concluded, reminding me again of just how far we'd come since we were boys, plagued by fears that we didn't understand.

Still, Trevor was always going to be Trevor.

'I'll fetch my new Capri tomorrow,' he called, over his shoulder. 'After I've sorted its insurance.' He laughed, doing a jig, which left me bold about my next move.

Marcus: this time I was going to get things right. I was not a limp-wristed cissy. I was a young man eager to share with the man who loved me as much as I did him. I had lost my war against being queer and it was the biggest win of my life.

# 31

The bottom of the stairs at number twenty had a lip that I liked to press my spine into while I slept. In the days when both sets of twins were at home I was often trodden on but now that I was old, the kid was mindful in case I got hurt. This occasion was different. He tore into the house via Ginger's liquorice allsort, flicked on the light and leapt over me, creating so much redness that my dodgy bowel threatened to open. Old dogs and excitement do not always mix well.

Still I was soon distracted by another returning wanderer: the spook was back yet again and, far from being his normal grey self, he glittered all over. 'It's happening with young Marcus!' he exclaimed. 'At last it's happening, Brucie!' he added, cocking an ear to where Craig moved about with urgency on the floor above.

I stood four-square and trembled, the ancient rescue dog and the spook, both eager for a happy end to the kid's tale of love discovered, love denied and love waiting to be rebooted.

'Please,' I prayed to Her Hoityness, 'make it right that

Craig has accepted his queerness. Please, please make it right,' I added, relieved that my bowel was behaving after all.

Two days before, a reunion between Craig and Marcus had seemed impossible but I dared to believe that it might now occur and certainly the spook had no doubts. His silver glitter grew even brighter, showing he was near the end of his time. All we needed was for things to go well and peace would come to us both. The moment was huge and I must have looked a sight.

The hair along my spine had bristled, and when he came tearing downstairs Craig was all spruced up, with a scent that made my nostrils flare like those of a horse. I offered my biggest blue moons and was unconcerned that because my tail was going like crazy my seal-wiggle was strong. The only thing that counted was for Craig and Marcus to be together. That was my job. That was why Ginger had rescued me. That was the point of my life – to help her youngest child find his way in the world.

It was good to feel that I was not a rescue flop and, as if to underline his faith in me, the spook was suddenly gone and I knew it was final.

He had picked his moment well. Things were so clear.

Craig was on the roll of his life and I had to be fully committed to sharing it. 'C'mon Brucie-Wucie-Lucie-

Darling!' he cried, striding towards the back door. 'Us've got a date!' he declared, as a wild mix of colours sent me giddy with joy, which Picasso shared: his big round eye had a shiny grin of its own.

'Us've got a date!' he mimicked, making me bark.

'Us've got a date!' he repeated as the kid topped up his water, and I saw that without the parrot's watchfulness, I would have been a useless rescue dog. He had often kept me right, and I shook my spine in gratitude. Parrots were the best.

Two seconds passed while he cocked his head at me and I became calm. That was part of his gift. He could soothe with ease, and after closing his eye, he left me to complete my mission. Exactly as Her Hoityness would have expected me to do.

Craig had unlocked the back door and we passed through Ginger's moonlit forest of ferns to where the pink, grey and black rear door of the workshop was wide open. Everything inside was a mess and his disregard for this showed that his time of hiding away from life was over. The stars were bright, the shiny red Capri was undamaged, and my success as a rescue dog was to be sealed by the reunion of the two young humans who had decades of togetherness before them.

The kid drove the Capri fast, and after we'd passed the long strip of hotels where Trevor was, we neared the lighthouse, whose island was marooned in the sil-ver-yellow sea. That said it for me: truly big stuff was happening, and the cornfields, as we turned inland, were luminescent.

The kid was born to drive, and as the Capri was put through its paces, I felt the presence of Her Hoityness, who I knew would take nothing for granted. Craig had a lifetime of queer-hating to overcome, and because things might still go wrong for him and Marcus, I had to be alert.

Everything was in the balance, and fifteen minutes later I stood at heel as he knocked on the blue-painted door of a downstairs flat that was part of terrace with tall bay windows. Here was the moment that Ginger had brought me into the family to make happen. The door was torn open and Marcus stood there. He had thick blond hair, olive skin and eyes that were even bluer than Raymond's had been. He was beautiful, his scent was perfect and red was all around him, making me yap like a pup.

'You took your time!' he cried at Craig, who did not have a moment to reply before they were kissing and I knew for sure that everything was how it should always have been, their two hearts beating as one.

Thrillingly Marcus's gaze became fixed on me. 'Brucie-Wucie-Lucie-Darling,' he teased, sending my tail into a frenzy, both young men laughing as I barked and turned circles on the short path. Soon I was tired and Marcus cupped my chin in his right hand, facing me in the exact way of Ginger after my rescue from the kennels.

'Look after him for me, Brucie,' she had said then. 'Look after my younger boy,' she had stressed, making me feel that I was the most important dog in the universe. Possibly Marcus thought the same.

'Thank you, Brucie, for looking after this rat-bag idiot,' he said, throwing a grin at the kid, who looked at us both with love that calmed my heart. 'Wise old dog,' added Marcus, stroking my flank with care, which showed he was mindful of my aches and pains.

Looking into his face I confirmed the openness of spirit that proved what I had always felt. Marcus Wright was the most genuine young human that any rescue dog could have wished for as the companion of their number-one charge.

'You brought him back to me,' he concluded, which told me that, despite my years of being a lazy-bones, I was the successful rescue dog Her Hoityness had ordered me to be, and my treasured Ginger had needed. We were almost at the finish for me, Brucie-Dog.

Could I have asked for better? I didn't think so. A washing-up bowl was filled with water, and Marcus made a bed of coats in the corridor that led to the bedroom where he and the kid went. That was great and soon I would sleep. But first I had to sniff out my surroundings. Just like day one with my rescue family, in fact.

# 32

I nosed into the big front room which, with its white marble fireplace and fancy plasterwork, echoed number twenty. It was obvious that Marcus was in the middle of moving in. Books were piled up, and because the curtains were yet to be hung, the moon came in through every pane of the wide bay. What I saw bathed within this light was so welcome that I had to fight against the howl that tried to escape me.

Next to a red racer – I guessed it was Marcus's grown-up bike – the twelve-year-old yellow Raleigh Chopper was on its stand, gleaming, as if ready for the day when my role as Craig's protector was over. It made me totally sure that he and Marcus were safe together and, for the first time ever, I did not dream as I slept. My second sight was done, my heart was slowing. I craved to rest in peace.

# Epilogue

All rescue dogs know of the Final Event, but because it's post-life no mutt can prove its substance when living. But I, Brucie–Dog, can see its truth now. With his wife Karina at his side, fifty-seven-year-old Trevor stands before the guests at the marriage celebration of Craig and Marcus, who are bathed in red, which the gathering rightly sees as joy. Trevor is silver-haired and I smell his pride at being best man. I love him for that and I do not need a second sight to know that his own long marriage has been good. He clears his throat and I realise that because he will speak from the heart, written notes are unnecessary.

'Forty plus years ago,' he begins, with a look at Craig and Marcus, 'I was a boy in this very hotel' – he gestures at the room – 'and my father was not a kind man. Somehow that unkindness spread through me to my friends, and with all my being I want to thank Craig and Marcus for forgiving me, and more so for becoming lifelong friends to myself and Karina, whose love for me has been life-saving.'

My doggy ears are pricked hard, the company applauds, and soon Trevor resumes.

'The early 1970s were not good for boys who fell in love with other boys. The youngsters of today' – he looks to several red-haired great-grandchildren of Ginger – 'may not know that boys were routinely attacked and driven to terrible actions, all because of whom they loved.'

The room has gone dead quiet and I wish that Jack, Vanessa and Rachael could see the wag of my tail. I love them hard but my focus must stay on those who were at the heart of my mission when I was alive: Craig, Marcus and even Trevor. Still, the nearness of Craig's big brother and his two sisters makes my skin silky, and I'm even happier to hear Trevor speak.

'What I really mean to say,' he continues, perhaps fearing that he is being too heavy, 'is that Craig and Marcus – head teacher at our old school – have not just survived, they've thrived, making life better for us all. Right from the start they were meant to be together and it feels correct, to me at least, that theirs is the first gay marriage this town has seen. All their parents – and Craig's stepfather Big Eddie – are long gone, but if they were alive, I believe they would be proud of their boys.' He fixes a look on Craig, adding, 'Not least your old man.'

The applause is thunderous, and as Marcus and Craig

stride to embrace Trevor and Karina, I, Brucie–Dog, see beyond the big windows that front the hotel. The moon leaks silver onto the sea, and beneath the white marble figure of Sir Winston Churchill, Her Hoityness and her tiny white pup are waiting. I am happy to go. I was Brucie the Rescue Dog. I loved my humans and they loved me.

# Acknowledgements

Fifteen years ago Arts Council England gave me a writer's award, which helped open the door on my Winston Tails project. Much has happened since but I have not forgotten their help. Thank you, Arts Council England.

In 2011 Constable took over the publishing of the first 'tail', Barking at Winston, from Zircon Press. It would be remiss of me not to thank Andreas Campomar for keeping the book in print.

I am indebted to my friend and publisher, Mike Wallington. He has consistently challenged me and helped to improve my work: thank you, Mike. Equally I must pay tribute to Mike Davis, who designed and typeset this book. As usual, it was a pleasure to work with you, Mike.

My editor Hazel Orme came to me via Constable and I could not have asked for a wiser guide or a better friend. I cannot thank her enough. Thank you, Tony Russell, for doing the proofreading.

Dr Pauline Hadaway and Professor Margaret Lewis critiqued the manuscript for this publication and I am deeply grateful for their encouragement. I also thank Pauline for her endorsement.

Peter Lawrence and several other older veterans shared their experiences of the Navy and war with me. Their honesty was powerful, and I also need to acknowledge the neighbours, teachers and others whose experiences of both world wars influenced me as a boy and youth. Little did I know how much I was soaking up from these men and women.

I must also thank Helen McManners, Gill King, Tom Ross and Lisa Harris for reading Winston Sees All in manuscript form. Their insights were more helpful than they know. Tim Dickinson's clear-sighted advice on the cover was uplifting, and so, too, was Ellie Whitworth and Ben Stone's drawing, 'Celebrating Bonzo'. It touched my heart.

Steve and Kim Davey and my old pal Tommy were there when I needed help with my computer. Without them, I would have been lost many times. Thank you, Kim, thank you Steve, thank you, Tommy.

My accountant Lynn Bennett has helped keep me on track throughout the Winston Tails years, and I thank her and the team at MooreBennett Ltd. Likewise I thank Martin's The Printers for their excellent service over many years.

David Haldane thank you for being generous with your time and expertise.

For ten years I toured the country, signing Barking at Winston and Winston and the Canny Lass at high-street and retail-park outlets. I found booksellers and their managers to be hard-working people and, with their help, forty thousand signed copies were sold. I thank them for their role in a long journey.

My husband Paul Simpson has been my partner for forty years and has never complained about life with an optimist who ditched the security of PAYE to be a writer. I love you, Paul.

In 2016 Barry Stone married his partner Paul Simpson, putting a seal on the relationship that began when Barry gatecrashed Paul's twenty-seventh birthday party in 1983. They have clocked up thousands of miles while exercising the adored and none too well behaved dogs that have been a major part of their world. They have a charming brown Labrador called Zac. Or 'the little so-and-so' when misbehaving.

*Photograph by Gabe and Cez.*

*Contact Barry: Barry Stone Writer on Facebook.*